Tudor Spy

**Book 2 in the Tudor Warrior series
By
Griff Hosker**

Tudor Spy

Published by Sword Books Ltd 2022

Copyright ©Griff Hosker First Edition

A CIP catalogue record for this title is available from the British Library.
Thanks to Design for Writers for the cover and logo.

Dedication

Adam Pendlebury- you have been dealt a rough hand but your grandad would have been proud of how you dealt with it, as am I. Hang in there, kid and know that the family is all with you and we are a powerful force

Contents

Historical characters

King Henry VII of England
Arthur Prince of Wales
King Henry VIII of England
Queen Elizabeth (Woodville)
Jasper Tudor- Duke of Bedford and the uncle of King Henry VII
Margaret Beaufort- wife of the Earl of Derby and mother of King Henry VII
Margaret of York, the Dowager Duchess of Burgundy
Richard de la Pole- the last claimant to the Yorkist/Plantagenet crown
King Philip of Castile-Lord of the Netherlands and Duke of Burgundy
Lord Thomas Stanley- Earl of Derby
King Louis XII of France
Sir Henry Clifford- Lord of Craven
King James IV of Scotland
Donald Dubh -Lord of the Isles
Lord Huntly- A Scottish noble
Lord Home- a Scottish Border lord
John 'Bastard' Heron of Ford- a Northumbrian knight
Sir Robert Kerr- a Scottish Border lord

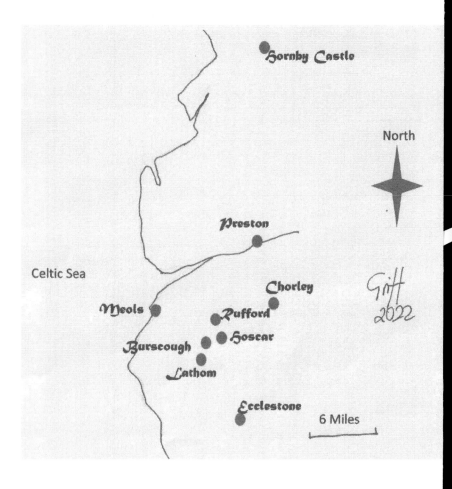

Prologue

Ecclestone 1500

After the rebellion of Perkin Warbeck had been quashed, I returned to life as a billman serving Sir Edward at Hedingham. I had a good life. Stephen, my best friend in the world, was my sergeant and my old comrade in arms, Sam and his wife, not to mention his children, lived so close that I was able to enjoy their lives too. Stephen and I were like favourite uncles who could drift in, be adored and then leave again without any of the effort or duties of a parent. Sir Edward was a bachelor in a bachelor's house and the visits to Sam were a visit to a family and that did both of us good.

We drilled our men and I became even more skilled with the billhook. My father had fought for King Henry at Bosworth Field and had been a renowned billman. I had a good reputation. Not all of us had the same type of billhook. Some liked the simple pole with a curved blade and a hook while others favoured one that had a spike in addition to a hook. Some thought that was like a poleaxe without the hammer. I preferred the small spike as it gave me an additional weapon to use in battle. I had money enough and I had the blacksmith make me a langet to protect the head of my weapon. The wooden shaft was vulnerable to slashes and hacks from bladed weapons. The langet helped to protect. Stephen and I worked well together but I felt guilty that I was the captain and he was just my subordinate but he did not seem to mind. I had learned my trade under Sam when we had fought against the Yorkist rebels supporting Perkin Warbeck and Lambert Simnel. I knew the value of training and Sir Edward's company of billmen and the men from his manor were amongst the best-trained billmen in the land.

It was a sad day when I left Hedingham and the service of both Sir Edward and the king. I was sad to leave my friends but also because my mother sent me a letter to tell me that my father, Walter of Ecclestone, was ill and that she needed my help. He had been a billman for King Henry and fought at Bosworth Field. As with all such warriors, there are wounds and hurts that cannot be seen. He was an old warrior and my mother's missive suggested he was close to death. Sir Edward was understanding for I had done both him and England a great service when I had helped thwart the foreign governments that tried to ferment rebellion in England. He was sad to see me go and I could see that in his face. Stephen and I were as surrogate sons. He would be lonelier when I left. My dearest friend, Stephen was appointed Captain of Billmen in my place and the night before I left for my home in the north, I enjoyed one last night with my two former comrades, Captain Sam and Stephen.

"When my father is well again, I shall return and ask for a place here."

Stephen shook his head, "We both know that you will not return but if you should then I will stand aside for you. You are the superior leader in battle. I can wield a billhook as well as you but I cannot lead as you do."

Sam was older and wiser, "You cannot do that, Stephen. James here is quite right to go and I do not think he will return here to Hedingham but you are your own man and must become a leader." He waved a hand to the north, "I think our old friend has more adventures left in him. After all, he was the one who spent years in Flanders and France as a spy. This life," Sam was very expressive with his hands, especially when he had been drinking and he made a grand gesture, "this manor is too small for James. Besides, he has money."

I nodded, "And I will use that money to make my home more comfortable for my parents. As for my life of adventure…I have had enough of playing the part of spy for the king. You may be right and it might be hard for me to return here. I will fight for him and my country but I need no more adventures. I would have what you have, Sam, I would have a wife and a family."

I left the next day with the gift of a fine horse from Sir Edward, Calliope, and with a chest of coins I had accumulated. I was a frugal Captain of Billmen and I had saved my earnings and treasure well. With armour on a sumpter I bought, I rode north able to stay in inns and enjoy stabling for my animals and comfortable beds for myself. I had left my home in Ecclestone many years earlier and tramped to war almost as a pauper but I would return as a man with money. When I had been Perkin Warbeck's companion I had dressed and lived as one of the nobility and I could not change my past. I knew I was not yet a gentleman but I had lived the life of one and that had changed me for I knew the good life and wanted that for me and my family. I had never even courted but I knew that one day I would wed and my life had shown me what I wanted. I had left Ecclestone as a wastrel but I would be returning as a chastened and changed man.

Chapter 1

Ecclestone

My father had been laid low by some affliction that had the doctors mystified. He could not use his right arm and the right side of his face appeared almost frozen. His speech was slurred and, at times, so was his thinking. I was shaken when I saw him. I had left him money when I had last visited so that he and my mother were comfortable but the smallholding had been allowed to deteriorate. That first night, as I sat before the fire in the house of my parents, I spoke with them about my life and what I had done. The last time I had been too close to the rebellions of Perkin Warbeck and Lambert Simnel but now I could talk. I was as honest with them as my oath to King Henry would allow. My mother took it all in but my father's illness meant it was difficult to tell the depth of his understanding.

"Have my sisters and their husbands not offered to help?"

My two sisters had left home some years earlier. They lived at Parr and Pendlebury. Although not on Ecclestone's doorstep, they were much closer than Hedingham.

My mother shook her head. "Your sisters made their bed and they have their own families. I was loath to ask you for help, my son, for I know you have a good life in Hedingham but when I wrote I thought that your father did not have long for this world." She shook her head and smiled, "He is a tough old man, is he not? If you wish to return to Hedingham then we would understand."

Her words belied the look on her face and I shook my head, "I will stay at home now that my adventures are done and make improvements to the smallholding for it needs much work."

My mother flashed me an irritated look, "Your father has done all that he could, James."

I smiled, "And I do not criticise but you are not trying to tell me that my father is happy with the state of his land?" In the short time I had been home I had seen how much the smallholding had been neglected. He had not grown new crops and the ones that were in the ground had gone to seed. The few animals he had were thin and undernourished. Had I not come then they would have struggled to eat. I was needed here.

I knew my father had been aware of my words when he attempted a grin but it came out as some sort of grisly grimace. His words were slurred but I heard my old father beneath the words. He was still a great man in my eyes, "You are right, James. Do what you will for this is all the inheritance that I can leave you."

"You have given me more than that for Walter of Ecclestone still has a reputation and men know what you did for the king, the country and this land."

My father shook his head. I could see that it was a real effort, "That is the past and those that commanded me have now forgotten that I even exist. Most of those alongside whom I fought are now dead and soon I will be."

My mother shook her head for she had to have the last word, "You will not and you, James, now that you have stopped your gallivanting when will you seek a bride? We would have grandchildren!"

I laughed, "Let me get my feet under the table first. I have come home to be the son you deserve and I will put this home back on its feet." I hauled my chest of coins onto the table. "I have made money while I served Sir Edward but it will not last. This is where I shall invest it. I intend to buy more land and hire men. I am no farmer but I know how to command men. I shall hire men who are young and ambitious. When we are in a better position and my father is well again then I will give thought to marriage but for the moment my plans are to become the owner of the best farm in Ecclestone."

I opened it and I saw both my parents' eyes widen when they saw the number of coins within. I had been frugal in my spending and saved. I was a successful warrior and such men always collect coins and treasure from their fallen foes. It was a fortune for people such as us. I doubted that the coins of everyone who lived in Windle and Ecclestone would equal half of what I had accumulated serving the king, the Earl of Oxford and Sir Edward. I spoke with both of them about my plans. On my way north I had visualised the property and the village and, after I had seen the state of the place, I had modified my vision of the future. My mother did not really understand what I planned but I saw the twinkle in my father's eyes. He did. I believe that he began to improve from that moment. He did not regain the use of the right arm and his voice remained slurred but he became, somehow, more alert and, as my mother commented, he ate more and his frame began to look healthier.

That night as I lay in my old bed, I actually believed my words. Those were my plans but many hundreds of miles away there were events that would shape my life. I could do nothing about them. When I had first left my home and started my journey the steps I took would form the rest of my life. I had, through the intervention of fate, become not only a billman but also a spy for King Henry.

I had never been lazy even when my parents had despaired of me and thought me, as the rest of the manor did, as a wild and wilful youth. I began as I meant to go on and I went, first to the steward of the Earl of Derby, Lord Stanley to seek land purchases. All the land in a manor was owned by the lord of the manor or the church. Ultimately it was the king who owned almost everything. The lord of our manor was the earl who had changed sides at the Battle of Bosworth and gained the throne for King Henry. The earl was one of the most powerful men in the land and the stepfather of King Henry Tudor. I went, therefore, with some trepidation to Lathom, where he lived. Thankfully, my name was known by the steward and I was received with more kindness than most men who were yet to be made gentlemen could expect. The steward listened to my request. I had thought it all through and made what I hoped was a worthy request. Most of the land was already farmed and owned. There was however one farm without owners and I managed to buy the derelict farm in Ecclestone. It had belonged to a foolish farmer who had followed Perkin Warbeck. Whilst fighting him had brought me riches, following that misguided youth had cost the farmer and his family their farm. Once he had been executed his family had been ejected from the land and they had headed to Chorley where they had family. As the farmer had also neglected the farm when he fought for the pretender, I was able to buy it for less than its true value. Of course, one never truly owned the land one farmed. It was always the property of the lord of the manor and a tenant farmer, no matter how prosperous, could lose his land on the whim of a new lord. You had taxes to pay and service to give.

I returned to Lathom where, a week after steward, Thomas Crouchley, had listened to my request he handed me the deeds. The deed cost me coins as did the purchase of the land. The steward, who seemed to me a kind man also gave me a warning, "This is all dependent upon his lordship agreeing to the price. When he returns to Lathom I will send for you so that he can confirm the sale. I know that thanks to your service to the king, he thinks highly of you and I am confident that he will concur with my decision. He would have loyal men owning his land but I cannot guarantee that you will be allowed to farm."

As I headed back to the farm, I knew what he alluded to. The earl's brother had foolishly sided with the rebels and had been executed five years earlier. Families had been divided in the civil war that men now referred to as the Wars of the Roses. I had been close to the rebels and knew that it was not as simple as Lancastrians and Yorkists. Families were torn between supporting one of the many claimants to the throne. Henry Tudor had put an end to that but he was still threatened by enemies, foreign and domestic. I knew what the steward meant by loyal men. Each of us would have to serve Lord Stanley and the king. We could be called to war for forty days each year.

The farm was close enough to our smallholding so that I did not need to move to work the land. The house although much larger was in a worse condition than ours and so I decided to demolish the poorer parts of the building, leaving just the living quarters and to put up more buildings for animals. With my shirt removed I laboured alone to move fences so that I had larger fields. The work was exhausting and, when I collapsed into my bed each night, I knew that I had to hire men to labour for me. I could not improve my father's smallholding and clear the new fields without help. The best place to do so would be after weapon practice on Sunday morning. My mother and I attended Christchurch and then I stayed to work with the billmen. My experience meant that they had elected me captain upon my return. My father might have been forgotten by the nobles of England but the men of Ecclestone knew what he had done. Although none knew of my life as a spy all knew that I had fought at Stoke Field and that I had been a captain of billmen in Hedingham. There was, thankfully, no resentment from Old John who had commanded the company. In truth, I think he was glad to be rid of the responsibility. There were more archers than billmen and I was soon elected as captain of the billmen. That was partly because my father had been my predecessor but I liked to think that I had a reputation too. The fact that I still carried what I called the Perkin Warbeck sword, also made me seem like an officer. As we practised, I watched and studied every one of the billmen. I was looking at their skills as a billman but, as a landowner, I was looking for workers and I knew what I sought. I wanted younger men who had few prospects. They would be as I had been before I left home on that fateful day all those years ago. I did not care if they were wild for none had been wilder than I had been.

There were two men who seemed perfect: Thomas Blundell was the third son of a farmer who had a smallholding the same size as my father's and lived in the village at the far end. Robert Mawdesley and his widowed mother lived in the smallest and meanest house in the village. Thomas' father's farm barely generated enough money and food to feed him, his wife and his family while Robert worked as a casual labourer when farmers needed extra hands at harvest time. That they were both poor was an understatement. Both young men were aggressive and had been in trouble for drunken behaviour. They had been hauled before the local magistrate and punished on more than one occasion for riotous behaviour. I had been the same. I had got into fights in Windle and learned to use my fists. While such behaviour put many prospective employers off, I knew that I had the strength of mind to overcome the behaviour and put them on the right path. There were few farmers who could afford to employ men and the only hope for the two men was for them to leave Ecclestone and seek their fortune elsewhere. For all their wildness they both loved the village. I believed that I could change their lives. I smiled to myself as the thought came into my head. I was glad that I had not voiced such a statement before Captain Sam. I know what he would have said, *'What an arrogant man you are, James!'*

After our second session, I invited the two of them for a pint of ale in the local inn. It would be their first test. They could, of course, refuse. Some men have stiff necks or they could abuse my hospitality. I needed men and the two, though they had problems that I could clearly see, had broad backs and looked like potentially good workers. They passed the first test and accepted my invitation for an ale and then somewhat flattered me by asking, as most men did upon first meeting me, about my work for the king and my part in the Perkin Warbeck affair. I had two versions of that story. The one for my family and Sam and the one for the public. I gave them the public story. When I had done, we were on our second pint. This was another part of the test; could they hold their ale and would they abuse my generosity?

"I am a man who likes to come to the point and not waste time in words that mean nothing. You know that I have bought old Jack's farm?" They nodded. "Well I intend to make a going concern of it and I need two likely lads to work for me. I had thought to offer you two the position. Before I waste more words and coins on ale, tell me if the prospect and the rigour of hard work appeals to you."

Thomas said, "That depends, captain, on the pay."

I laughed, "Thomas if you are paid more than three pennies a week at present then I will be surprised and you, Robert, live from hand to mouth." I already knew that a yeoman, such as Robert's father might earn £30 a year from his land. A labourer might be lucky to earn £9 and Thomas far less. I hoped that with my new land I might make £40.

Robert coloured and said, defensively, "I did not ask about the pay, Captain, but there is no need to demean a man so."

My honesty and my brusqueness had struck a nerve but I believed it was better for a man to know what he could expect, "If offering a man employment and pay, not to mention a better house then you have been demeaned. But I do not see it so. I speak truthfully for that is my way and if you do not like such honesty then refuse my offer, I will not be offended. You, Robert, live with your mother in the meanest house in the village."

"But we own it."

"Aye and I offer you the farmhouse at Jack's farm for you and your mother so that you could sell your house. What say you to that?" The house was a burden to his mother. She was still expected to pay taxes although I knew that the earl had not asked for them since Bosworth. If she died Robert might well have to pay taxes and work the fields.

His expression changed and he grinned, "That I had misjudged you, Captain James." I smiled back. The smile disappeared and a frown took its place. "But who would buy the house? There is little land and what there is consists mainly of tares and weeds. The house is almost falling down and the wind whistles through the wattle."

I nodded, "I will buy it and demolish the house. There is a hedge around it and I have a mind to have a small flock of sheep." On the ride home, when I had stayed at inns twixt Hedingham and Ecclestone, I had been made aware of the prices that wool was now commanding. It seemed to me that sheep were a better investment than pigs. True, pigs were easier to feed but once you had eaten them you needed to wait for them to produce young again. With sheep, you could harvest their wool each year and eat them when they could no longer produce young. Open grazing did not suit them but Robert's mother's house was perfect as it was already enclosed.

"You have planned this out then?" I saw Robert realise that while I was young, I had an old head upon my shoulders.

"I have. Now if you are agreeable then you will need to speak to your mother and to answer your question, Thomas, it will be sixpence a day and I will find the food for you both. If I like the way that you work then that might increase to nine pennies a day at the end of the first month. It depends on you. What say you to my offer and my honesty?"

Thomas looked happy and said, without hesitation, "I am your man, Captain James."

Robert nodded eagerly, "As am I. I will ask my mother directly and I know that she will accept the offer."

"Good. You start work on the morrow. Fetch your goods to Jack's farmhouse and have your sleeves rolled up ready for a hard day's work."

When I returned home, I told my mother and father all. I was still unsure how much my father could take in but the twinkle in his eye told me that he approved and my mother thought that giving the widow and her son the farmhouse was a Christian thing to do and showed her that I was reformed. I had, of course, changed but the real reason for my efforts was to make up for the damage I had done in my youth. Then my mother had been ashamed of me and quite rightly so. Now I hoped to make her proud.

The young men and I spent a week on the two new properties. I was gambling that the earl would condone my purchase of the widow's house but even if he did not it was the widow's and she was more than happy to live in the farmhouse that was, to her, palatial. I would still be able to use her field. As Thomas would be living there too, he worked as hard as Robert and we had the house ready for their occupation in three days. The last days of the week we spent demolishing the old wattle and daub dwelling and making the fences and gates secure.

On Saturday we worked on my father's smallholding. Now that we had the adjacent property of Jack's it was more like a farm. When he took it over, he had just grown food for himself and my mother. The fowl they had kept produced a few eggs and with the vegetable field that was all. I set about organising it. I took my two workers to survey the fields. The purchase of Jack's farm had enabled me to gain three fields. With my father's and the widow's and the improvements I had made, I now had five fields. Two would be for sheep and one for wheat. One, the smallest one, would be for greens and smaller crops to sustain the people who lived on the farm. I had doubled the number who would need to be fed.

I used my finger to point, as I went around the various fields. When I came to the fifth one, I said, "And that one shall have peas and beans. Then, when we have harvested it, we shall let it lie fallow until we plant wheat and we shall grow beans there." I looked at Thomas, "Who has the best oxen in the manor?"

He smiled for he knew the purpose of my question. We would need oxen to plough the field for wheat. "There is only one pair, Captain James. Edward Marley has the only oxen and so he charges what he will for their hire." Edward Marley thought

17

himself important and was most unpopular. He was not a billman but an archer although I knew he was not a very good one and far from diligent. At the Sunday practice he rarely managed to hit anything but the shortest of targets.

"Then we shall have to pay him for this year."

Thomas had heard and seen the pigs we had in the small hogbog. My father had one and Jack's farm had come with a brace of them. "Do you intend to keep the pigs or eat them?"

"Jack's farm has a hogbog already behind the cottage. When we go to Ormskirk to buy the sheep we will see if we can pick up a third sow and we can put them all in there. I will demolish my father's and add new rooms to the house." I had listened to my mother and knew that one day I would need more rooms for a family. That was in the future but I knew if I did not plan then my dreams might not come to fruition.

Both had more knowledge of farming than I did but I had spoken with Captain Sam before I had left. He and his wife, Katie, knew farming and had advised me. The two men were impressed by my knowledge. They did not know it was recently acquired.

"There is one more thing. You are both billmen in my company. You are also my workers. I expect high standards from you both. Your days of wild and wilful behaviour are now behind you. You drink within your ability to hold your ale and you keep your fists unclenched."

They nodded and I saw in their eyes that they meant it. I had given them hope of a better life. Both would be earning far more than they had before I had spoken to them and my promise of a roof and food took away two of the greatest fears of the time: hunger and homelessness.

The market at Ormskirk was a good one and as I had two men with me, I took more than half of my money. I was gambling I knew but I was confident that if I ran short, I could always hire on as a billman and earn more. I had never been to the market and did not know what might be on offer. I was prepared. Thomas had brought with him, from his father's farm, one of the sheepdogs. Nipper was Thomas' and they were close. He would marshal the flock on the walk back to Ecclestone. We took him with us with the expectation of buying a flock. We all rode for

Goliath was still with my father and I had brought another sumpter. I dressed as a gentleman and rode a gentleman's horse, Calliope. My time with the pretender had given me a wardrobe that was better than most men's. With my good sword strapped to my side, I was accorded the respect that my father would not have enjoyed as I jostled with yeoman farmers. My time with Perkin Warbeck had given me many skills and habits that marked me more than a simple billman: I could read and write. More importantly, I could speak better English than most men as well as both French and Flemish. That gave me an advantage for the words you use affects men's perceptions of you.

We spent the morning examining the sheep. There were two main types, the long-haired variety and the shorter-haired one. The latter were cheaper but as I could get more money from the long-haired types I had decided that I would buy a flock of longer-haired sheep. It would cost me more but I would simply buy fewer and rely on the fecundity of the ram. I spied the sheep I intended to buy and when the auction began, I bid for the ram I had my eye upon. He had but one horn; it looked as though he had lost one in some battle for a ewe and so I bought him for less than I expected. I hoped that he would be fertile. The ewes were, however, more popular. I was lucky in that I had more funds available. I lost out on the first ewe but I had the price now in my head and I managed to buy the next five ewes. Money was in short supply and each ewe cost me less. The other farmers seemed to want the cheaper short-haired varieties. I was well pleased. I paid the coins out and had my two men gather the tiny flock in a pen while I watched the rest of the auction.

I had not gone there to buy oxen but when the small pair of animals were brought before us, I waited to see what the price might be. The farmer who had the oxen to sell looked as though he had not eaten well for he was thin. His animals, too, were not only immature but I could see bones beneath their skin. The result was that there was only one bid and that was from a slaughterman who wanted the hide and the bones. I suppose I have a sentimental streak in me for I felt sorry for the man who had to sell the animals. I also had a practical side and I saw that as I had one fallow field, I could fatten up the oxen. I would not only save money, for I would not have to pay Edward Marley, but when the oxen were grown, I would have an income from their hire. I bid far more than the slaughterman but still below their true value to me. They were mine.

The farmer was grateful for the coins. He knuckled his forehead for my clothes and swords made him think that I was a gentleman, "Thank you, sir. I have fallen on hard times. My crops failed and I lost the land. These are all that is left to me."

I nodded, "And what will you do now?"

"Hire out as a labourer I suppose. I have a wife and a bairn. We still have a house over Meols way and I know how to farm."

I nodded, "I am Captain James of Ecclestone. If you cannot find work then I am seeking men to work for me."

"That is a kind offer, Captain, but my wife and her family all come from Meols. I shall try my luck there. If I fail then I may take you up on your offer." He nodded to the two animals, "They are called Hercules and Caesar. They are castrated and good animals. It has hurt me to let them go but I can see that they will have a good home. Anyone who can afford fine clothes such as you wear will be able to provide for two such oxen."

"Do not be deceived by clothes my friend and what is your name?"

"Giles Sharrap, Captain, of Meols."

There was little point in my riding home as I had to lead the oxen. I let my men ride their sumpters as they learned to work with Nipper to control the small flock. They had to ride back and forth to keep the flock under control. The ram proved to be an obstinate beast and Nipper had his work cut out with the animal. Hercules and Caesar seemed happy for me to lead them with the tether through their nose rings. It was dark when we reached our home. I was just glad that Jack had a good barn where we could house the oxen. There was enough hay left to feed them. The next day I began my life as a yeoman farmer.

It was autumn when I received the summons to go to Lathom and meet with the earl. By then we had managed to plough a field and plant winter barley. The ram, despite his behaviour on the way from the market where he had been so awkward, had proved to be fertile and had managed to impregnate the whole flock. As a result, I hoped to double the number of sheep by the spring. The beans had grown well as had the greens we had planted. There were enough wild rabbits around for us to have meat of some type to eat and we even caught enough fish from the small fishpond in the village to have fish every Friday.

I rode my horse to Lathom and made sure that I had on my finest clothes. My mother inspected me before I left and I saw the pride in her eyes. The prodigal son had changed his ways.

Lord Thomas had aged since I had last seen him and I did not think he was long for this world. He was a rich and powerful man but two of his sons had already died young and the steward had told me on my last visit that his eldest surviving son, George, Lord Strange had consumption. The earl and his family, despite their position, appeared to have ill luck.

He did, however, remember me. He beamed when he saw me, "I was surprised that you left Sir Edward's service, Ecclestone, but I am pleased for me." I wondered at that. Why should my arrival here make him happy? I just bowed my head and nodded as I knew not what to say. "Before we begin to discuss our business in earnest I can confirm my steward's decision to allow you to buy the land in Ecclestone."

"Thank you, my lord, and can I ask permission to buy the land of Widow Mawdesley in Ecclestone?"

He frowned and turned to his steward. I knew that Thomas Crouchley would have the information. The steward answered, "The land and house have fallen into disrepair. The widow and her son have not been able to pay your taxes for the last few years." He shrugged, "It is a small and mean property and brought in but two pounds a year, my lord. I did not think it worth our while to collect especially as she was a widow whose husband fell at Bosworth." I saw then the generosity I had ascribed to Lord Stanley was, in fact, the steward's.

The earl nodded, "Just so. And you believe that you can make this small and mean land profitable?"

"I hope so. I have plans."

He laughed, "You are a resourceful fellow. The king thinks highly of you. Make it so, Thomas, and have the deeds drawn up." He waved a hand at his steward, "Leave us and have some wine sent in."

I was surprised that the king even remembered me. He had struck me as a cold fish but so long as it kept me in the Earl of Derby's favour then I was happy.

The wine came and I sipped it. My time at the court of Perkin Warbeck had allowed me to develop a taste for good food and wine. I was still able to eat poor rations and drink vinegary beer but I enjoyed good wine and food. The wine I had been given was a good one.

"You may wonder, Captain James, why I was pleased that you have come back to your home."

"Yes, my lord, for I know that even with my improvements the land I farm will be but as a drop in the ocean of your income."

He waved a dismissive hand, "That is nothing. You are a soldier and a damned good one too. Sir Edward had high expectations of you. You know that my son, Sir Edward, Baron Monteagle is High Sherriff of Lancashire?"

"I did not, my lord."

"Aye, the king himself appointed him and charged him with keeping the Scots at bay."

"I thought we were at peace, my lord."

He laughed, "Peace? With the Scots? That is an illusion. All the while that good King Henry fought the Yorkists the Scots raided farms and lands whose warriors were fighting for the crown. They still do. The first King Edward had the right idea; make the Scots part of England and control them with castles. I am pleased that you are here for I am giving you command of the billmen of my manor. You are young but skilled and I believe you will make my billmen a potent force. There are one hundred men in total."

"I am flattered, my lord, but when will I have the time for I have a farm to manage?"

"I need you for once a month in the summer and once a fortnight in the winter. You will come here and train the billmen of the manor. It will be in place of their Sunday practice." His eyes narrowed, "This is not a request, Captain Ecclestone, it is a command. There will, of course, be a payment. You shall be paid £10 per annum."

I kept an impassive face but it meant I had security from financial ruin and, in truth, I wanted to be a soldier again, even if only on a part-time basis.

"What say you to this more than generous offer?" His words had a threat behind them. I had to obey.

"I am honoured that you have chosen me to help guard Lancashire, my lord, and I will do all in my power to lead your men well."

"There will be livery for you. I want all to know that it is my men that you lead." He spoke at some length about the make up of his billmen. It seemed that the twelve I led from Ecclestone was a typical number. Standish, Ormskirk, Meols, Burscough and all the other manors provided similar numbers. I could see why he wanted them trained together. As I left, he said, "There will be an invitation for you to dine with my son at Hornby Castle. Are you married?"

The question seemed incongruous and it confused me, "Married, my lord?"

"If you were then your wife should accompany you but I can see that you are still a bachelor. You should be married, Ecclestone. It keeps a man's feet on the ground."

As I headed home, I reflected that it was not just my mother who wished to see me wed and I would have to begin work on new buildings sooner rather than later.

Chapter 2

The invitation came in November for the feast of Epiphany, held on January the 6th. The liveried messenger who brought the invitation also told me that I would be expected to stay overnight. That was a relief as Hornby Castle was on the Lune and the short days of January would have meant a hard journey otherwise. My mother, of course, was all of a fluster as she fussed over me. She ensured that I packed all that I might need. By the time I left, I was happy that my two new men would be able to not only watch over my lands but my family too. Both had given up on their wild ways and even begun courting, now that they had money, two girls from the village. Once more the clothes bought for me when I had been a spy meant I had a more comfortable journey. It was over fifty miles to the castle which lay north of Lancaster and I broke my journey at an inn in Garstang.

I arrived at the inn after dark and as my horse was stabled, I could not help smiling. When I had run away from home to join the army fighting the rebels it had been summer but now that I had coins in my purse my journey was more comfortable. My sword, hat and cloak marked me as a traveller with money and heads were knuckled when I entered. I would be charged more than the real rate for the room unless I let them know I was aware of their attempt at rooking. When the price for the room was given, I gave a thin smile, "So, innkeeper, when I arrive at Hornby Castle tomorrow to dine with the High Sherriff of Lancaster do you think he would approve of your overly high prices?"

The ingratiating smile left his face and he paled, "Baron Monteagle?"

"Aye, for I am to become the captain of billmen of the Earl of Derby and shall be using this road more often. Perhaps I should seek another inn that does not try to rob honest travellers."

"No, captain, my first price was a mistake. I was not thinking." He gave me a price that was half of the first and I was taken to a room that was far better than I had expected in such a rural location. I had much to thank the rebels for. They had taught me confidence. The boy who had walked north had been changed when they had tried to use me for their own ends.

Hornby Castle had fine defensive qualities but the baron had made it a large comfortable home as befitted the son of an earl and the High Sherriff of Lancaster. Liveried servants took my horse and my bags and I was whisked into the Great Hall where a wave of heat and perfume hit me. I had become used to the fashion at Perkin Warbeck's court. The great and the good had bags of herbs secreted beneath their clothes. Called swete bagges, they made everyone smell slightly better than they might have otherwise. However, such a collection of smells made me slightly nauseous when I entered.

A liveried footman approached me, "Captain James?" I nodded, "You have arrived a little later than we expected. The first feast will begin soon. I fear you will not have time to change."

I was well aware that I stank of the sweat from my horse. "Have you somewhere I can freshen my clothes?" He led me to a small antechamber where there was a jug of water, a bowl and some towels. A jug with herbs stood in the corner of the room. He waited without and I began to use some of the tricks I had been taught in Flanders. I washed not only my hands and face but also used the cloths to wipe over my hose and boots. The servants would need to change the cloths but I had learned that the great and the good never minded making work for servants. Then, taking some rosemary, I dipped it in the water and used that to wipe down the sleeves of my tunic and my hose. It was not perfect and my clothes were slightly damp but I had taken away the majority of the smell of horse. The servant smiled when I reappeared, nodding his approval.

The Great Hall had been rearranged in the time I had been in the small antechamber and chairs and tables were now in place. Servants directed the guests to their seats. There was, as I well knew, a hierarchy to such things. I was not even a gentleman and, as I expected, I was seated at the lower end of the table with some local yeoman and their wives. I was, it seemed, the only bachelor. The couple opposite me were from Preston. He was a yeoman farmer and I could see that he was uncomfortable in the clothes he wore. His wife also had the ruddy features of one who spends long hours out of doors. They were in direct contrast to those closer to the baron and his wife. They were peacocks. The man next to me was a clerk. He had ink-stained fingers and his wife was a thin-faced nervous looking woman. I spent more time speaking with the farmer opposite. The clerk did not see me as important enough to warrant a conversation. I had learned that such feasts were a way for those who had social aspirations to rise. The clerk sought someone who might give him more financially rewarding work.

There was silence as the baron's chaplain said Grace and we all bowed our heads. Servants brought cloths that they draped over our left shoulders to wipe our hands upon. I had been unsure if knives would be provided for eating and I had brought the one I had used in Flanders. It was beautifully made of silver with inlaid mother of pearl but I did not need to fetch it forth for the servants provided us with the means to slice food.

The yeoman farmer, Thurston Bythell, was a blunt man who came to the point and he began to question me as soon as the servants left to fetch in the food, "So, sir, what brings a bachelor I do not know all the way north of the River Ribble to a feast with the High Sherriff? You have travelled far today."

His wife, Sarah Ann, asked, "How do you know husband?"

He chuckled, "I can smell horse. He might have used herbs to disguise it but I know the smell."

I laughed for I liked the man immediately. I appreciated honesty, "You are right, sir. I have travelled from Ecclestone where I have a farm."

"That is a long journey and means that you must have been accorded a room here in the castle."

The clerk turned when he heard the statement. I was suddenly a person of interest. "I have been given a chamber, aye. The High Sherriff has business with me."

The servants had brought the food while we had been talking and my fellow diners' attention was drawn to the array of delicacies on offer. They were tempting and well presented but I had eaten better at the court of the duchess. There was silence at the lower end of the table as the delicacies were devoured. The pike was well cooked and well flavoured. In contrast to the clerk and the farmer, I ate sparingly for I knew there would be more food to come and eyes would be watching to see if I refused any of the courses. As we awaited a second course the farmer wiped his hands on the napkin which lay over his shoulder and said, "So what business brings a farmer fifty miles in the middle of winter to speak with the High Sherriff?"

"I am the Captain of Billmen for his father, the Earl of Derby."

At that point, the clerk, not to mention those higher up the lowest of tables looked up. I was suddenly of more importance for I had mentioned the earl.

"You are young for such a position if you do not mind me saying so."

I nodded, "I know it and yet I have fought many times. I was at the battle of Stoke Field."

The simple statement was enough and I saw the farmer's face. He beamed, "And yet you farm. Do you mind me asking the size of your farm?"

I laughed, "I am a soldier who has taken to the plough and my farm is small. I have a pair of small oxen, a flock of sheep and five fields. I employ but two men."

His wife leaned over, "And I can remember a time when my husband and I were the same. It is good that you start small for that is how you will learn."

"Aye, but keep your billhook sharp, young sir. I now know why his lordship has asked for you to stay here. We provide an income for the county but it is you who will have to defend it against the Scots."

For the first time I was surprised, "I was not aware that there was danger from them."

The farmer laughed, "King James is ambitious and has an alliance with the French. He encourages his men to raid across the border for cattle." Slicing a piece of pork, complete with crackling from the pig that had been brought in he added, "The border is not clear and only Carlisle acts as a defence. There are many passes that can be used by raiders who descend upon farms, take cattle and sometimes kill farmers."

"As far south as the Ribble?"

"Once they came regularly. Now it is less frequent but the Lune is often attacked and the lands to the east of Carlisle suffer

every year. Farmers have complained. The Sherriff of
Westmoreland cannot hold back the Scots and Baron Monteagle
has promised that he will add the weight of Lancashire against
these intruders. I hope you have good men working your farm
for you may be absent more than you are present." My face must
have fallen for he continued, "What?"

"My two labourers are billmen in my company. If I go to war
then they will be with me."

His wife said, "You need a couple of boys to be shepherds.
They do not cost much and if you have someone to supervise
them then you can leave your farm for a short while."

"Aye, my wife is right. You will only have to be away for
forty days and your billmen will be paid for their service. I am
now too old to be called to war and employ others to do my
service."

"Thank you for your advice. I am glad that I was seated here.
A billhook is a more familiar weapon to me than a plough."

"And yet I can see by your fine sword that there is more to
you than meets the eye. I too am grateful that I was seated here
for I now feel that my lands will be safer."

I did not get to speak to the baron that night. I realised that I
had been invited to the feast merely to facilitate a talk the next
day. I was awakened before dawn by a liveried servant and taken
down to the Great Hall where the baron was dining alone.

"Sit Captain James, for we have much to talk about."

Servants brought us food. Most of the fare consisted of the
leftovers from the feast but there was freshly made porridge
which I ate before the meats and fish.

When we were alone the baron said, "My father has told me
of your past, Captain, and I am impressed. When I spied you last
evening I was surprised at your youth. Know that I will be
calling upon your services once the winter is over. You will need
to give me the forty days of service you owe my father and
England. You will need to make arrangements for your farm."
The earl, of course, knew that I had spied for King Henry and
been party to the capture of Perkin Warbeck. That news did not
alarm me but the thought that I might have to leave the farm
unattended did.

"My lord, it is not just me who will need to make arrangements. If I bring the billmen from your father then who will work the fields and tend to the animals?"

He nodded and wiped his mouth, "The men you lead will have to make sacrifices and your men will be paid. Last year the Scots came in spring and they raided many farms. The wealth of this part of England lies in sheep. You are a farmer?" I nodded, "And how many sheep do you have?"

"A small flock, less than ten sheep, my lord."

"North of here there are flocks in their hundreds and last year a third of the flocks were taken."

"I thought that it was cattle that were taken, my lord."

"It was but the greater number of animals that were taken were sheep." He stood, "Take food with you if you wish but we ride today and I hope you have a good horse for it will be dark when we return."

Sir Edward's choice of horse had been a good one. Calliope might have been named after a Greek Muse but she was a stout horse with the heart of a warhorse. She was slightly smaller than Sir Edward's warhorse but had the same sire and I was more than happy with her. Wrapped in my good riding cloak and with my beaver skin hat on my head I was ready for the elements. Two of the baron's men at arms rode with us as we headed north.

"We ride to Sedbergh for it was there that the Scots came last year. I need you to see the land where we will fight them."

"My lord, it will take me more than four days to march my men from Lathom."

He turned and smiled, "And the same to march back. I know what you are thinking. That will leave just a month to deter the Scots." The baron was a clever man and I nodded. "The Sherriff of Westmoreland has men watching for the Scots. He cannot stop them for there are too many places they can cross the border for, as you know, there is no firm border here. The old Roman wall is merely a rough marker. We will have a warning of their arrival and our bill men and archers will be needed merely to hold them until the men of Westmoreland fall upon them. That is why we use men from the south of the county. The billmen I could use will be needed to defend their farms. Your billmen and the archers who will come with you will be our only defence.

You need not bring all your billmen, just the best. I shall lead you all but the two hundred billmen and archers that you bring from my father will be the ones who face the Scots."

"Then we shall do all in our power to resist this incursion."

The land through which we rode became increasingly wilder. The road we travelled was rough and I saw many places that could be used for an ambush. We reached Sedbergh by noon and the baron was welcomed in the village. It was not a large place and I saw that there was nothing that could be used to defend it. It had neither a wall nor castle. There was not even a tower that could be used as a refuge. The headman of the village, a red-headed farmer fed us and then took us on a tour. It did not take long. He showed us the large farm that had been raided and destroyed in the last attack. I spied the remains of a derelict wooden castle that had not been used for some hundreds of years. He also pointed out other farms that had suffered.

"As his lordship knows, we lost more than two hundred sheep and four cattle. Our village cannot afford to lose more."

I shook my head, "I am surprised that you have stayed so long. The loss of so many animals would have broken both my heart and my spirit."

He gave me a grim smile, "You are not from around here so I will explain. My family has farmed here for generations. We were here before the Normans came and I can trace my ancestors back to the Saxon, Thurston of Sedbergh. I may not have a title but this is my land and no hairy-arsed Scotsman is going to drive me from it. His lordship has promised us that this time we will fight fire with fire and I thank God for that."

The baron nodded, his agreement, "And that is why, Captain James, you and your men will wait here, in Sedbergh for the marauding brigands who will come to take the new lambs and calves in the spring."

When I returned home, three days later, I had much to do. I sat with my father and two labourers to tell them my news. I had learned to read my father's fallen face and knew that despite his affliction he could understand everything that was said.

"Our families will be safe here, Captain?"

"Aye, Robert, but we need to make arrangements so that our livestock does not suffer."

Thomas said, "You know I am courting Ellen Tildsley?"

"Aye and a comely maid she is."

"She has a brother, William, and he knows animals. He is but twelve years old but he has an old head on his shoulders. I believe he would relish the opportunity to watch the sheep while we are away."

"But it will be in lambing season. I had hoped to be here to supervise the births. It will be our income."

My father spoke. His voice was slurred but he spoke slowly so that we could hear every word. "I can watch the boy and the sheep you have bought need no man's hand to help them birth. I can do more, my son, than sit here and be as a stone. My face has slipped and my arm is not as strong as it once was but the heart within me still beats. You go to defend this land and I am proud that you do so. Let me be a man again for however little a time God allows."

My mother put her hand on his and said, "And I can help too. You have made our lives better with your return. We can cope for forty days."

And so it was settled. William was, indeed, eager and he moved in directly. Over the next weeks, I trained hard with my billmen and worked even harder on the farm. There were not enough hours in the day for all that I had to do. When the call came from the earl for the muster the farm was as ready as we could expect. I did not take every billman, just the youngest. We still had enough men and the village would not be robbed of every man. With our billhooks across our backs and blankets and helmets on Goliath, I marched my men to Lathom. I also led the archers. They would be commanded by another but the men of Ecclestone marched together.

The earl had erected tents for us but Captain Richard and myself were invited into Lathom Hall to both dine and to speak. Captain Richard came from Burscough and had all the hallmarks of a master archer. Shorter than I was he had the barrel chest and the mighty arms that marked all great archers. He was dour but I liked him immediately.

The earl gestured to me with his knife as we ate, "Captain James has already visited Sedbergh, Captain Richard. He will explain your purpose."

I told the archer what we had to do and the nature of the land. "So we are waiting for the Scots to come and we fight them?"

I nodded, "The village is the bait and we will be hidden so that we may ambush them."

"And how many men do we face?"

"From what I can gather the Scots come with large numbers. The warbands will just be twenty or so in numbers but there will be twenty such warbands that filter down from the border. They gather and then attack."

The archer nodded as he drank some of the earl's ale, "And that is why they cannot be stopped further north. Then we shall stop them at Sedbergh." He looked at the earl, "And if they do not come in the allotted time we shall give, my lord?"

"They will."

The archer persisted, "But if not?"

"Then you shall stay there until they do."

"And be paid."

"And be paid."

The archer seemed satisfied with that.

"And if they come early, my lord? In the first days, we are there?"

The earl smiled, "Why, Captain James, then you can come back and still have the payment for the forty days."

That was good news to my ears and I would pray that they did, indeed, come early.

Chapter 3

The march north, in the teeth of bitingly cold winds, was a good opportunity to get to know the men we led. Not all were happy to be going to war. In fact, more than half were reluctant to be so far from their homes and they complained all the way to the Ribble where we camped. It was at the camp that I had the first threat to my authority. One of the men from Chorley, George Hayward objected to my order asking him to do sentry duty. We were taking it in turns and the night when we camped at the Ribble was Chorley's turn. It merely meant losing an hour of sleep and thus far none had objected. George was a huge brute of a man. With a broken nose and scarred knuckles, I knew that he was also a bully who liked to fight. He was not the leader of the Chorley men but he had their leader cowed.

"We are still close to our home and do not need a sentry and no pretty boy with a fancy sword is going to make me do a duty."

He did not say the words to me but to the men around his fire however, it was clear to whom he alluded. Ralph Appleton, the Chorley captain, had made the request. George made sure that I could hear the words and they were a challenge to my authority.

"Captain Ralph, is all well?"

The man shook his head, "Some of my men say they will not do their duty."

I nodded and kept an impassive face. "Yet the Earl of Derby has put these men under our command and they are dutybound to obey our orders." I whipped around to face the loudmouth. "Is there any other man except for this tub of lard who objects to standing a watch as all the other men have done?" That did two things. It made the giant rise to his feet and his comrades laugh.

"Who are you calling a tub of lard?"

I shook my head, "Stupid as well as insubordinate. Why you, of course. Now either you do a duty or you can head back home and await the punishment meted out by his lordship for failing to fulfil his sworn service."

I knew I had angered him enough and when he suddenly roared and launched himself at me, I was ready. I had been handy with my fists as a young man and knew how to fight. It was simple enough to step to the side and punch him hard in the ribs as he passed me. Roaring like a castrated bull he turned and came at me again. This time I did not move out of the way but when he swung at my head I ducked and hit him with my right hand at exactly the same place I had hit him with my left. I heard the bone break and then I punched him hard in the stomach. He had not had time to tense the muscles and he was winded. He doubled up and I brought my right fist under his chin. It was a well-struck blow and he fell to the ground, unconscious. Men applauded.

"Now, men of Chorley, you will all do a sentry watch this night. Every man in this contingent will lose, while we are on this duty, two hours of sleep. It is a small price to pay for safety. Does anyone else object?"

They shook their heads. I turned to see a grinning pair of faces behind me, "Thomas and Robert, you must have things to do and if not, I can find tasks for you."

Shaking their heads they hurried off. Captain Richard came over, "You are handy with your fists, James. I thought he would have demolished you."

"Bullies like that are easy to defeat but it has shown me why he is not the leader of the Chorley men. He has not the wit. I will speak with Captain Ralph on the way north. We cannot afford dissension when we face the Scots."

George was in too much pain for him to cause trouble. I spoke with his captain as we crossed the Ribble and headed for the Lune and gave him advice. George was in so much pain that he struggled to keep up and I knew that his days of dissension were over. Captain Ralph explained that he knew George was a bully but he was a fierce fighter.

"Captain Ralph, when you are a leader then lead. In battle, the men must obey you instantly."

He smiled, "You are far younger than I am, and yet you seem to have a greater knowledge of the role than do I."

"I served in a professional company of billmen and so I have seen more war than you. This little campaign may be just what you need to show you how to lead in battle and not just in practice."

The rain that struck us just before Sedbergh was a foretaste of what we could expect. Whilst winter had gone, this part of England was never warm. We were given the derelict fort as our home. I had persuaded Captain Richard on the way north that this would be the best place for us to use as despite the fallen and rotted wooden walls there were ditches and it was on a high part of ground. We made hovels from timber in lieu of tents and we settled down to wait. I had the men cut brambles to lay around the ditches. They would not stop an enemy from trying to surprise us but they would give us a warning. The thorns were still sharp.

The red-headed farmer, Henry Gilbert, invited Captain Richard and me to dine. It was plain fare for his purpose was to tell us news. "We have twenty men in the village who can be called upon to fight. I only have three archers and three billmen but the others know how to fight. I will place myself under your command."

I nodded, "The baron should be here in a day or so."

Henry said, "I am surprised he did not come with you."

I had already discussed this with Captain Richard and we knew the reason, "He will bring our only horsemen and I suspect will spend as short a time as he can here in this exposed piece of England. Do not worry, it will be the men here that have to face the foe."

The baron arrived three days later and his arrival coincided with the messenger from the Sherriff of Westmoreland who reported that the Scots had crossed the wall and we could expect them in days. They had raided isolated farms already and he had mustered the fyrd. The baron had us prepare our defences. We would be hidden in the houses and the farms to the north of the village. The baron and his riders would shadow the Scots when they were close and let us know when they were near enough for us to ambush them. The Sherriff of Westmoreland would be bringing his men to slam the gate and destroy any Scots who escaped us. Henry and his villages were to be the bait. They would wait in the walled yard of Henry's farm. He had told us that was where they had attacked the last time they had come. He warned us that the Scots like to come at dawn. That did not surprise me and I took the leaders of the different groups of billmen to give them my plans.

"The archers can rain death from a distance but we need to be in a solid block to face them. If it is still dark when the Scots come then the archers will not be as effective. We must be prepared to bear the brunt of the fighting. When I have the horn sounded then every billman gathers close to me. We will have two ranks and my intention is to fall upon the rear of the Scots when they attack the farm."

"I thought you said that the men of Westmoreland would fall upon their rear."

"They will, Ned, but if the Scots come at dawn, then the men of Westmoreland will still be marching to our aid."

To be truthful, and a man is always true to himself, I was looking forward to this fight. My last fight had been against mercenaries. This would be against a more traditional enemy, the Scots. Did I still have the skills to kill? That would be the difference between me and many of the men I led. I knew we had to kill and kill quickly. Some of those who had yet to slice their bill into an enemy might hesitate. That could be the difference between life and death.

It would be an uncomfortable night. The men I led were not the company I had led in Hedingham. There Stephen and I had drilled the men so that they acted and fought as one. The ones I led, Thomas and Robert apart, were of differing standards. Some were slower and some were faster. I had not had the time yet, with the few practices we had managed, to hone them into a weapon that was keen. I did not sleep but prowled amongst the houses and walls where my company sheltered and slept. I walked on one side and Captain Richard on the other. He, at least, knew that his men could stand, draw and release with monotonous regularity. They did not have to change formation and for them, the killing was almost remote. They would not see the man their arrow slew. Indeed, I knew that a good archer did not even need to look at his target. Once he had the range his arms drew back the bow almost as though by magic.

We heard the Scots as they moved towards us in the hours before dawn. They were trying to be silent but some of them wore mail and metal scraping along metal could be heard. They came, not only down the main road in Sedbergh but I heard them to the east and west, flanking the village. I had miscalculated. Henry Gilbert had thought that the last time they had come the Scots had followed the main road through the town. Either he had been wrong or they had changed their tactics this time. I was with my own contingent when I heard them and I roused my men and donned my helmet. We had a low wall before us. The enclosure in which we stood was normally used for sheep but they had all been taken south of the village. The archers with us strung their bows. I took my horn and placed it close to my lips. The sounding of the horn would be the signal to attack. The archers would rain death and we, the billmen, would hold off the Scots when they tried to get to the archers. That was the plan and, as plans go, it was a good one.

However, it relied on every archer and billman remaining silent. Someone, on the far side of the road, spoke. I still know not why and a Scottish voice shouted, "Ware, ambush!" The result was that shields were raised as arrows fell and the Scots at the sides turned to charge us. Gilbert and his villagers would not be needed. Baron Monteagle and his horsemen were also sleeping on the farm and they would need time to saddle and mount their horses. Worse news was to come. The men behind the village, on both sides, heard the cries and they came to their comrade's aid. I sounded the horn, late though it was.

I had placed Captain Ralph and his men close to us, for obvious reasons and I said, "Captain Ralph, you and your company deal with these Scots. Billmen of Ecclestone, follow me."

I led my men through our archers who parted to let us through. Behind me, I heard the cries as men were struck with arrows and then the clash of metal as their swordsmen duelled with Captain Ralph and his men. Thomas and Robert were at my side. We had benefitted from far more practice than the rest of the company. We would often spar at night and as we left the gate at the rear of the enclosure and came upon the Scots racing to get at our ambush we acted as one and caught the raiders by surprise. The three billhooks stabbed together in complete harmony. The heads were splayed in an arc and the three men we struck all suffered mortal wounds. Even more important was the fact that it allowed the rest of Ecclestone to form a small double line before the gate to the enclosure.

"We hold them here!"

As I looked down the line, I took great satisfaction in the men at the two ends of the line. Walter Hope sliced his billhook through the legs of the Scot trying to climb the enclosure wall while at the other end Jack Wheelwright disembowelled the Scot who tried the same thing there.

A man I took, by the plume in his helmet, to be a chief roared something in what I assumed to be Gaelic and his men formed into an untidy knot and ran at us. They held a variety of weapons. Most had vicious-looking broad swords favoured by such raiders but a few had long spears. The chief came for me with his sword and small buckler. He was flanked by four men with spears and they jabbed their spears straight at me. There might have been a time when I would have been afeared but I now wore a breastplate as well as a helmet and I had trained Thomas and Robert well. The billhook has not only a sharp head but a well-honed blade and the two men swept their billhooks to hack the spears in twain. I lunged at the chief. He was an older warrior and he deflected the head easily with his buckler. He then tried to skewer me with his sword but I had spent many hours with Sam and Stephen. I swept the billhook back across him and the metal scraped and scratched across his sword. I saw that he wore a breastplate and as we both pulled back our weapons for the next strike, I chose a move he was not expecting. I used the hook on his breastplate and instead of thrusting, pulled. As he lost his balance and came forward his sword struck not my body but the side of my head. My billhook was held diagonally across my body and while the hook was still caught in the breastplate the edge of the bill was not and I pulled it hard across his face. He wore a helmet but there was no protection for his cheek and the edge bit into flesh. Blood spurted and he tried to roar. The billhook had taken off his nose and the scream seemed unreal and not human. I tried something then that was a trick taught to me by Sam. I brought the shaft of the billhook up between his legs. I struck him so hard and so unexpected was the blow that he doubled up. Robert saw his chance and his billhook took the chief's head.

Rather than disheartening the Scots the death of their chief enraged them but in that rage came recklessness and well-used billhooks can make what looks like an easy space to use a sword or a spear suddenly become a death trap. They came without order. I know not if they simply sought to get their chief's body or wished to wreak revenge on the three of us in the centre. We had to fight furiously simply to defend ourselves. It was the men in the second rank, whose billhooks poked, prodded and stabbed between our heads who did the real damage. The Scots did not see the billhooks coming for their faces and they fell.

Suddenly I heard the sound of horses and heard the baron's voice, "For King Henry, St George, and England!"

Of course, the Scots could not know that the baron led barely a handful of riders. All that they heard were the hooves and the cry of a knight. They turned and fled which was exactly what the Sherriff wanted for as they turned the spears of his horsemen exacted a terrible revenge.

I saw that, as the horsemen pursued the Scots, we had thwarted their flanking attack, "Back to the village."

Dawn was breaking as we rejoined the fight on the main road through Sedbergh. The fight, it was hardly worth the name of battle, was over. Gilbert and his villagers had joined the fight and the Scots had fled. Billmen lay dead. Captain Ralph had done his work well but six of his men would not see their homes again. The bully George lay dead. I wondered if the broken rib had contributed to his death. Any weakness can be exploited by a determined foe. I could not go back and change what had happened and given the same circumstances I would do it all in the same way.

Captain Richard was unstringing his bow, "At least we can get back to our homes earlier than we might have expected. Did I hear the Sherriff and his horsemen?"

I pointed to the north and west, "Aye, he will chase them to meet the Sherriff of Westmoreland. Few Scots will reach their homes and the ones that do will rue the day they chose to raid Sedbergh." I turned to my men, "Come let us see what we can take from the dead." I smiled at Gilbert, "When the bodies are burned you will have fine ashes to put on your fields."

"Aye, good will come of this. We are indebted to your men, captains, we will ever be in your debt. Lords and kings may decide what must be done but it is the likes of us that have to do the fighting."

He was right. We reached the gate of the enclosure as the sun broke behind us. Already rats and foxes were trying to get at the bodies and they fled when we approached.

I pointed to the dead chief, "You killed him, Robert. His helmet and breastplate are yours. Thomas, you may have the sword." I turned to my men, "Take what you can from the dead for the bodies will be burned. Better that we benefit from their deaths than the earth. I found a purse in the chief's belt and took it. I would share the bounty with my men. He also had a fine dagger, they called them a dirk, in his boot. That too went into my belt. I let my men collect all the rest and, as we had lost not a man, we were in good spirits when, after lighting the fire beneath the corpses, we headed back to Gilbert's farm. I was in a reflective mood for I had learned valuable lessons. One was that our billmen needed more training and another was that a village was not the place to use billmen and archers. You needed an open field. We had been lucky and I knew it.

The handful of prisoners were all hanged when the two sheriffs returned. They were all given a brief trial but their fate was already sealed. There was great satisfaction amongst our leaders for this was the first time that such cooperation had been attempted. As we dined with the two sheriffs on Henry Gilbert's farm, we were told that we had ended the threat from the Scots.

Baron Monteagle said, "This was an expensive foray for Lancashire but it has taught the Scots a lesson. They can no longer simply raid across the border for England is no longer at war with itself and we can defend ourselves." He leaned over to me, "And you have proved yourself to be every bit as resourceful as my father said. I shall not forget your service."

We marched back to Ecclestone the next day. Now that we were going home, we had no need to stay in one company. Men were eager to get back to their own fields. We would be paid by the Sherriff for forty days of service but we had completed far less than that. The Scots had not been rich but every warrior had a few coins in their purses and so every man in my company was

richer. The chief had even had silver in his purse and my
company each enjoyed the equivalent of a week's wages. With
the money earned from the Sherriff, the men of Ecclestone had
done well from the action. Poor Goliath was the one who
suffered as we had Robert's metal haul as well as my armour,
helmets and weapons. It took a week to reach our home and I
was relieved that all appeared well when the mill and the village
hove into view. We settled back into the life of farming and
training quickly and I had almost forgotten the skirmish at
Sedbergh when, in August of that year, a pair of shepherds drove
a small flock of long-haired sheep up to my farm.

The older shepherd knuckled his head, "You are Captain
James of Ecclestone?"

"I am."

He nodded, "We have come from Master Bythell, he sent you
these ten sheep, all good breeding ewes to thank you for what
you did at Sedbergh."

My mother had come to the door and she frowned, "Master
Bythell?"

"A farmer from up Preston way, mother. I met him at Hornby
Castle."

She shook her head, "Thomas, Robert, see to the sheep and
you two poor men have walked many a mile, come inside and I
will feed you." She shook her head at me, "And you, James,
need to learn to be hospitable!"

The shepherds smiled at me as she led them inside. I could
not win.

The two men stayed the night and spent some hours with
young William, my shepherd. The lessons they gave him proved
invaluable. I also learned a lesson. The skirmish at Sedbergh
would never be recorded by monks and nobles but for the people
of that part of the county, the action had been as important as
Bosworth Field. Thurston Bythell had shown that by his
generous gift. It also told me that he was a successful yeoman
farmer for as his shepherds told us, the ten ewes we had been
given were a tiny part of the flocks he kept on the fells. As the
first year of the new century came to an end I had ceased to be
King Henry's tool to be used when he saw fit. I was a farmer and
almost a gentleman and I had a position. I was well thought of

not only in Ecclestone but also in the county. The High Sherriff knew me and the Earl of Derby thought well of me. His gift of a pair of sheepdogs was also a thoughtful one. I thought that my days of war were over.

Chapter 4

Lathom 1502

My next visit to the earl was two years after my first although
I knew, from the visits of his tax collectors, that I was well
respected. I was invited to a feast at his palatial home. I left a
farm that now had eight fields, for I had bought more and we
now had pigs as well as a large flock of sheep. My two labourers
had married the girls they had courted and although Robert's
mother had died, my father, sick though he was, soldiered on. I
had taken on another boy, Michael, to help William who was
now almost a man and a skilled shepherd. I had a company of
billmen that were the envy of the rest of Lancashire. The
skirmish at Sedbergh had honed them and they were now the
equal of the one I had trained at Hedingham.

The earl was not a well man and I wondered at my invitation.
His messenger advised me to bring clothes for a stay of some
days. When I arrived, I was taken to a fine room and that
surprised me for I was not, in my view, important enough to
warrant such a room. I was then accorded a rare privilege, a
meeting with the earl in private chambers. He looked genuinely
pleased to see me. "Captain James, you come here too rarely.
You and I have shared in some of the greatest events in the
history of our country. Men know my story but yours remains
hidden and I find that sad."

I could tell he was in a maudlin mood. My father also
suffered such melancholy and I took it as a sign of age.
Impending death will do that to a man. "I am content, my lord,
that I was able to serve and I am content with my life."

"And yet, Captain, you are single and England needs your
blood to continue. You know I have had eleven children?" I
nodded, "When I am gone, they will continue to serve this great
country. You need to look to your future too." He leaned
forward, "I have invited some guests this night to meet you. Like
you they are not nobles but as I have learned over the years many
who are nobles have not an ounce of nobility in them and there
are others, like you, who reek of honour. Enjoy yourself this
night and get to know others who will shape this part of
Lancashire for years to come. It will be my grandson, Thomas,

who will be the next Earl of Derby and I want him to have men around him who are loyal Lancastrians and Englishmen."

I could tell that he wished to talk and I was honoured that he was confiding in me. He had been unlucky with his children and more had died than had survived. That one of his sons was High Sherriff and another was Bishop of Ely spoke well of the man and his power but it seemed that he wanted one of them to speak to and I was the nearest thing he had. This man was the stepfather of the King of England and yet he was speaking to a simple farmer, a billman, of his hopes and dreams for England. When his steward came to gently remind the earl that we were dining in an hour or so he nodded, "I will come." He turned to me, "Now one thing more, James. I have a mind to make you a gentleman. It is little enough for the service you have done England and I dare say that if he was not consumed with affairs of state then King Henry might have granted you the title. If you wish to buy more land in Ecclestone then I am more than happy for you to do so. You have shown that you take something and make it better. I like such men."

"Thank you, my lord, I know not what to say."

He waved a dismissive hand, "Now tonight you shall sit on the top table." My eyes widened, "My son meant no disrespect when he put you on the low table but he has important men whose loyalty he must assuage by such acts. The feast this night is for those people whose company I enjoy. It is just a pity that you cannot tell the true tale of Perkin Warbeck. Still, as one of those who fought at Stoke Field as well as Sedbergh, you may spark interest in my guests. They are all old friends."

Knowing that I would be dining with the earl my mother had ensured that all my finest clothes were cleaned and in perfect condition. She had also trimmed both my hair and beard so that I looked, as she put it, 'half decent'. Faint praise indeed.

I waited in my chamber until summoned. There was a minstrel gallery. I had seen many such galleries in Flanders and musicians played melodious music. Rushes had been placed on the floor and the table was festooned with sweet-smelling herbs and vases filled with flowers. I discovered from the servants that this was an important feast for the Queen Mother was present. Margaret Beaufort was the wife of the earl and she was a formidable woman. The earl was her fourth husband but she only had one surviving child and that was Henry Tudor, the King of England. I knew that it was rare for her to be at Lathom. She had taken vows of chastity and lived in Northampton in a tiny village called Collyweston. I wondered at her presence but, when I entered a lady in waiting came to me, "The Queen Mother would speak with you, Captain James. Follow me."

I was taken to a small antechamber close to the Great Hall. I was fearful and wondered at this meeting. I bowed but continued to stand. I had lived at court long enough to know that one did not sit in the presence of such personages. She had piercing eyes and reminded me of a hunting hawk. "You, I believe, were the man responsible for helping my son to rid the world of the threat from Yorkist Pretenders."

"I played a small part, Queen Mother."

She snorted, "More than a small part from what I have been told." She nodded to the lady in waiting who gave me a purse, "I know that you have been rewarded already but this is from me for my son is the dearest person in the world to me."

The purse felt heavy but I knew it would be churlish to open it. I took it and nodded, "I am most grateful, Queen Mother."

"You may not know, Captain, but I rarely leave my home. However, the earl has not been well lately and when I heard that you farmed close by, I thought it convenient to visit with my husband and to meet you. I asked him to invite you. I can see that you were groomed well to watch the Pretender. Was that Margaret of Burgundy's doing?"

I knew that the two women hated each other and I did not know what to say.

"Come sir, the truth. I have outlived three husbands and all those save Margaret of Burgundy who has tried to thwart me are dead but you were closer to her than any man alive so I would know about her. Answer my question."

Had she been an inquisitor in the Tower I could not have been more afraid. "She did groom me, Queen Mother."

"And did she know that the Pretender was just that, a false hope of Yorkist power?"

I sighed, "I believe she did but..." I paused.

"Speak. Truth is all!"

"I think she hated both the Lancastrians and your son so much that she would have done anything in her power to end their rule."

For the first time she smiled, "We share the same Christian name and I believe that we have much in common. There is nothing more important, Captain James, than family and much as I hate her and her family, I cannot help but admire her motives. They are like mine." She stared into my eyes, "And you are a fine young man. It is time that you were wed."

Had she added, '*And I order it so,*' I would not have been surprised. I was out of my depth and I merely nodded and said, "I will endeavour to find a wife, Queen Mother."

As she waved a hand to dismiss me, she smiled again, "Then look now for that is my command." I was taken from the antechamber and led to the Great Hall. One or two of the guests were being seated already. I was not late. The earl and the Queen Mother would be the last to take their seats.

Although I was seated at the top table the presence of the Queen Mother meant that I was not close to the earl. I was at one end and close to a landowner, his wife and his daughter. Roger de Clifton was seated alone when I was taken to my seat. I smiled, "Are we two bachelors alone at the end of the table, sir?"

He smiled, "I fear not, young sir. My wife wants everything to be just so as we are meeting the Queen Mother. She and my daughter are making sure that they are perfectly presented. I just pray that they are not late for it would not do to offend the Queen Mother. I am Roger de Clifton and I have land close to Preston on the Ribble."

I nodded, "And I am James of Ecclestone. I have a small piece of land not far from here."

He smiled, "You are too modest and I have heard of your name. It does you great credit that you do not accord yourself your title of Captain of Billmen." He leaned forward, "Thurstan Bythell is a friend of mine and he told me of your action at Sedbergh. My daughter will enjoy your account of the battle. She likes to hear of battles. My wife has tried to curb her interest for she believes it is unladylike but you cannot change a child's nature, can you?" He looked beyond me and I saw the relief on his face, "Thank goodness, they are here before the earl."

I turned and looked. His wife, Mary, looked like a galleon under full sail. She was not a small woman and she had affected the dress popularised by Joan of Portugal, the farthingale. It made her look even bigger. Such was the effect that for a moment or two I failed to see her daughter but as the galleon veered off course, I spied the most beautiful creature I had ever seen. Jane de Clifton stole my heart the moment I saw her. It was only later that I wondered if everything had been engineered by the earl and the Queen Mother. The words I had enjoyed with both of them had already made me think that I ought to seek a bride but when I saw her then I was smitten.

Mary de Clifton was impressed that they were seated at the top table and assumed, I think, that I was more important than I was. We were introduced by her husband who gave me the title, gentleman. He added that I had fought at Stoke Field and Sedbergh. Jane de Clifton's eyes lit up when she heard that, "You must tell me all about them. I am fascinated by such matters."

"It is not seemly, daughter."

"Mother, I do not say I would like to fight in them for I know that I am a woman but our men go to fight for our land and I think it is important that we understand what they do."

And so I spent the whole of the meal talking of life as a billman. I confess that I could not even begin to make a list of the food we ate. I am sure it was all perfect but I was conscious of trying to impress this young woman whilst hiding my secretive activities. It was as hard as being a spy in Margaret of Burgundy's court.

It was the Queen Mother who left the feast first. Looking at the platter I could see that she had pecked at her food like a bird. Her ladies in waiting flanked her and we all stood as she passed. To my amazement and the delight of Mary de Clifton, she paused next to me. She inclined her head and said, quietly, "I shall be gone before you rise, Captain James, but you should know that your work for England is not yet done. My husband and my stepson will do all in their power to advance you but know that there is a payment for such favour and that payment is that you do all that is asked of you by your king."

"Of course and thank you for your kindness."

I meant her words and the generosity of the purse but she misunderstood me or perhaps I misunderstood her for she smiled and said, "Playing cupid is a whim for an old lady. Do not hesitate."

The whole conversation was spoken so quietly that I know no one else heard the words and then she was gone. I never spoke to her again as intimately as that night and I felt honoured. It will be many years before England sees her like again.

We sat and Mary de Clifton gushed, impressed by the intimacy of the exchange "You are obviously a star in the rising. Husband, you must invite the captain to our home so that we may get to know him better."

Roger de Clifton sighed and said, "Yes, my dear."

I was still bemused by the words of the Queen Mother and they rang in my ears. The evening ended all too soon and I went to my bedchamber wondering about the events of the evening. I rose as early as was polite and went to the Great Hall for breakfast. The earl was eating and he waved me over. "You and the de Clifton girl seemed to be getting on well last night."

He had a glint in his rheumy eye and I gambled, "And was that planned by your lordship?"

"Let us say that for one like me who is concerned with matters of state it was a pleasant diversion to put the two of you so close together. You are not unhappy about our intervention, are you?"

"Of course not my lord, but I am but a lowly farmer and she is a lady."

"She has no title and you are now a gentleman. Roger de Clifton has land but he is no farmer. He just has money. Believe me you, young though you are, have more innate skills as a farmer. His wife is an ambitious woman who drives her husband to be more than he is."

Things were clearer now. Mary de Clifton had been the obstacle and the attention shown to me by the queen had removed that obstacle.

After breakfast, the earl insisted that we ride together. "I am too old to hunt but if I ride with a young warrior like yourself then the days of my former glory, like Bosworth, will come back to me. Come, I shall show you, my lands."

As much as I wished to stay and speak with Jane de Clifton, I could not refuse such a request and we went to the stables where his horse was already saddled. We rode all morning and he stopped at Burscough Priory. He was well known and welcomed. The monks gave us wine and warm bread and ham. As we left, he said, "That is where I shall be buried. I have already made my wishes clear." I cocked an inquisitive eye at him. He shrugged, "I am almost sixty and my life should have ended many times 'ere now. A man should prepare for death but live each day to the full. Two days ago I felt as though I was at death's door but riding with you makes me think I could live forever." He shook his head, "I shall not and it is an illusion but a pleasant one."

We arrived back at noon and although his face was flushed with the joy of the ride, I could see that it had taken much out of the earl. "I shall spend the afternoon in my chamber but I thank you for the ride. It was a joy."

After he had gone to his room I went to the Great Hall in the hopes of bumping into Jane. The steward came over, "The other guests have all departed for their homes, Captain James. You are welcome to stay for the earl thinks well of you."

The implication was clear, the feast was over and a good guest would depart, "Of course, Thomas."

He smiled, "The earl had me prepare the documents of title and deed for you. I shall await you with them at the front of the hall."

I went to my chamber and saw that my bag had been packed already. Poor Calliope would have more exercise than she was used to. I mounted my horse and the steward handed me the deeds. "I was told to tell you, Captain James, that an invitation to Clifton Hall will be on its way to you. The young lady was most unhappy to have missed you."

My heart sang as I headed home but, as I neared Windle, which meant Ecclestone was not far away an air of disquiet came over me. As much as I had the prospect of happiness with Jane de Clifton, I could not help but feel that once again I was being manipulated. The Queen Mother did not leave her home and travel many miles merely on a whim. The earl was too practical a man to let sentimentality rule him. I was needed and the one common factor was King Henry. What was now required of me?

My mother was the one who bombarded me with questions. However, when I mentioned the Queen Mother then even my father took an interest. Although I tried to hide the news about Jane I could not. I might be able to spy for King Henry and adopt a false face but my parents were a different matter and I could hide nothing from them. She was delighted when I told her. Even the news of the extra piece of land and my title seemed less important to her.

The extra land consisted of four adjacent fields. They were of varying quality and had all lain fallow since I had come back. Thomas told me that they had been farmed by villagers who had either died in the wars or had left to seek employment elsewhere. Now that the divisive war between Lancaster and York was over there was more stability in the land and prosperity meant higher pay, especially in some of the larger towns. Grubbing a living on a thin strip of land was hard work. Of course, for me, it meant I had to employ more men. Our flock had grown and William, now almost a man had proved to be a sound investment which was why I had already employed an assistant for him. I sought similar youths from the village and my reputation not to mention my title drew the best to me. Thomas and Robert were seen as the model. Mothers were quite happy for their youngest sons to come to me as labourers knowing that I would look after them and they would prosper. My store of gold and silver had grown rather than been diminished. The Queen Mother's purse had been a full one. When I had shown the purse given to me by the Queen Mother my parents had been both shocked and impressed by the number. There were fifty crowns in the purse. It was a veritable fortune. Whilst I was as happy as my parents, unlike them I was suspicious. What was the purse buying? I placed the purse in the chest hidden under the floor of the kitchen and put the coins from my mind. I could do nothing about my position. The Earl of Derby was the lord of the manor and he could do with me anything he wished. The land I held was not freehold but leasehold. He could take the deeds from me at any time. What would happen when he died? All that I could do was live as best I could and make my farm, now more than doubled in size, as profitable as possible.

When the letter arrived, two days after my return, inviting me to Clifton Hall I found all thoughts of political intrigue and manipulation by the great and the good disappeared from my head. I rode Calliope hard on the ride to Clifton. The hall whilst not as grand as the earl's at Lathom, still made my home seem like a hovel and as I rode towards the moated hall, I began to doubt that my suit to Jane de Clifton would be successful. I had decided to propose marriage before I had set out. I had convinced myself that my new title and the good graces of the Queen Mother and the Earl of Derby would be enough to win me the hand of Jane de Clifton. In war and when I was spying for England, I feared no man but, as I threw my leg over the saddle and handed Calliope's reins to the stableboy, I was riddled by doubt.

Those doubts faded when I felt the warmth of her father's welcome, "We are all delighted that you have come. We shall dispense with titles. I am Roger and I shall call you James. Let me walk you around the grounds while we speak." He was a smaller man than I was and he looked up at me, "We need to talk, do we not?"

I was grateful for the honest look in his eyes, "That we do."

He had an ornamental garden. I had never seen one before. There was, of course, a kitchen element to it with herbs and salad crops but he had roses, intricate hedges and plants, that, so far as I could see, would serve little purpose other than to look pretty.

"I am no farmer, James. I have a reeve who manages the land for me. I do, however, like to grow plants. I have an orchard and the delight I get from eating my own apples and pears is beyond words. I am that sort of man. There is no ambition in me and I am content with the one daughter that God sent to me and the land I inherited. I have no son to leave it to and I want my daughter cared for. You understand?"

"I think so but all of this is a little sudden."

He had a fish pond and I saw the bubbles from the fish as they came to the surface. I envied him the pond. It meant he could eat fish every Friday. In the village, the pond was so overused that sometimes it was sticklebacks we ate. I determined that now that I had more land, I would build one.

He picked up a stone and threw it into the pond. "Do you see how that tiny stone, insignificant though it was, has affected the whole pond? The ripples might be smaller when they reach us but they are still visible." There was a rose arbour with a bench beneath it. "Come let us sit for the perfume from these roses is pleasant." We sat. "They do not flower all year and so when they are in flower, I like to enjoy them. They are transitory. Here but briefly and then they are gone. They are a metaphor for life."

I nodded, "You should have been a poet."

He looked shyly at his fingers and I saw that they were ink-stained, "And you have found my weakness. My wife does not understand it but Jane does. We are close, my daughter and I. I love my wife but she is a force of nature." He became more business-like, "You say this is all sudden. It is not. Last year my wife wished Jane to become a lady in waiting. I took her to Northampton for King Henry and his queen were visiting with the Queen Mother. We arrived after the royal couple had departed but the Queen Mother was much taken with Jane. She asked why we wished her to be a lady in waiting." He gave a chuckle, "You have met the Queen Mother and know that a man does not try to deceive her. I was truthful and gave my wife's reasons. Margaret Beaufort is the cleverest woman I know. She said that it was better to find a good husband for Jane."

I could not help but interject, "Jane was there when this was said?"

"My daughter and I are close. Aye, she was there. She is clever too. The Queen Mother said that she would seek one who would be worthy of my daughter and that we were to wait for a summons from her. That was enough for my wife but I think she thought it would be some great lord or knight who would ride up to Clifton Hall on a white courser. My daughter and I were greeted by the Queen Mother when we arrived. The earl gave my wife a tour of his home and we were warned of your presence. Unlike you, James, we knew what to expect. As soon as we were seated close to you, I saw the purpose of the earl and his wife. When I saw the love that flashed between your eyes, I was content. I am a poet and I have read the poems of Dante Alighieri. You know them?" I shook my head. "He fell in love with Beatrice when he was nine and she was eight. He married

52

another but he had one true love. I believe in that true love." His eyes held mine. "Do you wish to marry my daughter?"

I found myself fearful for this was a mighty decision and seemed to have come too quickly and then I remembered the feeling of breathlessness when I had first met her. I nodded, "I would and yet I feel that I am far beneath both you and your daughter. I come from common stock."

He smiled, "We all come from the same stock James and from what I have heard about you my daughter would be lucky to have you as a husband and I will have someone to whom I can leave this hall."

When we returned to the hall and Jane and I greeted each other all was confirmed. I think the only one who was surprised was her mother. When I asked Jane to be my wife she answered in the affirmative almost before my request was made. The surprised mother recovered when Roger asked her how we should organise the wedding. Any doubts Mary de Clifton might have harboured disappeared as she began to plan a wedding which she thought would rival that of a king or queen. In the end, it was a smaller affair than she thought. The guests she invited were, in many cases, far too grand. I knew that the Queen Mother and her husband would not be able to attend and whilst the Sherriff of Lancaster sent a fine glass goblet as a present, he did not attend either. My parents attended but not my sisters. I cared not for I had a bride and I looked forward to a comfortable life as a farmer who had a past that would give colour to a dull and predictable future.

The marriage was only marred by one thing. Prince Arthur, King Henry's eldest son died a week after we were wed. In the grand scheme of things, it should have had little effect but it was another stone thrown into the fishpond. Jane and I were happy and she loved our little farm. She and my mother got on well and Jane doted on my father. As she had truthfully said when we had first met, she loved hearing of wars and my father's bravery at Bosworth Field was a story she never tired of hearing. I was not lord of Ecclestone but I was the most important man in the village thanks to my title as gentleman and captain of billmen. When we walked the village ladies curtsied and men bowed as we walked by. Jane was the kindest person I ever met and always had soft and gentle words. It was good that we were prosperous for Jane was always giving coins to those less well off than we. She loved riding and one of the wedding presents given by her father, along with a fine dowry, was a hackney that Jane loved to ride. We rode every day and it was then that we got to know each other.

It was four days after we had returned to the farm after the wedding ceremony that Jane began to open her heart to me. The first four days and nights were spent enjoying the company of each other and even had I not been in love with her already those four days and nights would have made me do so.

As we rode towards Billinge, the highest point close to our farm she said, riding up the steep slope, "I know of your past, James."

I nodded, "It was little enough that I did at Stoke Field and Sedbergh."

She had the cheekiest smile I knew. She looked like some sort of pixie had materialised in our world, "The Queen Mother told me of your past. I know the service you did for King Henry. Do not hide your past from me. I loved you from the moment I saw you but the knowledge that you helped to secure the crown for King Henry and did so without any thought of reward makes me love you even more."

We had reached the top and as I held her hand to help her to dismount, I said, "This reward is greater than any title I might have been given."

She stood on tiptoes to kiss me, "And you are so modest. Your mother told me that you were not always so."

I nodded as we looked back towards the farm, many miles distant, "I did things of which I was not proud and then I was chosen to be the king's spy."

"Tell me of your life as a spy."

And so, as we sat beneath a benign autumn sky, I gave her an account of my life at the court of the Duchess of Burgundy. I did not tell her all. I had done things that were not for the hearing of a lady but I told her the most important parts. When I had finished, she looked thoughtful.

"You now think less of me?"

She shook her head, "No, I am even more admiring of you. I was just thinking of Perkin Warbeck. I knew the name of course. I was a young impressionable girl when he revolted and I thought of him as some sort of monster. From your words, I can see that he was not. He was misguided and used."

"Aye, we are all pawns in the game of life. We are used and discarded. It is better to concentrate on family."

"Then let us do so."

As the next year dawned, we discovered that Jane was with child. The news pleased us all. My father had worsened since the wedding. It was nothing to do with the wedding but his ailment. However, the news that he would be a grandfather again gave him a new lease of life. We prepared for a family and I started work on a new house I would have built on the new land we had been given by the earl. We did not know it but the ripple from the stone was about to touch us and would change our lives again.

Chapter 5

Lathom 1503

The king came to Lathom to visit with the earl who was not a well man. The arrival of the court could not be hidden and we all knew that the king and his son were not far from our home. What came as a surprise, however, was the invitation to ride to Lathom. King Henry sent for me and I felt trepidation as I mounted Calliope and bade farewell to my pregnant wife. The message only reached us at noon and I left directly for it would not do to keep King Henry waiting. It meant I reached the hall in the late afternoon.

The home of the earl felt different as I rode up to what was, in effect, a royal court. It was not just that the king and queen as well as the heir apparent were present, there were all of King Henry's officials as well as senior lords. This was not simply a royal progress and he had brought officials from London with him. The steward, Thomas, met me at the entrance, "If you would lead your horse, Captain James."

I dismounted and followed the steward around the back of the palatial house. Usually, a servant would take my horse to the stables and I wondered what this meant. There was one large block of stables with the horses of the earl and his family but we did not go to that stable. Instead, he led me to a smaller and meaner stable filled with sumpters and working horses. He smiled apologetically as he helped me to unsaddle Calliope, "The main stable is full, Captain, I am sure that you will understand."

I did and only too well. "And let me guess, Steward, I am not to sleep in the main house."

He had the good grace to nod and add, "Aye, Captain James. Every room is taken." He shuffled his feet and was clearly embarrassed. He pointed to the hayloft, "I fear that this is the only accommodation we have at the moment."

"And where do I dine?"

He pointed to a low building attached to the rear of the hall, "You will only be here for one night, captain, and the servants' hall will have to do. The food will be wholesome, I can assure you."

I was beginning to become impatient, "Then why was I invited?" He shook his head, clearly ill at ease. I lifted down my saddle, "Thank the earl for his hospitality and tell him that I will spend this night with my wife under my own roof."

He reached out to arrest my movement, "It is the king, captain. He wishes to speak to you but in private. None must know." He nodded towards my bag, "You will need no fine clothes, Captain. I will fetch you when it is time to meet with the king until then if you could keep yourself away from the public gaze." I stared at the man who was as old as my father and must have been attending to the great and the good since before I was born. He nodded, "Matters of state, Captain James, override all of our expectations and rights."

He was right of course and I knew I was paying the price for the purse of gold, the land and my bride. I would have to swallow my pride and accept it. "I will wander and explore the grounds."

He looked relieved. "I will find you, fear not."

If I was to be in disguise, I thought it best to adopt a different gait and pull my hat over my face. I was glad that I had ridden to the hall in the working clothes I had been wearing when the message had arrived. I had hoped to change in my chamber but now that would not be so. I had explored the grounds with his lordship and I went to his fishpond. My men and I had begun to dig ours out on the poor piece of boggy ground on one of my new fields. I was looking for ideas on how best to finish it. The earl's pond like many fishponds was fed by a small stream. I saw that there was a wooden sluice at each end. It made sense. That way fresh water would constantly seep in and yet the fish would not escape. In times of flood then the gates could be opened. I could do the same with the small beck that soaked into the boggy ground. It would mean that the field would be drier and I could put animals there without fear of their hooves being damaged by wet ground.

I was bending over one of the gates when I heard a voice behind me, "You must be Captain James of Ecclestone."

I turned and saw a red-haired youth of about twelve or thirteen. I stood and said, "I am but you have the advantage of me, sir."

He smiled and I warmed to him immediately, "I am sorry, I am the king's son. Prince Henry. He asked me to find you so that we may talk." He pointed to the main hall, "He awaits us in the chapel. I am guessing that you know where that is to be found."

"I do, my lord. I am sorry that I did not recognise you."

He shrugged, "There is no reason why you should." I led the way and he said, "From what I have heard, Captain James, you are also something of a sheep in disguise. You do not look like the man who helped to thwart a Yorkist plot."

It was my turn to smile, "I was a spy, you see, and if a man is to be a spy, then he should not look like one. I merely played a part, like a mummer."

"And did it well." We neared the buildings and he said, "You know I am to be king?"

"I am sorry for your brother's death."

He shrugged, "His loss is my gain and I believe I have a stouter constitution than my brother. When I am king, I may call upon you. I shall need resourceful men around me and both my father and the earl believe that you are a man who can be trusted completely. That is rare."

I nodded and remained silent but my heart sank to my boots.

Two bodyguards scrutinised us as we entered the chapel but, apart from the earl and the king it was empty. King Henry did not look well. In fact, he and the earl looked like dead men walking.

"I hear you have married, James. That is good. A man needs a wife and children."

As something to say more than anything I volunteered, "And my wife is with child too."

He gave a thin smile, "As is the queen. Good."

He looked at the earl who said, "King Henry needs his spy once more, James. We are here in a sacred place and what is said here should be considered as the confessional." I nodded. It went without saying. "Princess Margaret has been betrothed to James, the King of Scotland." That was not news as I had heard the rumour the last time I had been at Lathom. They are to be married this summer in Scotland." He looked at the king who nodded, "We would have you go with the princess as a bodyguard. In reality, you will be a spy and report back to King Henry."

The king said, "I hope that this union will bring peace to my northern borders. When my son ascends the throne, he can cast his eyes to France rather than fearing a dagger between the shoulder blades from Scotland. He may need your services there too but I need to know if there is danger from King James. I have no doubt that he will soon dispense with your services as a bodyguard but I want you to discover if the Scots have any plans to do as they did with the unfortunate Perkin Warbeck and support strife and dissension in England."

I was aware that three pairs of eyes bored into me and that there was silence in the chapel. "Let me be quite clear, King Henry, I will be a spy but in open view. They will know my identity?"

The king smiled, "And that is how we will learn of their intention. I know that when you were a spy, you played a part. Play one now. As my mother discovered when she spoke with you, you are a personable, witty and intelligent young man. We would have you play the part of a dull, unimaginative warrior. It is why you were chosen when this marriage was arranged. If anyone can see to the heart of a plot against England then it is you. When you are dismissed then you will return to Lathom and give your information to the earl."

I looked at the earl and wondered if he would still be alive when that happened.

"And when do I leave?"

"The marriage is due to take place in August. You will travel to Greenwich on the 1st of July and take ship with my daughter."

"And what does she know, King Henry?"

"Nothing. She will be glad of an Englishman with her for she does not wish to be wed to a Scotsman but we all make sacrifices for our country. To her, you will be just that, a bodyguard. You must play the part with her too. Are there questions?"

I could not think of any except one, "And if I am not dismissed as a bodyguard?"

The earl smiled, "If you have not discovered a plot in six months then there will be none. Flee."

"In that case, I would not use my own name. I will adopt one as I did the last time I served you as a spy."

"Is that really necessary?"

"Your son has already asked me to serve him. Thanks to the earl and your mother I now have a family. I would not bring harm to them." I was thinking on my feet and I improvised a name, "I will be Thomas of Burscough. My accent will fit and if there are questions about my background then his lordship can corroborate my story."

I heard Prince Henry laugh, "You are both right about this man. He is a born spy."

King Henry nodded, "Then you shall be Thomas Burscough. Earl, make him a gift of a piece of land from Burscough. It will add to the deceit." He stood, "We will see you at Greenwich," he smiled, "Thomas of Burscough."

The prince did not smile as he said, "And remember, that I also have calls upon your time and when the time is right, I will use them."

The king and prince left us. The earl shook his head sadly, "I am sorry, James, you are just too good at what you do."

"There seems little point in my staying here this night for I may be recognised. I will fetch my horse and ride home. It will give me the chance to make up a story for my wife."

"Give her the truth, James, I am sure she can handle it."

He was right. When I arrived back, late at night I told her all. I would tell no other but it was a relief to have someone with whom I could share my secrets.

"This is an honour and we shall have more land."

"But I will be leaving you and our child."

She laughed, "And how much use will you be when there is a baby Your mother is already looking forward to the child and Thomas and Robert's wives are both mothers but the new house will need to be finished. This one will be too crowded."

"Of course."

"And we will need servants for the new house."

The dowry would be diminished by the expense but it would be worth it.

It was as we were fitting the roof when the messenger came from the earl. It was the deeds to a small farm close to

Burscough in the village of Hoscar. There was no lord of the manor and the dozen houses made it an insignificant place. There was not even a church or a chapel and that was unusual. The farm was almost derelict and I would need to invest money if I was to make a profit. I spent two days there and hired a local man, John of Hoscar, who agreed to be my reeve. He had a wife and two children to support and his small holding was not big enough. It would mean investing in more sheep but it would give me a story to use in Scotland. I was serving as a bodyguard to gain the money I needed for the farm. My time in Flanders helped me to plan ahead.

My son, James, was born on June 25th. I had been worried that I would miss the birth but Jane had been confident the bairn would arrive before I left. My father saw the baby and then died on the 26th of June. He had been ill and I know that he had hung on to see the child. My mother and I held his hands as he silently slipped into eternal sleep. My mother just said, "Farewell Walter, I shall not be long." The birth and the death seemed to be somehow linked. One man of our family had passed on and a boy was born. I liked to believe that my father's spirit was in my son or perhaps that was wishful thinking.

Jane, despite her upbringing, proved to be a natural mother and was up and about in time to attend my father's funeral which came the day before I left for London. I left a tearful mother, a wife who was fighting back the tears and a son whose tears were for his mother's milk. I felt tears pricking my eyes as I left my home and took the road south and I was glad that I was alone on the road with my thoughts which were as confused as the world I would soon enter. I would be a spy once more.

The journey south was a hard one. The funeral meant that I left myself just three days to get to London. Calliope would have been sorely tried. I was glad that I hired a horse. If I ruined it then it would not matter. The ride allowed me to make my story more believable. I began to adopt the character I would play in the inns at which I stayed. I stopped smiling and scowled more. I needed people to dislike me. It was hard to do and I realised that I was now older than when I had spied before and this would be a much harder task. By the time I reached Greenwich my mouth was almost permanently set in a scowl and my poor horse would take a week to recover. The king was at the palace of Greenwich but his face was filled with sadness. The love of his life, Queen Elizabeth had died ten months after his son Arthur. He had been smiling when, at Lathom, he had told me that his wife was pregnant again. She had died in childbirth and a more distraught man I had yet to meet. He clearly loved his wife. Prince Henry was not at the palace and Princess Margaret was with her ladies preparing for her imminent departure. I was invited to dine with the king. He ate sparingly but I knew why he had invited me to dine. He wished to talk.

"Your first child is healthy, James?"

"He appears so but he was born less than a week ago and so I pray that God will watch over him."

He made the sign of the cross, "And that is what we all pray. I have been robbed of two in the last year and I wonder if I am to follow them soon."

I shook my head, "Do not think that way, King Henry, you will have many years ahead of you."

"You know that Thomas, Earl of Derby is unwell?"

"Yes, King Henry, but he is older than you."

"That seems not to matter to God." He leaned over. "You are going to Scotland as a spy but while you are with her I would have you protect her. You will, won't you?"

"Of course, King Henry."

King Henry was known as a hard and cold man but that night showed me that while he could be ruthless, he loved his family and that was no bad thing.

I met the young princess the next day and it was hard to maintain my cold manner. I was heartened by the fact that King Henry must have adopted such a façade for I had glimpsed the real Henry Tudor. The princess was just pleased to have a bodyguard when she was going to a new land many hundreds of miles from her home. She did not want to go and I had to force my dour demeanour as she wept and begged her father not to send her north to be with a man so much older than she was. Margaret was barely out of her childhood. That she had known for a year she was to marry the Scottish king did not help. I suppose she must have hoped that it would never happen. Her brother had been due to marry a Spanish princess and he had died.

The next day her face showed her distress but she had been brought up as a princess and knew her responsibilities. As the cog set sail, she jabbered nervously to both me and her ladies. It helped me as all I needed to do was to remain silent and watch the shore as we sailed down the Thames to head for Edinburgh and a new life.

I liked the young princess from the first moment I met her but I was not able to show that through smiles and pleasant words. I sympathised with her situation and wished I could offer kind words but that was not my character. Instead, I had to maintain a dour aspect. I did not enjoy it. The young woman had known for a year that she was to marry the much older Scottish king but she had still to meet him. There were rumours, and they had even reached Ecclestone, that the king was a womaniser and had illegitimate children already. King Henry had been a very faithful husband to the queen and his children had been brought up with the highest morals. His only wild child was Mary Tudor but Margaret was a model of propriety. She loosed question after question to me as we sailed down the Thames. I knew the answers to some of the questions but my flat answers were in direct contrast to her lively and animated questions.

The princess and her two ladies had been given a cabin at the forecastle of the cog. They had the luxury of bunks. To get to their chamber they had to pass through a smaller opening where chests could be stored and the door of which was a loose one made of hide. That was my bedchamber. With a hammock slung across the door, I would be a chamberlain and none could enter without disturbing me. It was not as though we expected danger, this was a king's ship, but it was as well to get into good habits. As luck would have it, we reached the mouth of the estuary and the open sea after we had retired. The squeals from the cabin told me that the ladies were enjoying the wild motion. I wondered if it would last.

I rose in the night to make water. The first mate was at the helm and he had a watch of five men. The black night could not hide the white flecked waves of a livelier sea than the one that had struck us when we left the Thames. The seas were stormier and I hoped that the ladies were asleep for if they woke then the squeals of delight might be replaced by screams of terror. I struggled to get back to the cabin. James of Ecclestone might have waved to the crew and exchanged words with them but Thomas of Burscough just clambered back into his hammock and tried to get warm again.

The storm worsened and the captain himself came at dawn to tell us that unless the seas abated, he would be forced to put in to one of the ports on the Lincolnshire coast.

Princess Margaret was young but she knew the right things to say, "I am sure that whatever decision you make, Captain, will be the right one. I am confident that God will watch over us and that we are in good hands."

The captain smiled at her words. Thomas of Burscough remained impassive. I was already finding it hard not to be myself.

The storm did abate and by the evening we were approaching the mouth of the Humber. Once more, after they had eaten, the ladies questioned me about the land. I knew it, of course, for when I had first joined the company of billmen I had travelled down the Roman Road to Stoke Field. "Is this Scotland yet, Master Thomas?"

"No Princess Margaret, we are still in your father's realm. We pass another two great rivers, the Tees and the Tyne before we leave English waters. Once we pass the mighty castle of Bamburgh and the islands of the monks, then we shall be in Scottish waters and the realm of your future husband."

When, the next day, we passed the mouth of the Tees and the basking seals, the ladies were all for asking the captain to reef the sails so that they could view them for longer. Their pleas worked and we bobbed about the estuary for a good hour before the captain ordered the sails loosed and we sped north again.

"I have never seen those creatures before Master Thomas. They were almost human. Were they mermaids? They looked to have tails like mermaids."

One of her ladies, Lady Alice, shook her head, "I do not think they could be, my lady, for they had flippers instead of arms and they had whiskers."

Princess Margaret looked deflated, "I should like to see mermaids. Have you ever seen them, Thomas?"

I shook my head, "Those are the first seals I have seen. I believe they are hunted for their oil and their flesh."

She looked shocked, "That is terrible. Do they have seals in my new home?"

King Henry had told me a little of the politics of the land and I had more information now than I might have had. "I believe that to the north of Scotland, in the Kingdom of the Isles, there are seals and the men there, descended from the Vikings, hunt them."

"The Kingdom of the Isles?"

"It is a disputed realm, Princess Margaret. Your future husband sees it as part of Scotland but the warriors there refuse to acknowledge him. King James has been fighting them for some time."

She nodded, "A little like Wales used to be." I saw her eyes light up as she remembered something, "Did I not hear that the Isle of Man belonged to such warriors once?"

"That is right, Princess Margaret and the lord of Man is now the Earl of Derby. Perhaps King James sees the isles as a prize he can now grasp."

It was after we had passed Lindisfarne and Bamburgh that the Princess became more withdrawn. It seemed to me that she now realised that she was leaving her own comfortable world and entering a new one. Had I been James of Ecclestone I might have offered advice. The young princess had recently lost her mother and might never see her father again. Thomas of Burscough, however, was a dull bodyguard who stood impassively by as the princess gripped the gunwale while the ship turned up the Forth.

I realised later that the Scots must have had some sort of signalling system for King James and his knights were waiting to greet us when the ship docked at Leith. I almost had to put the princess from my mind for I knew that from that moment on I was a spy once more. I was being placed as close to the King of Scotland as I could to enable me to discover the plots that King Henry and his son feared.

Servants came aboard to carry the bags of the ladies ashore. My leather bag stood out as different but I pointed to it and said to one of the servants, "And take that with you. It is mine." I adopted an imperious growl and the man knuckled his forehead and picked it up.

I followed the three ladies down the gangplank. Princess Margaret had been gracious and she gave the captain a small purse of silver. Her grandmother's influence was clear.

I was not certain of the reception that the princess would receive. The king, instantly recognisable from the deference of others and his magnificent apparel, knelt to kiss Princess Margaret's hand. It flustered her as she had been ready to curtsy to the king.

"You are even more beautiful than the portrait I was sent. Our children will all be handsome. Are these your ladies?"

She recovered well, "This is Lady Alice and Lady Elizabeth. Master Thomas is my bodyguard."

The king's smile briefly left his face as he turned to look at me, "You need no bodyguard for this is Scotland. England might be filled with cutpurses and outlaws but Scotland is civilised."

It was an insult and intended to see how I would react. I played the part, "King Henry was concerned that Princess Margaret should have protection on the sea voyage north for there are still pirates out there."

The king looked a little mollified at my reasonable explanation but I could see that he did not like the hired English sword being so close to his presence.

"As you can see, Master Thomas, I am well protected by the finest knights in Scotland and your services will not be needed."

Princess Margaret put her hands on her husband's, "I beg your majesty to allow Thomas to stay. I am sure there will be times when I will have to be apart from you and he is a comfort to me. He might look like stone but I trust him."

King James relented, "Very well. Angus, find a horse for this English sword."

When the weary and ancient-looking hackney was fetched for me I saw that my time at the Scottish court would be hard. The looks of disdain on the faces of the Scottish knights were a measure of my position. This would not be as easy as spying in a court where I was looked upon as an ally. Here there would be suspicion and my every move would be closely watched. I wondered, in light of King James' comments, how long I would be tolerated. I had to find out as much as I could before, as I suspected, I would slink back to England with my tail between my legs. I kept my face stoically serious as I mounted the hackney and rode as close to the horse of Princess Margaret as I could. The wall of steel that was the Scottish knights meant I was at least twenty paces behind her. As a bodyguard, I would be singularly useless.

The newly built palace at Holyrood had been decked out for the wedding which would take place on the 8th of August. The building was next to the abbey and was incomplete. The king's chambers and the Great Hall were completed as was the great quadrangle but the rest of the palace was still unfinished. It smelled new.

Until that time my bedroom would be behind the door to Princess Margaret's bedchamber. She and her ladies had been given a large bedroom with three beds and an antechamber that was intended for a chamberlain. I would sleep across the doorway. Princess Margaret was a kind lady and she had not liked the way I had been treated. She had Lady Alice bring me extra cushions and a spare fur. "I think it is a shame the way that you have been treated thus far and I am sorry that it is on my account. When I am married, I will try to persuade the king to have you accorded more honour."

The dour Thomas replied, "Thank you, Princess Margaret, but I am, as your husband-to-be says, a hired sword. My purpose is to defend you and to die doing so if that is necessary."

Her hand went to her mouth, "I pray it will not come to that. Who would wish me harm?"

"I know not, and that is why I view everyone with suspicion."

I discovered that not all those in the palace had such an aversion to the English. There were two serving women who had been taken captive in some border raid in the past and, having been freed, now worked in the palace. As they spoke English well, they were assigned to fetch and carry for the three ladies. Agnes, the elder of the two, seemed to find me attractive and she was the one who brought me food and ale. She intimated, after our first few encounters, that she was not averse to a liaison. I was not flattered enough to be deceived. I was her hope of freedom from Scotland. If I took a fancy to her then when my time as a bodyguard was ended, I might take her with me. I had no doubt that once in England I would be abandoned but I played along with the deception. I played patty fingers with her without making my face crack into a smile. She and, Joan, the other servant, became a mine of information. When they brought me food or helped the princess, they divulged information without being aware that they did so. As servants, they were almost invisible and while I might be viewed with suspicion if I loitered close to a conversation between nobles, they were not. It was from them I learned that the king, as soon as the wedding was over, planned to complete his conquest of the isles. That gave me hope that I might be allowed to stay with the princess just a little while longer.

Apart from my brief daily contact with the princess, my life was lonely. Agnes and her attention became something to which I looked forward. Perhaps my face occasionally broke into a hint of a smile for Agnes became encouraged.

The day of the wedding would be the last one where I would sleep behind the door. King James would never countenance an Englishman sleeping close to his chamber. I was just two paces from the princess when we entered the church but I was quickly moved away from the couple once the ceremony began. I used the opportunity to scrutinise the knights. I now had names for many of them and knew that Alexander, the third Lord Home, was the senior lord. He was one to watch for I learned that he had aspirations to be king. It seemed to me that King James was keeping his enemies close to him. Lord Home was the most powerful lord in the borders and I knew that if there was an attempt at insurrection in northern England then he would be part of it. I began to watch those who were close to him. Flanders had taught me patience and as the wedding ceremony dragged on I was storing information about the knights and nobles I saw before me.

At the end of the service one of the king's knights, Sir Andrew Buchanan approached me, "The king has sent me to allocate you quarters prior to your return to England."

"I am still the bodyguard of the princess."

He sneered, "She has no need of you." He leaned in and I could smell the drink on his breath and the sweat under his arms. "The Queen," for the ceremony had been long as she had been crowned too, "has asked that you be retained. It will not be for long, Englishman, and then you will be sent home. Come, your gear has been taken to the chamber you have been allotted."

It was another insult. Although a new building they had stored beer and wine in the cellars in preparation for the wedding. While the rest of the palace was of the highest quality the cellars were rudely and crudely built. They were not intended to be seen and were purely functional. Its newness was marked by the lack of rodents. Over time they would discover their way in but I had a new door, and hinges that did not creak. The storeroom close to the beer cellar still smelled of the barrels that had been removed to make way for me. A tiny opening allowed a little light in. There was a straw paillasse, a chair and half a barrel were the only pieces of furniture.

The knight took great pleasure in saying, as he left, "Make yourself comfortable."

Sir Andrew did not like me. I think his family had suffered in the border wars and he blamed the English. He certainly delighted in the humiliation he heaped upon me.

Despite the chamber and its damp walls, I was happy with the position of the room. It meant I had to pass through the kitchen to get to my room and my movements around the castle would be less suspicious. I knew from the court of the Duchess of Burgundy that the kitchens were the best place to gather news and information. Often, they knew of important events before even knights and nobles. I would bide my time.

Chapter 6

Edinburgh 1504

I learned many things in my first months in the palace. For one thing, I worked out why King James had agreed to the marriage. King Henry now had just one male heir, Prince Henry, and if anything happened to him then the next in line would be his wife. He was gambling that he could become King of England without a fight. I also learned that marriage had not changed his nature. He often left the queen's chamber to ride to one of his ladies. I, of course, could not follow him but Agnes named at least three ladies who enjoyed the king's favour. A telling piece of information I gleaned was that he always rode alone. The king was a brave man and feared no one and I knew King Henry would wish to know that.

However, the most vital information I gathered was a result of the position of my chamber. I had retired early and doused my candle. I heard footsteps coming from the kitchen. The passage led nowhere except to more of the cellars and I was used to servants fetching more beer but this time it was not a servant for there were two voices and that alerted me. I listened and deduced that there were two men. I vaguely recognised the voice of one as an assistant butler but the other was an unknown voice. Before my days as a spy I would have just turned over but my new position meant that I slipped from the bed and waited behind the door, the better to hear the conversation. Such clandestine meetings might reveal some information I could use.

I heard the end of a sentence, "And you are sure that this night the king visits the inn on the mile, the Golden Swan?"

"I am and he left but ten minutes since."

I heard the chink of coins. "Here is your payment. Forget that you have seen me."

I heard the coins jingle as the assistant butler said, "You are a memory already."

The footsteps passed my door again and headed back towards the kitchen. Thomas of Burscough might be happy if the King of Scotland came to harm but he was married to Margaret Tudor. The words were sinister enough to warrant an investigation. I quickly dressed and slipped on my cloak. My beaver hat completed my dress and with my sword on my belt, I slipped out. The corridor was empty and in darkness. I saw why they had chosen such a place for the meeting. I did not know who else might be involved in what was clearly a conspiracy nor did I know what might ensue. I could guess but I had to be sure. I was King Henry's man. I headed for the side gate. There was a sentry there but as it was still early and the gates had not been locked, I was allowed out and I headed for the inn that had been mentioned. I knew that on the main street of Edinburgh, referred to by many as the mile, leading as it did to the citadel, there were many inns and whorehouses. King James' appetite meant that he had a taste for such women. I used the shadows to head to the inn.

The inn had an entrance on the main thoroughfare as well as another that led to the rear and the stables. I saw no one acting suspiciously at the front entrance and so I slipped down the dark alley that led to the rear of the property. The light from the rear entrance showed three figures lurking on the stable side. When King James emerged, he would go for his horse. There had to be an ostler and I wondered if he was part of this conspiracy. I waited in the shadows. If anyone came down the alley then they would find me but I was lucky and no one came. I heard the watch on the street as they marched down calling the time. The gates to the palace would be locked soon but I had embarked on a course of action I would have to see through to its end.

The flash of light told me that the door to the inn had been opened and I drew my sword and made my way down the alley. The shadows which left the inn door had all moved to the stables. I hurried down and wondered if I should shout a warning. The noise from the inn, however, would have masked all but a shrieking scream and even that might have been explained as some overly active whore. If King James was in danger, then silence from me would be his best hope of survival. As I neared the stables I heard the king's voice, "Know you that I am the king!"

I heard the clash of steel and hurtled into the stables. The ostler lay dead with his throat cut and the king, his back to the wall of the stables had his sword and dagger to defend himself against the three attackers. It was the time to announce my presence for I was behind them, "Hold your treacherous hands. That is the King of Scotland you are trying to kill."

One of them, a huge man with the biggest beard I had ever seen, turned and I saw that he had a sword and a short sword in his hands, "We know and you will die with him, Englishman." He swung both swords at my head and had they connected then I would have been decapitated. I had quick reactions and I ducked, slashing with my sword as I did so. My sword hacked across the thighs of the bearded giant. The king was holding off his foes but they were wearing him down. The noise from the inn meant that all were oblivious to the assassination attempt. As blood dripped from my blade, I took my dagger from my belt and lunged at the face of the man I fought. It was an easy blow to avoid but in doing so he had to step back, bringing both weapons up to block the blow and that had been my intent. I was able to pull back my sword and stab the would-be killer in the middle. The sword slipped through the leather jack and into his flesh. I pushed him from my blade. He was not yet dead but it was a mortal strike and I saw, out of the corner of my eye, that the king had lost his dagger. Stepping over the bearded killer's body I lunged with my sword into the back of the man who had raised his sword to end the life of King James. His companion was distracted and King James' sword slashed across his throat.

The king seemed to see me for the first time, "You!"

The bearded man was tough and he had pushed himself to his knees. He used both hands to try to drive his sword into the king's middle. King James knew how to kill and his sword almost took the head from the giant's shoulders.

The king's eyes narrowed, "Was it fortune brought you here or are you part of this conspiracy?"

I sheathed my sword and my dagger. The king swung his sword until the tip was at my throat, "I was in the luxurious chamber you gave me when I heard someone from your palace tell another that you were coming here this night," I paused and smiled a thin smile without a hint of humour in it, "to visit a lady. Money was exchanged. The men sounded suspicious and so I left the palace to come here. I was unsure what was planned. I am Queen Margaret's bodyguard and you are her husband. You may not like me or want me but King Henry paid for my services and I am a good bodyguard. I did not wish the husband of my charge to die."

After what seemed like an age the sword was removed. He looked at the bodies, "I know not these fellows but from their voices, they come from the borders. Who did they speak to in the cellar?"

I shook my head, "I know not his name but from his voice, he was one of the under butlers."

He grabbed the reins of his horse and pulled himself into the saddle. "Come with me. I want you within a sword's length until all is revealed."

I walked ahead of him and we headed down the almost deserted street to the main gate of the palace. That he was expected was clear but my presence was not and halberds were readied. "Captain, have four men go to the Golden Swan. There are dead men there. Have their bodies brought here then seal off the palace. I want none to leave. I want all the servants brought to the Great Hall so that I may inspect them. Guard this man." The captain went to take my sword but the king said, "Leave his sword for the present. He has been of some service to me this night."

The noise that was made was a great clamour and the whole palace was awakened and in an uproar. I stood with the captain and the king in the Great Hall and we watched as sleepy servants, who had little enough sleep as it was, were driven into the Great Hall.

The steward had managed to dress in his livery and he came to the king, "King James, what is amiss?"

"An attempt was made on my life this night and one of my servants sold the information. This man does not know the name of the servant but he will recognise him. He was one of the under butlers."

"I will see if they have all arrived, my liege." The steward turned and looked down the line of servants, "Where is Robert?" The other servants looked at each other and the steward turned to me, "You do not see the man here?" I shook my head. "King James, one man is missing. Robert of Coldstream."

The king turned to the captain. "Find him." Queen Margaret and her ladies appeared and the king flashed a look at me that told me to hold my tongue. "My love, go back to bed for this does not concern you. Your bodyguard has been of some service to me this night and I need to have words with him."

She looked from me to her husband and then nodded.

After they had gone the king leaned into me, "Now listen carefully, Thomas of Burscough, while I am grateful to you for your actions this night unless you swear an oath of silence then you will rot in the dungeons of Edinburgh castle until your body is weary of life and succumbs to the eternal sleep. You will simply disappear."

I was Thomas of Burscough and playing a part. I shrugged, "I am a sword for hire. I care not what a man does but I am paid to protect Margaret Tudor from all enemies. Are you an enemy, King James?"

His eyes narrowed and his hand went to the hilt of his sword and then he smiled, "No, I am not an enemy but I am a man with an appetite for a certain type of woman. I will pay for your services. Whatever King Henry pays you I will equal."

I nodded, "Then my silence is bought."

It was a short while later that the captain returned, "He has fled the castle, my lord. We found the sentry at the rear gate. His throat was cut and a horse stolen from the stable."

I knew that we could have taken him had there not been such a clamour. The king nodded, "Then Robert of Coldstream is declared an outlaw and none shall give him succour in my land."

The steward and the captain of the guard nodded.

The king continued, "And Thomas of Burscough needs accommodation that matches his status as bodyguard to the Queen." I noticed then that he looked at me differently. Had I ingratiated myself into his favour or made him wary of me? I had followed my instincts and for good or ill, I had to live with my decision. I was also aware that I had thwarted an attempt on the life of King James. Those who had planned the assassination would not be very happy with me. I would now have to watch my back.

I was given a new chamber. From the looks of the room, it had been occupied not long before I was given the room and I wondered who had been evicted. I was not in the wing of the palace with the king's chambers but I was centrally placed.

The next morning it was as though nothing untoward had happened. All the servants must have known that something had gone on but no one mentioned the attack. I learned, through Agnes, that the servants had all been sworn to secrecy and the bodies had been removed from the inn. King James did not want the world to know that there were people who wished him dead. My life became marginally easier from that moment on. I was hardly welcomed but the scowls were no longer there and King James and his steward appeared to go out of their way to be pleasant to me. I dined in the Great Hall, albeit on a lowly table but I was more confident that none would spit in my food now that I was seen as someone who was not an enemy. The steward, when he brought me the promised purse from King James, even volunteered the information that the three killers had been identified as men who were also from the borders. To me, that suggested Lord Home was behind the plot but as he was still welcomed at court by King James either the king was a consummate actor or he was keeping Lord Home close to watch him.

Queen Margaret asked for me to walk with her one afternoon. It was the first time since the wedding that we had been alone. Her ladies walked behind us.

"Master Thomas, what went on the other night? The king had blood spattered on his tunic and the servants will not talk of what went on for they are all frightened. I command that you tell me."

I was in a difficult position. I wracked my brains to come up with a way out of it. It seemed to me that the king just wanted his infidelity hidden and I devised a believable story that would not compromise me.

"Some men mistook the king for another and attacked him. I was fortunate enough to be walking close by and I came to his assistance. That is all. I was doing my job as a bodyguard."

"But why was he alone? He visits me in my chambers but he never spends the night with me. Where was he?"

I shrugged and was grateful for the Thomas persona, "I was taking air for the room I had been given was not a good one. I know not why he was alone and outside the palace but he was not far away. Perhaps he too wished for air."

We walked in silence for a while. The quadrangle was a pleasant place to walk and the potted plants were all fragranced so that the air was sweet. She stopped and looked up at me, "Thank you for saving the life of my husband. Perhaps he was taking a walk but I will try harder to please him and keep him in my bedchamber."

As I looked at her, I was aware of how young she was. She had seen just fourteen summers and was still little more than a child. James of Ecclestone might have wanted to put a protective arm around her and tell her that it was not her that was at fault but the king. Thomas just kept a stony expression on his face. Inside I sighed with relief for I knew that she would not tell the king that I had divulged at least part of his secret.

The one person who was not happy was Sir Andrew Buchanan. I heard, through Agnes, that he had tried to have me returned to the cellar but to no avail. That made him hate me even more and whenever I dined in his presence, he glared daggers. One day when I was walking along the corridor he attempted to barge me over for he was a big man. I was a billman with strong arms and the result was that rather than me falling over he reeled back against the wall.

His hand went to the hilt of his sword and then he thought better of it. "Why do you not go back to England? You are not popular here and the king only suffers you."

I played Thomas of Burscough once more, "I am a sword for hire and I fulfil my contract. So long as I am paid then I stay. I have learned to ignore the bites of insignificant insects."

"Beware, Englishman. I have a long memory."

"I too have a long memory but fortunately for me I have more skills than other men when it comes to weapons so feel free to test those skills any time you wish."

His face told me that he thought about it but he did nothing about it and carried on down the corridor.

Now that I was closer to their chambers, I was in a good position to see the comings and goings. The queen, young though she was, did manage to keep King James within the palace or, perhaps, he had been frightened by the attack. He would have been killed had I not been there. As I was now accepted as someone who whilst English, was not a threat, I overheard more conversations and parts of conversations. From them, I learned that King James wanted a military victory to ensure his name would be remembered when he was dead. His armies had helped to retake most of the isles but he wanted to lead an army to war and be accorded the title of victor. Unless the Lord of the Isles gave him such an opportunity then he would have to try his other neighbour, England. That news would not please King Henry who needed a distracted Scotland to allow England to square up to France once more. When they drank the Scottish lords were loose with their tongues and, as with Agnes and the women, I had become part of the tapestries that hung on the walls. I was almost invisible or they assumed me dumb. Thomas' character was dour and silent. I had chosen it well.

It was two of Lord Home's knights who gave me my first decent clue as to Scottish ambitions. Lord Home was a border lord and his knights were bemoaning the fact that England held more Scottish land in the east than in the west. The border, which had been in the same place for more than a century, ran from Norham to Carlisle. I heard them talk about how easy it would be to cross the river and ravage the land. "Norham has almost fallen many times. Now we have bombards and cannons it would fall easily. We could place our guns on the north shore of the Tweed and pound the castle into submission. That is the only barrier. The fertile land of Northumbria would then be ours for the taking."

"Lord Home could do that now. We have the bombards."

The other was slightly less drunk and he shook his head, "It is King James who wants the victory. We shall have to be patient. We will have a war but it will be with the wild men of the isles."

"Aye, and they have poor purses compared with the knights of Northumbria."

"Besides there is no honour in killing a wild Viking."

Everything they had said, despite their drunkenness, was true and I could have left there and then for I had the information I had been sent to find. Norham had been mentioned many times and was seen as the key to the back gate to England. Two things prevented me, Queen Margaret and the fact that if I tried to sneak away then I would be pursued. I worked out that I had three months to bide my time and then make an excuse to leave.

It was a fortnight later that the rider came in from the borders and I was summoned to the presence of King James and his senior lords. "Thomas of Burscough, the man, Robert of Coldstream was found with his throat cut in Berwick. We are no closer to finding out who paid him but his death so far from here finally vindicates you. There were lords here who thought that you were behind the attempt on my life."

That was the first time that I had realised that not only was I under suspicion but also that he had told his close advisers of the attempt. I now had the names of the men who would be the ones King Henry should fear.

He took a small purse of coins, which was smaller than the one given to me by the Queen Mother and smaller than the one the steward had given to me and tossed it to me. "Here is for your troubles and to warn you that your services as a bodyguard will be needed again. I am taking Queen Margaret with me when I go to bring the rebels in the north to heel. We shall all go to war." He did so in the presence of his advisers and showed me his cunning. He wanted them to think that he was paying me coppers. The first purse contained some golden coins with the silver. "You will need to watch the queen closely when I go to campaign in the west. You may need your sharp sword and quick wits."

It seemed to me more than a little reckless for the king to take his young bride on a campaign. James of Ecclestone might have objected, but Thomas of Burscough did not. To be fair to the king Queen Margaret was keen to accompany her husband. As preparations were made, I saw the method behind King James' plan. This would be a way to show those in the west of his land that he was their king and had a new queen. He was telling them that there would be children.

King James had defeated the old lord of the isles, John Macdonald and quashed the rebels more than ten years earlier. Now the grandson of his defeated enemy, Donald Dubh, had escaped from prison and was in Lewis with Torquil Macdonald and many rebels who wished a return to a ruler from the isles. The army was set to gather at Inverlochy Castle where the loyal Cameron clan would provide the bulk of the army. King James would travel with his one hundred knights and two hundred and fifty pikemen who used the long spears so favoured by the Scots. As armies go it would be a small one that marched across Scotland but, despite the presence of the queen and her ladies would be relatively quick. I saw then that King James was a clever leader who understood the needs of campaigning.

The queen would not have to ride, as we had wagons for the spears and armour, they were given a carriage especially fitted out. I was given a better horse and my position would be next to the wagon. The ride north and west used roads that had been first built by the Romans. They followed the valleys and passes. The first part, towards the Clyde, was the easiest but once we reached the Trossachs it became harder. As Thomas of Burscough, I found it hard to maintain my dour character for Queen Margaret was enchanted by all that she saw. She had enchanted the carters who drove the wagons for she never complained. Her ladies might have grumbled at the condition of the road but Queen Margaret who was still so young, giggled and laughed.

As we neared the coast, I began to see the myriad of islands that lay to the west of us. The soldier in me began to assess the problem for both sets of soldiers. Had the rebels chosen then they could have stayed on their islands and been immune from attack. They had ships and they were sailors. King James had few ships. However, if the rebels wished to challenge the authority of the king and regain control of the isles then they had to bring him to battle. It was an interesting problem.

While the castle at Inverlochy was old it was, at least, secure and the king and his queen were able to be accommodated there. There was no room for me and Thomas of Burscough had to live in a tent with the carters who had brought the wagons. My association with the queen meant that I was accepted by them and as I did not complain, as many who were given tents did, then I was able to share their food and their information. I had learned in Flanders that it is the little details that you learn that can provide the greatest intelligence. When the locals came to sell us food, they brought with them the news that the rebels were heading towards Achnacarry. The tiny hamlet was positioned on an isthmus between Loch Lochy to the east, and Loch Arkaig to the west. What amazed me was that no one had thought to tell the king. It was the following day that I delivered the news and I did so casually, assuming that he already knew.

The king was at breakfast and I approached the queen to ask if she needed me to escort her anywhere.

"I should like to see some of the lakes hereabouts. I understand there are two pretty ones to the north of us."

"That would be inadvisable, Queen Margaret, as I believe the rebels are heading there. Perhaps we could ride further south, towards Oban."

The king reacted immediately, "The rebels are heading here? How do you know?"

I shrugged, "I thought it was common knowledge. The carters with whom I share a tent told me and they had it from the locals."

He turned to the Cameron who was dining with him, "And did you know?"

The knight looked embarrassed and said, "There was a rumour but it was unfounded. I intended to send men this morning to scout out Achnacarry."

King James was a decisive man and he turned to Lord Home. The incident with Robert of Coldstream had not removed the suspicion about the border lord but intensified it. He was keeping him as close to him as he could, "Lord Home, muster the army. We march in an hour." He turned to the queen and smiled, "My love you shall stay within these walls until I return. I may have need of your bodyguard this day." From the look he gave the Cameronian knight I knew that he suspected treachery from his erstwhile allies. "Get your war gear, Thomas of Burscough. I need you and your sword." He smiled, "Do not fear, should you draw and use it then there will be payment."

James of Ecclestone would have done it for nothing but Thomas of Burscough was a professional and I nodded.

Chapter 7

It was unexpected but I would be in a battle once more and, this time, fighting alongside England's enemies. At least the men I was fighting would not be English. I rode with the king and his knights but the difference was that they wore armour and all I had been able to find was an old pot helmet. I was not too proud to wear it. We left the castle and headed north led by the Cameron clan warriors who were eager to get to grips with their ancient enemies, the Macdonalds. The two hundred and fifty men who were the most potent Scottish weapon, the pikemen, marched behind us. As I was at the rear of the column of knights and squires, I was able to turn and examine them from time to time. They carried their pikes over their shoulders. Eighteen feet long and steel-tipped they were a frightening weapon. The Swiss were using them even more effectively in the Empire and combining great phalanxes of men thus armed to become the dominant force in the battles taking place in the Empire. The Scots, whilst not as effective, were hard to beat and cavalry had little chance of breaking them down. Each Scottish pikeman had a helmet and some, the ones I presumed who would be in the front rank, also wore a breastplate. They had a variety of side arms from swords to falchions and daggers. They were King James' own men and I assumed would be his best.

My attention was drawn to the mob of men at the front of our army. Mob is the best word to describe them for there was no order to them. They had all kinds of weapons, armour and clothes. They were drawn from the land of the Camerons. Their chief led them on a horse and had we not been with them would, in all likelihood, have happily fought the Macdonalds on their own. They were loud and sang songs, none of which I understood. They shouted and jeered and I guessed that they were insulting their enemies before the battle was even joined.

There are some battles which are almost formal in their nature. The two sides line up, prayers are said, absolution is given and horns sounded to begin the fray. This battle, if battle it was to be, was not one of those. The two warbands, for there are no better words to describe them, of Highlanders spied each other as the two armies converged and with a mutual roar, they hurled themselves at one another. I knew that it took King James by surprise. It took him some moments to discover that events were beyond his control. The bulk of his army consisted of the Cameronian warriors. That they were outnumbered by the rebels seemed to make little difference to the highlanders. It was that day that I learned valuable intelligence for King Henry. King James was brave and able to think on his feet. He shouted an order for the horsemen to form on the right of the pikemen and for the pikemen to make a phalanx.

As I wheeled the borrowed horse, whose name I did not even know, I wondered how best to play this. James of Ecclestone would not desert his comrades but Thomas of Burscough might. The king made my decision for me, "Thomas of Burscough, stay by me and my standard." The standard was carried by a young knight, Sir Adam Foreman, and I placed myself on the opposite side of him. The king's intent was clear. I was staked to him and his colours. If they fell then so did I.

We had formed two lines and being in the front rank I had a good view of the battle. It was more of a brawl than a battle and men fought not with their heads but their hearts. It was clear to me that quarter was neither asked for nor given. Men hacked the bodies of their opponents when they had killed them, often resulting in they themselves being killed by enemies who saw an opponent who was temporarily defenceless.

The king turned to Lord Huntly, "We cannot have this, Huntley. We need order and control. The battle has barely begun and already I can see that we will be hard-pressed to escape with our lives."

"The men you have as a reserve, King James, are more than enough to deal with these rebels."

"Perhaps."

I was not so sure. I had fought in battles that relied upon serried ranks marching with weapons held closely together for self-protection but they had generally been over flat ground. This would not be flat ground. There were rocks and dips. There was hard ground and there were bogs and that was before the battle had begun. When the pikemen had to move, they would soon find themselves disordered. I was learning more and more about England's enemies.

The battle was the fiercest around the two chiefs and their banners. Guarded by the best of warriors the combat ebbed and flowed as fresh warriors joined the fray. It looked as though the Camerons, despite their lack of numbers, might just hold the rebels when both the standard and the chief fell. The defenders of the chief died to a man. Having seen their leaders and bravest warriors fall the will of the remainder weakened and they fled. It was inevitable and we could do nothing about it. I looked at King James. As ever he was decisive.

"Lord Home, hold the pikes here. Knights, we will make them think we are fleeing. We will ride to the east and draw them to our pikes. Follow my lead and when we wheel, we will fall upon their flanks."

The knights and squires who followed the king did not lack courage either. The knights each had a lance and it was just the squires and me that would have to use a sword. It was a clever strategy for as soon as we turned and rode to the east there was a collective roar from the rebels and they hurled themselves at the pikemen who stoically stood with a wall of steel-tipped pikes to receive them. I had been given a good horse but it was not a war horse. However, the king's plan to quickly wheel, meant that I was able to keep up with the king and Sir Adam.

The pikemen stood stock still and I saw how effective they were. The long spears meant that even those who were in the sixth and seventh ranks were able to bring their pikes to bear. It was not just the front rank that would be able to fight. With their helmets and breastplates, they were better armoured than the highlanders who did not bother with either helmet or armour. They relied upon the sheer ferocity of their attack and it was frightening. I had stood in a line of billmen and knew that if the highlanders had charged me when I was a young warrior then I might have been terrified enough to run. The highlanders had thrown all their efforts into charging the pikemen and that meant they were not looking to their left as they hurled themselves recklessly at the pikemen. Their wild attack might eventually succeed. I saw that some of the highlanders had used their swords to hack off the metal end of the pikes. Even a shattered pike was still an obstacle and the pikemen managed to hold off the frenzied attack. With the squires with us and the local knights who had joined us, there were more than two hundred of us but the sea of Macdonalds before us seriously outnumbered the Scottish horsemen. Sir Adam and I had no lances but the others in the front rank did and as they struck the highlanders every lance struck flesh. Those who were not lanced had a good chance of being trampled by our horses. I leaned from the saddle to slice my sword across the neck of one highlander. The mercenaries who had trained me in Flanders had done a good job. I used the edge of the blade to slash down at the backs of the men or, if they faced me, their necks. Without the brim of a helmet, a gorget or a mail hood, they were defenceless and my well-made sword had an edge that cut through to the bone each time I used it. It was well-weighted so it required little effort to use. Three men had fallen to my sword before the Macdonalds realised the danger they were in and they began to turn to face the threat on their flanks.

It availed them little for I heard Lord Home shout, "Pikemen, forward!"

Having endured the wild charge the pikemen, all as experienced as any billman I had led, began to march forward. Marching with serried pikes was, perforce, slow but it was steady. While the ones in the second rank back held their pikes steady the front rank warriors were able to jab. That they were well trained was clear as they all struck at the same time. It was as though they were punching the Macdonalds as one. The two-fold pressure on the highlanders began to tell. Their best and most experienced warriors were trapped between our horses and the advancing pikes. They fought bravely but they were outmatched if not outnumbered. A good leader would have organised them but their leaders were as wild and foolishly courageous as the men they led. Wounded and bleeding they fought on beyond reason. King James and his knights had now shattered their lances and the two lines had become one. We were sweeping their right flank towards the loch and when Donald Dubh and Torquil Macdonald wheeled their horses away from King James and his knights then the battle was over.

King James showed a ruthless side to him that day. We chased, harried and butchered every enemy we could find. In an attempt to flee us, many threw themselves into the loch. We only stopped when weary horses could go no further. The knights all cheered the king. It was a victory and although the rebel leaders had escaped, we had slaughtered so many that there was little chance of them defending the isles against an invasion. The work of the king was done. The capture of Donald Dubh and Torquil Macdonald might take time but their days of freedom were most definitely numbered and the men of the isles' power was broken.

We dismounted to walk our horses back to the castle. I did not intrude but walked behind the standard-bearer and the king.

One of the local knights, Sir Alexander Cameron, spoke to me. He had been close by me when we had charged and he spoke as one shield brother to another. "You fought well today, especially for an Englishman who had nothing to gain for his service."

I was still playing a part and I shook my head, "There you are wrong, my lord, for I was paid."

He nodded and waved a hand towards the west, "This is the end of the isles you know. The Macdonalds took it from the Vikings. There are still Norse who live on the islands and they will continue to fight the Macdonalds. Torquil Macdonald gambled and lost."

"Vikings? I thought that they were in the past."

"This was their domain and they still sail their dragonships. They are pirates to a man and you cannot change their nature. I fear there will be isolated farms and villages that will suffer when they raid once more. Once they lost Man then the pirates who remained found sanctuary on the isolated islands to the west." He smiled, "I have a castle and my people will be safe from the early morning raids. They will seek to profit where there are no castles."

After a mile or so when Lord Huntly and the other nobles had come to heap praise upon the king, he turned to me and said, "Thomas of Burscough, I can see why King Henry made you the bodyguard of my wife. You fought as bravely and as hard as any of my knights and nobles."

Sir Adam nodded, "Aye, he did that, my liege. He handles a sword like a condottiere. I would fight with you any time, Master Thomas."

The king shook his head, "I think, Thomas of Burscough, that, as an Englishman, you have done enough for both your charge and for Scotland. When we return to Edinburgh, I will find a Queen's Knight to guard the Queen and he will be a Scot for that is right and proper. You will be recompensed for your time and for the service you have done."

And with that, I was dismissed.

Despite my dour and serious manner, the queen had become fond of me and she begged her husband to allow me to remain. James of Ecclestone would have wished that but not Thomas of Burscough. It broke my heart to let her tears fall on stony ground but I had done all that the king had asked of me. I was given a good horse, a small chest of coins and passage on a ship that was travelling from Leith to London. The queen gave me letters for her mother and father as well as a signet ring. She was a kind lady. No one came to wave me goodbye and more care was taken to load my horse than to ensure that I was comfortable. The horse had come from the royal stables and Alexander was a truly generous gift. It showed me that I had managed to deceive King James for he was so pleased with my efforts that he had no inkling that I was a spy.

It was only when I boarded the ship that I discovered that The Earl of Derby had died. The sailors mentioned it and I realised that even though I had been in Scotland a short time I was far from news of England and my home. I had known the earl was unwell but I had honestly expected to see him upon my return. That would not now happen and I wondered how it would affect my status. I had been told to report to him but now I would have to find another to whom I could give my report and news. The letters from Queen Margaret would be just the excuse I needed. I had the long voyage down the east coast of England to ponder the problem.

I hated the voyage up the Thames as despite the fact that it was a relatively short voyage to Greenwich it seemed unending. There was much traffic on the river and with both adverse winds and a high tide the captain had his hands full. It took time to unload my horse and it was as the task was completed that I learned that the king and his son were further along the river at Richmond. I could have reloaded the horse but I did not relish the slow passage down the river. I had only ridden Alexander briefly and so I rode the sixteen miles to Richmond. The horse enjoyed opening his legs after the confines of the cog and I was able to shed the character of Thomas of Burscough and become James of Ecclestone once more. I had managed to end my contract early and I relished the opportunity to return to my home.

It was dark when I reached the palace at Richmond. In hindsight that was a good thing. I impressed Prince Henry who thought it had been a deliberate act on my part and made me look like a more efficient spy than I really was. Father and son had both changed. The king looked older while the prince, although not yet a man looked to have grown and was developing the perceptive hawk-like stare of his father.

Servants were dismissed and food fetched so that the three of us could talk. I had already decided upon honesty. I told everything, even about the king's infidelity. I even told the rumour, because I thought it was important, that I had heard from Agnes, that the king had secretly married a Scottish lady, Margaret Drummond. I did not believe it but as the rumour was circulating, I was honour bound to tell the king. I told them of the skirmish, it was not large enough to be called a battle, and I gave them my perception of the motives of King James.

When I had finished, I drank half a goblet of wine and waited for the interrogation that I assumed would follow. King Henry looked to have shrunk since I had first met him or, perhaps, I had grown. His eyes were sad when he spoke, "Thank you, Master James, I like your honesty, unpalatable though it might be. I have remained faithful all my life but I know that other kings were not so honourable. It is sad that I have had to sacrifice a loyal daughter for the sake of England."

Prince Henry said, "But could we not use this rumour of a wife to our advantage, father?"

"When you become king, Henry, you will learn that there is a moment for such things. Tell me, Master James, in your opinion is there any chance that the Scots will cause trouble on the borders?"

I shook my head, "Not for a year or two, King Henry. The claimant to the isles escaped and King James will be hard-pressed to catch him. There will be cross-border raids, there always will be, but the people who live there are used to them. What I do know is that when they do attack it will be through Norham and that they will use bombards to do so. They will not try to take Bamburgh or Berwick."

Prince Henry was intrigued, "Why not and how do you know?"

"When I became accepted as not being a threat to their king, his knights were looser tongued and on the ride to the isles, I learned that Northumbria is regarded as Scotland and Berwick, which we won, is regarded as a prize. They would not damage that prize but the thorn that has stuck in their side for many years is Norham. It has never yet fallen and they would destroy it and slight it."

King Henry asked, "And could they take it?"

I nodded, "I have not visited the castle but I believe that it is old and cannons could bombard its walls. King James is gathering a great number of guns. It is why they will not destroy the castle that they regard as theirs, Berwick. Norham, Etal and Ford are their targets."

The king smiled, "You have done well. You may return to your home, James of Ecclestone but know that I may well call on you again. You are a good spy and an intelligent one at that."

"We should reward him, father!"

The king shook his head, "The rewards given to him already were given by the Earl of Derby. If the King of England was seen to heap honours on a lowly gentleman from Lancashire, then attention would be drawn to him. The Sherriff of Lancashire may well reward him but we will let James of Ecclestone become anonymous once more."

The prince was like a dog with a bone and he turned to me, "When I am king," he looked at his father, "God willing many years hence, then I will need your services. I shall surround myself with warriors like you, that I can trust. Scotland will learn that England is too powerful a neighbour for them to try to ravage and rape its land."

The next day, as I left for home, I realised that my life as a country gentleman would be a brief interlude. I needed to make the most of my time at home in Ecclestone.

It was late afternoon when I rode into the village. I now regarded it not only as my home but as mine. I owned the most property in the village and more men now worked on my land than any other. So, as I rode through the town on my new horse, Alexander, men stopped work and knuckled their foreheads. They smiled as they said, "Welcome back, Captain." King Henry might think I was anonymous but there would be gossip about me and my absence from the village. I would have been missed at the weapon practice and that alone would have merited speculation. Now that I had returned, riding what was clearly a warhorse, the gossip would be fuelled. I did not think for one moment that any would connect me with the king. I smiled as I waved back. Only my wife and mother would know the truth. Even Thomas and Robert, close though they were would not be a party to my visit to Scotland.

The stables were at the rear of the new house and close to the hogbog. I rode through the rear gate and was almost unobserved. I reined Alexander in when I was in the cobbled yard. When I had acquired Calliope, I had realised we needed someone to look after our equines. With a couple of sumpters, it paid to have one who liked horses. John was only eighteen but he loved horses and when I had given him the chance to be my stablemaster he had leapt at the opportunity. The newly built stables, finished before I had left for Scotland, had room for him and when he saw my new horse his face lit up as though the present was for him, "Captain, that is a magnificent beast." He examined the horse as he held the reins for me to dismount, "and he has not been gelded. Captain, we could buy a mare and breed."

I smiled at his enthusiasm, "You think we could?"

"With a horse like this, it would be a crime not to." He nodded towards the newly built house, "Your mother has moved in with your wife. She was ill not long since." He must have seen the shock on my face for he shook his head, "She has recovered well but the mistress thought it better if she lived here."

The house had been finished just before I had left. I had not even spent a month inside its walls. It would take time for me to call it home. Everything looked new and freshly painted with whitewash. I entered the rear door. The change from the days when I had lived in the village with my parents and sisters could not have been made clearer than by the scene in the kitchen. My mother and wife were there but there was a serving girl from the village who helped and another who bounced my son, James, on her knee. The kitchen was four times the size of the one in our old home. I had been in the kitchens of the earl and the Sherriff not to mention King James and whilst my kitchen was tiny in comparison it still had many of the features of those kitchens.

As I stepped into the kitchen, I was able to watch the women as their conversation filled the room. They had not seen me and I basked in that moment when I was invisible. A good spy knew how to be hidden and I was. It was the girl, Mary, who was playing with James who spied me, "Captain James!"

The others all turned to look at me. Jane was at my side and hugging me in a flash. My mother moved more slowly these days and she wiped her hands on her apron as she came to me.

"Husband, we did not expect you."

I kissed Jane, "I returned as fast as I could. I would have overtaken any message I might have sent." She moved aside to let my mother hug me, "You have been unwell, mother. You need not work in the kitchen."

She squeezed me and I felt her bony fingers. She had lost weight and was thinner. "This is the kitchen and I am happy here. I have Jane and my grandson. Where else would I be happy?" She moved away from me, "And are you home now or will you go gallivanting off once more?"

"I am home and I cannot see when I will be needed again." I was mindful of the two village girls and I was careful with my words. "You know better than any, mother, that we cannot predict events outside our control. I am home and I am happy. Let us enjoy that."

I spent the first day with my son. He had grown in the time I had been away. Then I walked my land with my wife and son. It was slow progress as everyone wished to speak to me. I know that they were all curious about my absence but my wife and I managed to evade and deflect the questions as we commented on the land, their families and their homes. Thomas and Robert had changed beyond all recognition and I knew that they could each manage a farm for me. I was aware that I had a farm now at Hoscar. When one or the other grew restless it would be there as a way of keeping them happy. For my part, I was delighted with their endeavours. Our fields were now filled with wheat, barley and oats. Our flock of sheep had grown to more than a hundred. If I wished for more then I would need to find more land. The pigs' numbers had swollen and we could either sell or eat the excess. Meat as a meal was rare in a village like Ecclestone. The fishpond had been finished and Robert had managed to stock it with fish. We would not harvest the fish for a year but when we did then the whole village would benefit from fish on Friday. Life was good and with the prospect of war far from us, there was an air of optimism in the village and, indeed the county.

Chapter 8

Ecclestone 1505

The happy times ended, albeit temporarily, at harvest time when, a week after my daughter, Elizabeth was born, my mother died. She had never truly recovered from her illness. My return brought her respite and, I think, lengthened her life and the expectation of another grandchild made her cling to life like a drowning man will a piece of driftwood. I paid for the doctor from Lathom to attend her and he shook his head and gave us the news that he could do nothing, "She has a worm eating at her and her death is as inevitable as the arrival of winter. All that you can do is to keep her comfortable and happy. She has enjoyed a good life, Captain James, and speaking to her I know that she is proud of what you have achieved. Just continue to do as you are doing and she will be happy until the end."

My wife had been brought up almost as a lady but somehow she and my mother got on so well that they might have been mother and daughter. She was certainly closer to my mother than the woman I still thought of as a galleon under full sail. "She missed your father, James. They loved each other and when he was taken part of her died. I think she hung on while you were away." We never mentioned Scotland. We could keep secrets. She patted her ever-growing belly, "The new baby will keep her going but I think that you should be prepared for what happens after the birth."

I heeded my wise wife's advice and I was as attentive as a son could be. I made sure that I spoke to her each night and as often during the day as I could. Her mind began to wander and sometimes she addressed me as Walter. I took that as a compliment for my father was still my hero. It broke my heart to see her die a little more each day.

When Elizabeth was born her naming was easy and my mother's joyous face almost made me burst into tears. She passed away quietly in the middle of the night. It was my mother's way for she did not wish to bother anyone and I think that she chose the moment of her passing. I knew she would be happy for she would be reunited with my father. My wife and I sat on either side of her bed and each held a hand as she smiled at us and quietly slipped into eternal sleep. We sat there in silence, both wrapt in our own thoughts until Elizabeth began to cry for milk. My wife smiled for she believed, as I did, that part of my mother was in the bairn. She had given us some time to ourselves and the baby's cry was a reminder that life goes on.

We had my mother buried with my father. I had paid for a good stone for my father and the stonemason did a fine job of carving my mother's name. My sisters came for the funeral. Like me, they were now older. I had only seen them once since they had left home and that had been at my father's funeral. I did not know them but family is family and I gave each of them a gold crown. The farms were doing well and I wanted to show them that their little brother was now a man of substance.

Life then began to follow a predictable pattern. It was determined by two things, the seasons and the Sunday training. I still trained my billmen once a week and the billmen of the hundred once a month. The hundred was the number of billmen mustered in a group of villages. The training of the hundred took place at Lathom and that meant a hard march for my billmen. I think it did them good for we sang as we marched and it drew us closer together. Since the skirmish at Sedbergh, I had begun a stricter regime and our training was both hard and rigorous. My reputation had been enhanced by the battle and now the men obeyed every instruction without question. I had also learned from the pikemen at Achnacarry. We began to train in three ranks so that the bills of the second and third rank jabbed before the front rank. It was harder to do than one might imagine but we had persevered and become very skilled. Of course, the proof of that particular pudding would come in the eating and until we had to fight then we would not know how good we were.

The Sherriff came one Sunday to speak with me and to observe the training. His nephew, Thomas Stanley, was now the Earl of Derby and Sir Edward, visiting the family home at Lathom, was keen to see that his nephew lived up to his brother's standards. The Sherriff did not know of my last exploits and I did not enlighten him. His brother had been well able to keep secrets and I was not about to betray the old earl.

"I like the way you train your men, Ecclestone. You are a young man who is not afraid of change."

I nodded, "Of course, my lord, we will never know if what I am doing is right until we have to fight."

"Do not be so eager for war. If Sedbergh taught us nothing it is that danger can come not from some foreign foe but from those who wish to take from the people. Keep training and maintain your vigilance. I have to tell you that if the billmen of Lancashire have to fight again it shall be under your command for my brother had great faith in you." He smiled, "I hear you are a confidante of the Queen Mother too. For a gentleman farmer, you move in exalted circles."

He was right of course. I was a big fish in my own pond but even in larger patches of water, I was a fish who commanded respect. The nobles who lived at Knowsley, Windle, and Winwick often invited my wife and me to dine with them. I confess we refused more invitations than we accepted. It was not out of rudeness but we were happy in Ecclestone with my children. When the first Christmas after my mother's death came, I invited Jane's mother and father to my home. They had never visited and we had more than enough room. When the house had been built, I had ensured that there were quarters for guests and so James' and Elizabeth's grandparents got to see them. Mary de Clifton was not a natural mother and certainly not a natural grandmother. While my mother had never been happier than attending to James when he had been a baby, Mary de Clifton did not even want to hold my daughter. Jane's father, in contrast, was in his element and made funny faces, noises and rolled around on the floor quite happily with James. Mary was not happy with his display. The more I saw of Mary de Clifton the less I liked her. She had delusions of grandeur and aspirations to be that which she could never be, a lady. Even if she had been granted the title, she would not have earned it. My mother-in-law apart, we had a wonderful Christmas and when on twelfth night Roger de Clifton left for home I was sad as were my wife and son. Mary de Clifton would have left on St Stephen's day if she could. She had expected a house filled with nobles and not a happy family who just enjoyed each other's company. In fact, the only part of the new building of which she truly approved was the dovecote I had placed in the yard. It was empty as yet but she saw it as one sign of nobility. For me it was not a posturing gesture to impress people, it was a practical way to have meat and eggs all year round.

That winter was a hard one and not just in our part of Lancashire. We were lucky that we had food aplenty but some parts of the land endured famine and people died of both hunger and cold. We did not and I ensured that all the village benefitted from our prudence. The young James would not have done so but my mother and Jane had changed me and I was a better person than the one who ran away to war. The icy grip held the land for months. It was, we later heard, a cold snap throughout the land. I feared for those who had farms on higher ground for at least our sheep had stone walls where they could shelter and my labourers were able to clear snow so that they could feed.

As Jane and I sat in the warmth of my new home with the fine fireplace sending out heat to warm every nook and cranny I shook my head and gave a wry smile. "What amuses you, husband?"

"It is not amusement but wonder. This cold makes life hard for us but when it is over so many animals will have died that the price of wool will rise and we shall be better off. We have done little to make this so and yet we will be rewarded while others will not."

She smiled and shifted her position. "But you have done something. You put sheep here in Ecclestone and protected them. You had the foresight to do that."

"I am no farmer."

"Yet you are. I confess that there is more of a soldier in you than a farmer but you make the right decisions. Your mother knew that well. I did not know your father long but the two of you are so similar and show that the apple does not fall far from the tree. Keep doing what you are and all will be well." She rose and held her back.

"What ails you, my sweet?"

She shook her head, "My back is giving me trouble. I wonder if I am with child again. The last time I had this pain was when I carried Elizabeth and it was the same with James."

"So soon?"

She laughed, "We did not spend much time apart and Elizabeth is a good sleeper. It might well be. I shall consult with the ladies."

Thomas and Robert's wives were amongst a small circle of women in the village who were called upon as midwives. The knowledge was passed on from mother to daughter. Doctors were rare in places like Ecclestone and small injuries and ailments were dealt with by these same women. They appeared to have special powers and none could explain how they gained them save through blood. The women confirmed that my wife was expecting our third child. When I had built the house, I had done so with a large family in mind. The purses of coins I had been given had been put to good use. I had a little gold left now but what I had been paid could be seen in the large number of animals and the well-furnished and spacious hall.

It was late February when the thaw came and we had to open the sluices on the fishpond. The ditches I had built proved their worth and there was no flooding. When we inspected my fields and the village, I was gratified to see that we had lost neither animal nor villager. My mother would have been proud. I had shared our excess and the village had benefitted. I was now seen as the headman of the village. My title of gentleman accorded me the right to be addressed as master but I was happy when the villagers thanked me with my title of captain. That was one with which I was more familiar.

It was a week after the roads reopened that Thomas Crouchley, the Earl of Derby's steward, thrashed his horse into my yard. He threw himself from his saddle as I emerged. The clattering hooves had seemed urgent. "Captain, we need the men mustered."

I could tell from his lathered horse and his manner that something untoward had occurred, "What is amiss?"

He pointed to the west, "Warriors in dragonships landed at Meols and raided the isolated villages and farms."

"Vikings?"

He shrugged, "I know not. The boy from Meols who rode in with the news was terrified beyond belief but I think that they are Norsemen. They are raiders and are causing hurt but the earl is in

London and if men are not mustered to rid our land of these men then I fear there will be much hardship and death."

"You have sent to the Sherriff?"

"I did but the rider will take at least a day, maybe more to reach his lordship. You are closer. I have Captain Richard bringing his men to Burscough. That was a good rallying point." He suddenly looked nervous, "Was that right? I am no soldier."

"Aye, it is close enough and placed centrally. Go inside and eat." I knew that Jane would take care of him. He was no longer a young man and I admired his courage in making such a ride in the conditions. I waved over Thomas and Robert, "Muster the billmen and the archers. We march to war."

Sedbergh meant instant and unquestioning obedience. They both headed off and I went to the stable. "John, I need Calliope saddled and Goliath and the other sumpters readied. Fasten my billhook to Goliath and when my war bag comes then fasten that too."

"War, Captain?"

The steward explained to my ostler. I think he was trying to come to terms with this catastrophe, "War, John. I have raised the fyrd and ordered them to meet at Burscough. I sent a rider to Hornby Castle to seek help from Sir Edward but it is far from here and it is the men of this hundred who will have to try to stop these raiders from taking captives. Captain Richard has been informed but I wanted you to lead the men."

Jane had left one of the servants seeing to Thomas and she looked up at me, "Raiders have attacked Meols."

Her face fell, "But Meols is not far from Clifton."

"It is south of the river. Your parents should be safe."

"But who would attack? The Scots?"

I shook my head, "I cannot know that yet. They came in dragonships and so they could have come from Scotland, the Isles, Ireland or even Iceland. When they are taken, I will discover the truth. There will just be John and William left to watch over you. Will that be enough?"

"They are both good men, aye. You must do what you can. Send these pirates back into the sea from whence they came."

I went to my bedchamber and opened my chest. Rather than carry my armour on my sumpter I would ride to war ready to fight. I donned my padded jack, breastplate, backplate, fauld and greaves. I carried my helmet. My war gear was kept in a bag and I carried that to the stables. John had already prepared the animals and I handed him my war bag before fastening my cloak about my shoulders. I hung my helmet from my saddle. Men were making their way to my farm. Thomas and Robert were already organising them. With their bags hanging from their billhooks there were ready to march. Robert and the other men who had pieces of armour wore them but everyone carried their helmets from their billhooks. The archers were ready too and they had their bows in cases that they hung from their backs.

I waved a hand at the sumpters, "Fasten any bags and gear to the sumpters we may have to march more than twenty miles this day."

Thomas Crouchley joined us and my wife handed me a basket. "Here is food for the day." John fastened it to Goliath. She stood on tiptoe to kiss me, "Take care, my husband."

"I will be back as soon as the threat is gone. Watch over our children and tell them…"

She smiled, "I will but they know that already."

The men had formed the column as I threw my leg over Calliope's back. I saw my wife's eyes welling and knew that there was nothing I could do.

"Men of Ecclestone, let us march to war. We go to fight those who would make slaves of our people."

The men all cheered and that heartened me.

Chapter 9

The steward would not be able to ride further than Burscough but I needed him there to confirm my authority. I rode but that was because the steward was mounted and I needed to speak to him. We had twelve miles to go and passing through Rainford, Bickerstaffe and Ormskirk we could more than double our numbers. By the time we reached Burscough, it was gone noon and our column's tail was a mile from the front. We had but sixty men but that was more than double the number with which we had begun. The prior had fed the ones who had been sent ahead by the steward and I was delighted to see that Captain Richard was there. I needed his skills to direct the archers. We had one hundred and eight men. As an army it was small but it was all that I had. We ate but I chewed while in conference with Captain Richard, the steward and the prior.

"We have heard that these raiders are less than six miles to the west and another, much larger warband is heading for Rufford. Sir William Hesketh and his family are not there at the moment and they only have the fyrd to defend the village." The prior looked worried, "We cannot leave Burscough Abbey undefended."

I wiped my mouth and drank some of the priory ale, "There are men still on the road. Steward, you must employ those in the defence of this priory. I believe that we must head for Rufford. Those who are at Meols have already been raided and we can do nothing for them as yet. The larger warband will be the one from Rufford. We must bring them to battle and buy the time for the Sherriff to reach us."

Thomas Crouchley said, "But that may not be until tomorrow. What if you are defeated?"

I looked at Captain Richard who nodded, "Then we must ensure that we are victorious. We have one advantage and one advantage only. Thanks to the steward's valiant ride and early warning they will not expect retribution, not yet at least. I would hazard a guess that their intention is to take Rufford and then desecrate the priory. This is the rich prize." The prior made the sign of the cross. "It may well be that you have to defend Burscough from those to the west of us."

The steward stood taller, "The earl's bones lie in this priory and I will die before I allow any to damage his tomb. Fear not, Captain James, if you can hold the larger warband at Rufford then we will stop the other from achieving their end."

I would no longer need Calliope and I left the horse at the abbey. I would march with my men the three miles to Rufford. As we headed up the road, my helmet on my head, I looked at the sky. We would reach Rufford in less than an hour and there would still be enough daylight for us.

As we marched Captain Richard said, "We need intelligence as to the dispositions of our enemies. You are armoured and must move more slowly than we. I will take four of my archers and we will run to scout them out. I will send one back to give to you their numbers."

It made sense, "Then I will command all until you return."

He smiled, "James, you and I know that you have the mind that will dictate our battle. I am content to serve under you. My archers can stand off an enemy but you and your billmen will be the ones who have to face their fury."

He gestured to his men and with strung bows, they loped off.

I saw the spiral of smoke in the distance. It was too large to be the fire from a dwelling. Something had been set alight. The fyrd of Rufford were good men. I had led them at Sedbergh but there were only twenty-two of them, billmen and archers. Sir William, the lord of the manor had retainers who could fight but they would be with him and not in Rufford. I wondered if the fire was from his manor house. It would make sense. Once sacked it was what pirates would do. As we neared the village, the flames I could see told me that the fire was from a much more substantial building than a small house. The manor house was, indeed, on fire.

Captain Richard and his archers stepped from the trees and he held his hand up for me to stop.

"There are more than one hundred and twenty men in the village. They are Norsemen. Many wear old-fashioned mail byrnies and they have shields and helmets. I estimate three boats' crews. They are still ransacking the village and did not see us. We must hurry but how do we defeat them?"

I had passed through Rufford on my way north and I said,
"There is a ford across the river is there not?" He nodded.
"Could you and your archers work your way around the village
for I have a mind to drive them north towards you? If nothing
else you would be able to loose into their backs where they
would be unprotected by shields. We will march in a column up
the road and draw their weapons to us."

"You would be the bait?" I nodded. "Then we will be waiting
on the other side of the river. We will need some minutes to get
into position. God be with you."

As the archers headed off, I turned to my men. I had just
seventy billmen. I recognised many faces from Sedbergh and
that filled me with confidence, "I want to make a column seven
men wide and ten men deep. We will fight as a hedgehog. Let us
keep them from our front and sides. We march as one and drive
them to our waiting archers. I want all the ones with helmets and
armour in the front. Keep together and fight as a single body. I
want no one duelling with Norsemen. Two or three striking
together will reap a greater reward. We fight for Lancashire,
England and King Henry." The men did not cheer for they were
too nervous and the outcry might have alerted the raiders.

It was reassuring to be flanked by Thomas and Robert. Robert
had the armour and helmet taken at Sedbergh while Thomas
wore a helmet and my father's old breastplate. It was still
serviceable and meant the three of us could face our foes
together. There was a cacophony of noise ahead. There was still
the clash of metal on metal and the screams of terrified villages
and those who had been wounded. With the smoke coming from
the burning hall our advance was hidden from raiders who were
just intent on plundering and ransacking. As we passed one
warrior astride a woman, Jack of Rainford left our column to
bring down his billhook and smash it through the pirate's spine.
The woman screamed even louder but the man was dead. Jack
had disobeyed my command to do so but I understood why he
had done it. We reached the burning manor house before we
were seen and before we had to bring our collective billhooks
into action. Five raiders, wearing byrnies and with round shields
were carrying plunder from the hall. When they spied us, they

dropped their plunder and one shouted in a language I did not understand although his meaning was clear.

"Now! Charge!"

There were only five men but I knew we had to have a quick victory to give all my men heart. The five were still drawing their swords as we hit them. I rammed the spike of my billhook into the face of the one in the centre as Robert brought his blade into the next of the second. Jack, on the outside, had the luxury of a wide sweep and his billhook hacked through the thigh of the end warrior biting through to the bone, severing the limb and effectively killing him for his lifeblood poured from his veins. Thomas was able to use the same stroke as me and his foe had his face skewered. Peter of Parr had his strike blocked by a shield but Harold the Pig Man had a free swing and took the raider's head with a wide sweep of his bill. The men behind me gave a cheer and that, allied to the raider's shout alerted the rest.

I saw a well-armed warrior. He had a good helmet and the design on his shield had the three legs of Man upon it. This was not just any warrior this was the leader. I heard him shout something and it became clear that he had ordered a shield wall. It was an effective formation. The raiders locked shields in three ranks to bar our passage to the ford over the river.

"Reform!" I wanted a solid formation as we struck them and the men stopped to dress our ranks. It gave me the chance to assess the opposition and to allow Captain Richard and his men to get into position.

Their leader was a huge man. I saw he had bracelets on his bare arms and he held a war axe easily in one hand. His shield had a metal boss and I knew that he would use it offensively. His byrnie came below his knees and a blow to his legs was out of the question. The good news was that none of those we faced had a spear. It meant we would have the first strike. I counted on the seven of us having a one-in-two chance of striking flesh. All we needed to do was to break the cohesion of the shield wall and our longer billhooks would protect us. I was also relying on the archers.

"The Earl of Derby, England, and King Henry!"

The battle cry set us off and we were all in step. Billhook shafts rested reassuringly on our shoulders and we marched. We all held our billhooks slightly behind us so that we could thrust as one. It was clear that these raiders had never faced billhooks for many swung their weapons too early. The chief and the men who flanked him did not. The war axe was held menacingly over his right shoulder and I could see his eyes as he calculated the perfect moment to strike. Our billhooks were thrust when we were two paces from the raiders and our march meant that we struck the shields, byrnies and flesh when we were one pace from them. The axe swept across to chop off the head of my billhook. Mine was no ordinary billhook for, like a poleaxe, it had a langet of metal protecting the top foot and a half of the weapon. The axe struck the langet and deflected the head but it did not damage it. The spike of the head was driven across the right arm of the man next to the chief and drew blood.

It was at that moment that Captain Richard and his thirty odd archers released their arrows into the backs of the raiders. I could not see them but as there was a collective wail from the rear rank, I knew that his arrows had been sent from a close distance and every one of them had found flesh. The third rank disintegrated and the ones in the second rank tried to turn to face a new threat. Even the leader was distracted and I brought my billhook backhand across his head. We were still moving forward and they no longer had the reassurance of a second rank of shields to support them. The war chief could not help recoiling and he began to overbalance. As he did so, I rammed the spike of the billhook into his unprotected neck. He wore no armour and the necklet of silver did nothing to stop his death. Robert had despatched the raider I had wounded and Thomas and Peter of Parr ended the life of the third raider. As the arrows began to thin their second rank, the enemy broke. Their leader was dead and they were now outnumbered and attacked on two sides. They fled. The disadvantage of a column of billhooks is that it is unwieldy. We could not pursue as fast as they fled.

Captain Richard saw the dilemma and shouted, "Archers, pursue!"

I turned and said, "See to our wounded and finish off the enemy. We take no prisoners."

That said I knelt to speak to the dying man whose arm I had sliced and who had been stabbed by Richard, "Where are you from?"

In answer, he spat and Jack was so incensed that he chopped through the man's neck. We would learn nothing.

A wounded villager, his right arm bandaged, approached, "Thank God you came, Captain. They came after the sun was at its height and we had no warning. I was in my fields when I heard and I brought my men as fast as we could but by then the ones in the village were dead."

"You know me?"

"I fought with you at Sedbergh."

"Then organise your defences. I will leave my wounded here but Burscough Priory and the tomb of the Earl of Derby are in danger. Captain Richard pursues the ones who raided here. You should be safe."

He nodded, "We will do as you command and God speed."

None of my men had been killed but eight were wounded. I left them and then led the rest back down the road to Burscough. We were tired. Nay, we were exhausted but I knew how few men we had left at Burscough. If we took the time to rest then the steward, the prior and the monks might all be dead, not to mention the villagers. My men were of the same mind as me and with our helmets hanging from our bloody billhooks, we trudged back down the road from whence we had come.

It was dark as we approached the village and the priory. We could hear fighting from ahead. It was not the same sound we had heard from Rufford. There were fewer cries and the metal on metal sound was augmented by the sound of wood on wood. They were trying to batter their way through the priory's sturdy gates. Just as at Rufford we did not know the numbers so at Burscough we were, quite literally, in the dark. This time we did not have the advantage of archer scouts. I halted eight hundred paces from the village and gathered my men around me. One of the captains had been wounded but the rest remained and I planned on using that village unity to our advantage. Fighting in the dark it would be all too easy to hit a comrade.

"We attack them in groups from the villages. I will lead the Ecclestone contingent. As we are the largest I intend to attack the men who are assaulting the gate."

"How do you know they are attacking the gate, Captain?"

"Because, Lol, I can hear something striking wood and the priory has stone walls. They may be trying to climb the walls but it is relatively easy to keep men from the walls. The rest of you spread out and attack men that you outnumber. I want no heroics. We are the finest of billmen but in the dark, we are at a disadvantage. These raiders know how to use a sword and an axe. We fight not for honour but to kill as many of the enemy as we can. Surround individuals and butcher them like the animals they are."

I hoped I sounded ruthless for if we showed mercy then we would lose.

We passed men trying to climb the walls. They held a shield between two men while a third clambered on the shield to try to climb the walls. The defenders used anything to hand to push them off. We passed them for others could dislodge them. We had to get to the gate. As we neared it, I saw that they were using a log as an improvised ram and were smashing it against the gate. Some held shields above their heads while four men swung the log rhythmically as they chanted. Even in the dark, I could see the lighter marks of fresh wood where the ram had begun to crack the ancient gate.

"Spread out so that all our billhooks can find a mark."

There was too much noise for them to hear us and we were still hidden by the dark. I knew that would change when the first of them died. I swung my billhook in an arc and hacked through the byrnie and into the side of one of those holding a shield up. Robert skewered one of those holding the ram while Thomas used the hook from his bill to pull one of those holding the ram. As the warrior tumbled to the ground Peter hacked off his head. The ram dropped and the warriors turned to face us. The three we had initially killed meant we now were equal in number but as the two men who had been holding the log had to grab weapons the odds swung in our favour. As I faced a warrior with a sword and shield I knew that no matter what happened the tomb and the priory would be safe. Now I had to save as many of my men as I could. I was not only the captain of this company but the best and most experienced warrior. I used every ounce of experience that night. I feinted with the tip of the bill hook and as I had expected the warrior I faced used his shield to block the blow. I then used the hook to pull at the byrnie around his knee. He was unbalanced and he used his sword arm to try to get balance. I used my left shoulder to ram into his shield and the already falling warrior fell to the ground where he lay as helpless as a fish caught in my fishpond. He died quickly when my billhook found his throat. I whipped my billhook up and around for Jack was fighting a warrior with a war axe. The blade of my billhook hacked into his back. Thanks to his mail shirt it did not kill but it hurt and Jack ended the warrior's life with his next strike. I looked around and saw that the enemy warriors were all dead.

I cupped my hand and shouted, "It is Captain James of Eccleston. Rufford is saved and we have come to aid you."

The prior shouted, "Praise God, Captain James, for we were almost breached."

"Stay within until the danger has gone."

I turned and saw that my men were whole. If nothing else these two encounters had been the most effective form of training we had enjoyed for many a month.

I used my billhook to point, "We work our way around the walls. If they run then let them do so, I want no enemy alive and close to the walls when the sun rises."

That we were all weary beyond words went without saying but victory gives a man extra energy. I knew that the enemy would be as weak as we were but they had seen their comrades fall and die. Just as victory strengthens so defeat weakens. As we moved around the walls, the enemy fled for the largest single group had been at the gate. We outnumbered all that we found. It took time to complete the circuit for I wanted none hidden close by but by the time we had joined all my company together and returned to the walls I knew that there were none of the enemy raiders left alive. They had all headed west and I knew that they would head for their beached ships. I could do nothing about that. We were too tired and the thought of another march of miles could not even be contemplated.

I shouted, "All the enemy warriors are gone. You may open the gates." I turned to my men, "Thomas, take the weapons and the mail from the dead and stack their bodies. We will burn them and the metal can be used in Ecclestone by our blacksmith. Robert, come with me." I stacked my billhook against the wall and entered. The monks were tending to the wounded. I saw a pile of sheet-covered corpses. Burscough had paid a price.

The prior approached, "They attacked but an hour after you had gone, Captain. Luckily, the steward had ordered all the men in the walls after the last twenty billmen arrived. The steward placed them around the walls and their resolve stiffened our defence. Still, had you not arrived then it might have gone ill for us."

I looked around, "Where is the steward?"

"He was hurt and we had to take his left forearm." He saw the shock on my face. "He lives. Come I will take you to him."

I turned to Robert, "Find Calliope and the steward's horse. Saddle them."

The steward was in the priory with another four who were more seriously wounded. I saw the bloody bandage around the stump of the steward's arm. He gave me a weak smile, "I had not used a sword since I was a young man and it showed. The earl's tomb is safe and it is my left arm that was hurt. I can still write."

"And the new earl should reward you steward, for you have saved more than the earl's tomb. Your hard ride and our early warning made all the difference. We saved Rufford and it may well be that only Meols suffered heavy losses. We shall see."

A monk brought me a jug of ale and I emptied it in one.

"Will you not rest, Captain?" The steward had concern on his face.

I shook my head, "No, Thomas, you must rest but I need to ride to Meols. I want to know for certain that they have gone. Robert and I will ride there now. You and the brave defenders of Burscough can rest. You deserve all the honour for you were not warriors."

As I approached Robert, I saw that he had drunk some ale and he held two small loaves in his hand, "I am guessing, Captain, that you and I are to ride. Here is a loaf. It is yesterday's and, I do not doubt, more than a little stale but it will fill a hole."

I took it and nodded my gratitude. A moment or two of eating would not change things over much and we both devoured the bread. I mounted Calliope. I had chosen Robert as he also had a breastplate and a sword. I was not sure if we would meet an enemy but we two were the best equipped to deal with any. He mounted the steward's horse.

As we left the gate Thomas waved. The bodies had been stripped and I saw that he had ordered kindling to be gathered. Soon there would be a fire and the air filled with the smell of burning flesh. I was glad I would not have to endure it. We headed along the road to the village of Meols, along the coast. Behind us, the first hints of a new day could be seen in the sky. The two horses had rested during the day but there was little point in thrashing them to death. The glow ahead made me slow as I tried to work out what it was. As the first rays from the sun lit the land ahead, I realised it was a building that had been fired and the glow was the last of its timbers burning. Suddenly a pair of figures stepped out from the darkness and I drew my sword and prepared to fight for my life.

"Captain James, we were sent to take you into the village. Captain Richard sent us."

It was then I recognised two of the archers from my village, "Henry, what happened?"

"We will tell you as we walk." He led us down a track that passed the burnt-out building. We dismounted. As we followed I noticed that they had but two arrows apiece. "We pursued the warriors west. The captain was careful not to walk into ambushes and so our progress was not swift. They tried to defend Meols. It was when, a couple of hours later, more men arrived from the east that the captain realised you must have relieved Burscough and he pulled our men back."

Dawn had come and as we passed Meols to our left I saw the devastation caused by the raiders. Captain Richard and his archers were as weary as we and, like my two archers, had virtually no missiles left.

I dismounted and held out my arm to Captain Richard, "Well met."

He nodded, "Burscough?"

"Safe, although the steward has lost a forearm."

He nodded, "Aye and two archers are hurt too. I sent them back to Rufford." He pointed to the sea. "There are four longships there. We have neither the men nor the missiles to do aught about them."

"And the villagers?"

He looked down at the ground as though seeking an acceptable answer, "I know not."

"Then we must make them think we bring an army and stop them taking captives back." We both knew that such raiders wanted not only animals, food and treasure but also women and children to be kept as slaves.

"I have one arrow left and most have two or three at the most."

"But they know not that. What will happen when you nock an arrow and draw?"

"They will think we intend to rain death upon them."

"When the arrows fall and you nock again, they will run. We will get as close to them as we can before you release and Robert and I will remain mounted to act as a defence." He looked doubtful about the plan and I said, quietly, "Would you be able to sleep at night knowing that we did not do all that we could to stop our people from being enslaved?"

"You are right." He turned, "Hob, you have three arrows, give me one. String your bows for we go to war again."

I said, "Robert, draw your sword and when we ride stay to my right. I have fought from the back of a horse before now but you have not. You are there to protect my right."

He nodded, nervously, "Aye, captain. I can stay in the saddle and that is about all."

The raiders were still on the beach as were the captives. The beach at Meols was a large one. It was very dry as the tide did not come all the way to the houses. The ships were almost half a mile away and the raiders and the captives were still close to Meols. I saw that they had not had the chance to load and even as we approached, I saw another four raiders heading for them. They were the last of the ones from Burscough.

I heard a shout from the raiders when they spied us. We had to make them believe we were the advanced guard of a much larger army. I turned in my saddle and shouted, "Wave behind as though there are more men following. Robert and I will ride at them."

In hindsight it was madness but I put myself in the position of the raiders. They had been bloodied by, as far as they knew, two different forces. They had lost more than half of their men and if they saw horsemen and archers, both faster than men of the men of the fyrd, then they might believe that a column of billmen was behind. We had defeated them twice through billmen and I guessed we had killed their braver warriors. Those were the thoughts in my head as Robert and I galloped towards the raiders.

The four who had yet to join the main band simply ran for the ships. As Robert and I dug our heels in our horses leapt forward into the soft sand. The sight of their four comrades fleeing was enough for the bulk of the raiders and they simply ran. The captives were forgotten but some tried to carry small chests of treasure that they had taken. I risked looking behind me and saw that Captain Richard and his men were just thirty paces behind us and running as fast as the softer, dry sand would allow. I saw that there was wetter and harder sand ahead and that would enable Calliope to close with them.

I saw that the dragonships were not all the same size. There looked to be forty or so raiders left but some were wounded and supported by those without wounds. They were heading for the largest of the vessels for they could not take all the ships away. Someone must have realised that Robert and I would reach them before they could clamber aboard their ships. I saw that the tide must have been coming back in as the ships bobbed on the water. Two warriors turned and face us with their shields and their spears. They began to chant and sing. I had long ago guessed that the raiders were of Viking stock. Whilst not of the same quality as those that had raided five hundred years earlier, they still believed in the values of those Norse raiders. They intended to die with their swords in their hands.

I was no fool. I might be able to make a couple of good strikes with my sword but I risked my horse and it would be to no purpose. When I was just ten paces from them, I shouted, "Robert, wheel right!"

The two raiders were braced with their shields together as I took a route around them. Once I had passed them, I wheeled again to pursue the others. The ships were twenty paces from the shore and the water looked to be a couple of hundred paces from us. The sand was harder and that allowed more speed. I wanted these raiders to decide that this part of Lancashire was too large a morsel for them. I wanted them to board and flee, grateful that they had not died. I was a better horseman than Robert and he was ten paces behind me. That suited me for it gave me the chance to use my sword. I rode not at the nearest three men for two warriors supported a wounded man. Instead, I rode at the man carrying a chest on his shoulder. I leaned from my saddle and as he turned at the sound of my hooves, I swept my sword across his back. I had not yet used it and it was a well-honed blade. It bit through the leather byrnie and across his spine. His voice echoed like a sea bird's and made the men who had yet to reach the ships, turn. They saw him fall and those carrying treasure dropped their booty and hurled themselves into the sea. I reined in and made Calliope rear. I raised my sword and shouted, "This is the price you shall all pay for stealing from this land! Begone!" I knew not if they would understand the words but the gesture was clear enough.

The last three men boarded and one of the dragonships pulled away from the shore. I saw the deck crews of the other ships jump into the sea to swim to the one ship that had survivors aboard. I turned and saw Captain Richard approach. The last two raiders lay in the sand, their life blood pouring into it and their bodies pricked by arrows. We had won.

Chapter 10

We burned the dragonships. Their blackened skeletons would be left to mark, at low tide, the place where the Vikings' dreams of treasure and slaves had ended. It must have worked for, as far as I know, no others came to raid Meols. We took the treasure back to the villagers who had fled back to their village. Not all the men had been killed although all had a wound to mark their fight. John Burnell told us how the ships had come in the night and moored at sea. The long stretch of beach had afforded them secrecy and they had fallen upon the unsuspecting village. The boy who had brought the news to Lathom had been collecting wood for the day and he had seen them and had taken the one horse in the village and ridden to Lathom.

We were all exhausted but we made the village defensible. Our timely arrival meant that the animals of the village and most of the food had yet to be loaded onto the Viking ships. We were fed and then we simply collapsed and slept the sleep of the dead.

The Sherriff and twenty horsemen arrived the next day. We were still making order where chaos had reigned. The men we led, although still tired from the exertions of the past days were still able to help the villagers of Meols rebuild their homes. My decision to act swiftly had worked and the animals that they had gathered on the beach to board their ships had largely been saved. The coins that they had taken from both Rufford and Meols had also been saved. We had learned, from one of the Meols' villagers that the raiders had, indeed, come from the islands. The recent rebellion against King James allied to the hard winter had meant that they were starving and Meols appeared to be the easiest target to attack. Just a day of rowing from their island haven had brought them to an undefended piece of coast. We had been lucky.

Sir Edward took Captain Richard and me to one side, "I went to Burscough first for I feared my brother's tomb would be desecrated. The prior and the steward told me of your actions. For that I thank you. Now tell me what went on here."

We told him what we had learned and what we had done. I pointed to the burnt-out wrecks. "They will stand as a marker for any other who thinks that this coast is an easy place to raid." He nodded and I risked his ire by taking him to task, "My lord, Lathom has a fortified hall and can defend itself. Even Burscough has the priory as a sanctuary but what of the rest? Rufford was a rich prize that they might have taken had it not been for the efforts of the steward."

"But wars are over. This is the first raid we have suffered in a generation. Now that the civil strife is over what need people for castles and fortified manors?"

I sighed, "My lord, with all due respect, that is easy for you to say for you have Hornby. What of Sedbergh?" I could not tell him of my spying mission but I had to speak. "I do not believe that the Scots have given up on their ambitions to take back those parts of England that they regard as theirs. Could you not use your good offices to ask Sir William Hesketh to build a hall which can be defended? He will need to build a new home in any case and a fortified manor would be best."

Mollified by my offer of an answer made him nod, "Perhaps that would be wise."

I was relieved, "I have made my new home in Ecclestone stronger. It is not fortified but it can be defended. If raiders had come to our village, then they would have found it a more difficult prospect than Rufford was and we are a smaller place."

He smiled, "That you have ideas above your station is both gratifying and worrying. My brother thought highly of you and I can see why. Both of you did well. That you managed to defeat such a force without the aid of knights does you both credit."

"What of Thomas Crouchley, my lord?"

"What of him?"

"But for his action, there would be four dragonships sailing north filled with the folk from Meols and Rufford not to mention their animals. Your brother's resting place might have been destroyed and with it his legacy. We fought and held them but had he not summoned us as swiftly as he did then the end might have been a disaster for the county." He frowned and I sighed, "The raiders who escaped will tell others that Lancashire is not the place to raid. Had they been successful then this might have become a regular occurrence. I do not think we will see any more raids and that is thanks to Thomas Crouchley."

"You are right, James of Ecclestone although it is a little impertinent to take the Sherriff of Lancashire to task. I will speak with the earl and the steward shall be rewarded."

He turned the head of his horse around and we were forgotten. Captain Richard chuckled, "You are fearless are you not, James? You care not for rank at all."

I smiled. I could not tell him that I had lived amongst those who thought themselves above others and I knew them for what they were. "Perhaps, Richard, but a man must speak his mind or else he is a slave. If I lose favour by my words then so be it. I am my own man and I know my value. Sir Edward and the earl cannot do without the likes of us. If there is a war and a battle it will be their banners we follow and they will garner the glory but it will be us who wins the day."

"Aye, you may be right. The king has his crown thanks to men like your father. Aye, well I will head back to my farm. God speed and we shall meet again, I dare say."

I clasped his arm, "Aye, we will and it is an honour serving with you. You lead my archers well and they speak highly of you."

He nodded and left.

As we prepared to march the twenty odd miles home, I knew that we would be laden. The pack animals were at Lathom and until we reached it, we would have to carry our booty. We used Calliope and Thomas' horse as pack animals. The mail we had taken was of poor quality but it could be melted down and made into nails and horseshoes. The men now each had a helmet. Again, they were not the best but they afforded protection to those who had none. The swords and the daggers were the greatest of the prizes for they were well made and had been maintained over the years. Each of my company now had a sword and I knew from experience that the more weapons a man had the better his chance of survival. We also carried the Rufford treasure and I would leave that at Burscough. With helmets hung from billhooks, we marched to Lathom and were in such good heart that we sang as we walked. It made the journey seem easier and was a mark of the bond we all felt.

The steward was still pale but he was able to speak to me and thank me for my service. He was still the earl's man. Thomas

Stanley might be dead but the bachelor steward, Thomas Crouchley would spend his life ensuring that the memory of the earl who had made a king, was not forgotten. I found myself admiring the man more and more. We had little time to talk for we still had many miles to go but now we had more pack animals to carry our burdens and with full bellies, courtesy of the monks, we made better time as we finished our journey to Ecclestone. It was dark when we entered the village but the noise of our singing brought wives, mothers and children to the doors to welcome us. Sir Edward and his lack of gratitude were forgotten. The nobles of the land meant nothing to the people who worked it. The next day would see our lives returning to a predictable and pleasing pattern.

Unlike most ladies, my wife was keen to know about the battles we had fought. I was not as graphic with the details as I would be if I was speaking to her father but she deserved to know what the men of the village had done. My wife was often addressed as my lady despite her lack of title. The reason was clear, she behaved and acted as one. The women in the village all deferred to her. Most of the respect she enjoyed came from her own innate qualities but her association with my mother had helped. Having seen what had resulted from a poorly defended village my wife and I planned improvements that would see a safer village.

I realised that the small wall we had around the yard and the main house could be easily raised to be the height of a man and study gates built. When we had cleared the neglected fields we had found many stones and they had been preserved. We could now use them. By adding a fighting platform at the bottom of the inside of the wall we would be strengthening the wall as well as aiding the village archers to defend our walls. I still had my father's horn and we let the village know that three blasts meant all should come to my hall for protection. The drainage ditch around the outside of the wall was deepened and I felt, as the year began to draw to a close, that Ecclestone was better protected than it had once been. The animals we had nurtured were healthy and our flocks and herds grew. I now had to use the common for the excess sheep. The cheese we produced was highly prized and the mill that now ground our wheat was a great success. As the year ended we knew that if we had another hard winter then we would survive for we had prepared well.

It was in April that my second son, Walter, was born. It was a more difficult birth for he was a large baby. When the village women looked worried and asked me to send for the priest I determined that I would not put my wife through such danger again. In the end, the priest was not needed and, afterwards, when, with Walter asleep, she lay in my arms she told me that it was her duty to bear me children but she would make herself stronger to endure such danger in the future. I knew that I had been lucky that the Queen Mother had the foresight to put us together. Had she not done so I would never have met her. I might well have married but I know that I would not have been as happy and Ecclestone would have been a poorer place without her.

Life went on and it seemed that I had been forgotten by King Henry. That suited me. I knew that I had offended Sir Edward and as he was now the most important man in Lancashire that might have been a mistake but thanks to the good offices of my friend, Thomas Crouchley, the young earl did not share his uncle's views and I was not punished. I was even allowed to buy more land. Life was still hard and sometimes, despite all the efforts of my wife and I, villagers died. When they died without heirs, I bought the land. I was not trying to build an empire but I wanted Ecclestone to prosper and I knew that my wife and I were the best people to do that. We now employed labourers and servants from the village. They were well paid and well treated. Neither my wife nor I saw any purpose in saving pennies and making people's lives meaner. It was a false economy for the people we paid worked hard and we made more money from their endeavours. Thomas and Robert now acted as bailiffs for two of my farms. Their wives aspired to be like my wife and life was good. We had another daughter, Mary, and that birth was easier.

I wondered if I would ever have to use my billhook in war again. I hoped not but we prepared for war each and every Sunday. We had increased the billmen for more young men chose the billhook over the bow. Thomas and Robert told me that was my doing. They all wished to emulate me. The lessons I had learned at Sedbergh, Rufford and Burscough, stood us in good stead. We were now far more flexible. When we trained at Lathom, once each month, my well-drilled and disciplined company became the model for the others to copy. Thomas and Robert were my corporals and I raised them above the captains from the other companies. Such was our reputation that none objected. With their shiny breastplates, good helmets and the best of billhooks the two men looked like captains and were treated as such.

It was on one of our training days at Lathom that Thomas Crouchley, now nicknamed Thomas One Arm, out of respect for his bravery, took me to one side. "King Henry is unwell and we may soon have a new king."

"Prince Henry, whom I met?"

I was far enough from the court and London to be unaware of the succession.

The steward nodded, "He is not the same man as his father." Thomas was confiding in me and I cocked my head to one side. "His father, the king, is a most serious man. You know that." I nodded, "Prince Henry is a young man who enjoys sport, hunting and pleasure. England is rich and thanks to your efforts, and others, not least the king, we are a prosperous country."

I smiled, "You are telling me this for a purpose."

He nodded, "James, I like you but I know, from the old earl, that you have qualities that will be used by this royal family. The Queen Mother still lives and she is one who, despite living in isolation, will have a hand in moulding young Prince Henry. You can be sure that she will remember both your name and your service to England."

"But I am now just a simple farmer. True, I am now a gentleman but surely there are others who might be used first."

He sighed, "I was close to the earl and privy to much that, perhaps I should not have been but he trusted me. You can be confident that I do not spill secrets like water from a leaky pail." He had a wry smile on his face, "For one thing there is no one to whom I could divulge them. You are as close a friend as I have and as I meet you but once a month I am like one of those hermits who lives alone in a cell. I know what you have done for the crown and what better disguise for a spy than to disappear into a Lancashire farm. I say this because I am old and I know that my service to England is in the past. You are young and I tell you this to warn you that Prince Henry, when he is king, will call upon you."

His words cast a shadow over me for I knew he was right. When I told Jane she merely smiled, "And I have always expected this, my husband. Remember when I first met you, I told you that I admired you. I have enjoyed these years of peace but I have viewed each day that you were not taken from me as a gift from God. When you serve the king you serve England and God. Do not fear the future but embrace it and let us enjoy every day that we have while we have it."

I knew I was lucky in my wife and I heeded her advice. I threw myself into the running of the farms, the village and raising my children. James was now six and he was keen to be a warrior. I had learned much about weapons and knew that while wielding a billhook was a useful skill swordsmanship was also handy. I made us two wooden swords and we used those. It would be some years before he had the strength to use a billhook but the time spent with a wooden sword that was heavier than anything else he held would make James, or as we called him, Jamie, stronger and give him skills that could be transferred to the billhook. He endured bruises and the occasional cut without complaint and he showed natural ability. He had good reactions and teaching him when he was so young meant he learned how to use a sword without even thinking. He was desperate for a sword and knew that I had a couple of spares, captured during my battles.

"Jamie, when I deem that you are ready then you shall have a sword but it will not be one I took in battle. I will have one made for you and that time will only be when you have a beard. I am giving you skills. Do not be impatient to use them. I went to war when I was young but I had a beard and I was lucky. I was protected by men who were more skilled than I. I am giving you skills so that you do not need to rely on luck."

Jamie was a good boy and heeded my advice. He came with me to watch the weapon work on Sunday and when he saw the way that greybeards deferred to me I think he knew that it would be better to obey than to be as I had been, rebellious and ready to run away to war. King Henry died two weeks before Prince Henry was eighteen. We heard the news almost as soon as the king died for riders were sent throughout the land to tell all that the king was dead but we had a new one. Gone were the days of pretenders and Yorkists who sought the throne. King Henry had managed to make England so prosperous that none wanted a return to the chaos and anarchy of a civil war. I wondered if the new King Henry might need to do anything other than continue his father's work. When I next met Thomas at Lathom he told me that the Queen Mother had personally selected his advisers. She was not going to allow the same events to overtake her son as had imprisoned the ill-fated King Edward to a short life and a secret death in the tower, along with his brother. Her son would attain the crown and have every chance of survival. The Queen Mother, the great lady that she was, died just five days after her son's coronation but by then she had ensured his survival.

King Henry showed his ruthless side when he arrested, tried and executed, his father's two ministers who had imposed an unpopular tax regime. Edmund Dudley and Sir Richard Empson were victims of their own success. They had made the treasury rich and King Henry could now use the money whilst making himself popular with the people. It was a sign of what was to come. I kept waiting for a summons but none came. He obeyed his father's last command and married the bride of his brother, Katherine of Aragon. When the year drew to a close I began to think that Thomas Crouchley was wrong and that I would not be needed by the new king. Thomas was right and I was wrong.

Chapter 11

Ecclestone 1510

The king was on a royal progress with his new bride and visited Lathom. I did not expect an invitation but I received one. One of the earl's liveried servants rode to invite me to meet the king the next day.

"Do I bring my wife?"

The servant shrugged, "I was told to invite you, Master James, and no one else." He wheeled his horse around and headed back to Lathom. I had not recognised the man. The new earl had surrounded himself with new men. It was the way of the world. The old were often discarded. I just hoped that Thomas Crouchley was still employed.

Jane took it well and laughed off the implied insult, "Walter and Mary demand much of my time, husband, and bowing and scraping before the king and queen does not suit me. Now my mother would be in her element. If my father and she had been invited then his treasury would have been emptied to buy her the clothes that she needed." I laughed for my wife was right. "Will you be staying overnight?"

"He did not say so. I will pack a spare set in case but I hope it will be a courtesy. Perhaps he wishes to thank me for the action at Meols and Burscough."

Part of me was intrigued for I had only met the young king once or twice and that had been when he was still barely a youth. How had he changed? We had no choice over our king but his decisions would affect every man, woman and child in the land. I rode Alexander to Lathom. It was not to impress the king but Calliope had grown old and it would be a hard ride in one day. William had groomed him so that his coat shone and his mane looked magnificent. The gift from the King of Scotland had been a grand one.

No time had been given and so I left not long after dawn. Better to arrive early and be kept waiting rather than making a new king wait. As with every royal progress, there were far more people travelling with the king than one might expect. The stables were full but I was known well enough for the horse master to take care of Alexander for me and to keep him shaded.

Thomas Crouchley was still the steward and although he was busy he was a loyal friend and found the time to greet me.

"Captain James, you have made good time. The king and queen are at their breakfast. If you would come with me to the antechamber."

I leaned in, "What is this about?"

"The king said he needed to speak to the man who helped defeat the raiders from the north."

I was relieved. It was as I had thought and hoped. He would pat me on the back, like a faithful hound, and then I would be dismissed. With luck, I would be back home in but a few hours. There were others waiting in the antechamber but I did not know them. They had the look of young nobles. Perhaps they had been invited as I had or, more likely, they were attempting to gain some favour from the new king. My clothes were not fashionable enough and they ignored me and continued their conversations. There were many manors in this part of Lancashire. Nobles often had three or four sons and each would want their own land. The three nobles in the antechamber were three such. As I listened to them, I discovered their aspirations. None had ever fought with the billmen and archers. They would know how to use a sword but none would bother to witness the Sunday practice. When I had fought at Sedbergh, the knights there had all been from the northern part of the county. The Hesketh family of Rufford had not been at home when their manor was destroyed. I suspected that these young nobles would have had similar stories.

When Thomas Crouchley returned, an hour later, the others rose expectantly. The steward smiled, "The king has asked for Captain James. If you would come with me, Captain?" The three young nobles flashed me looks of pure hatred as I was led to the Great Hall. Breakfast had ended and the only ones remaining were the new earl, the king, an archbishop and a priest. King Henry was dressed, as one might expect, magnificently and he exuded both power and confidence. His father never had. The earl was also dressed in the latest fashion and I felt like a peasant in comparison.

The king beamed, "You are the man who saved this part of Lancashire. The earl is keen to thank you personally as am I."

121

The earl stepped forward, "Thank you for saving Burscough Priory, Captain James. Had my grandfather's tomb been desecrated it would have been a tragedy. I thank you and I confirm all that my uncle promised you."

My words to the Sherriff had not been in vain, "Thank you, my lord, I am pleased that I could be of service."

"Derby, I will speak in private with the captain and then I shall join you for the hunt. I am keen to see the nature of the animals in this part of my realm." With that the earl was dismissed and when the door was closed the four of us were alone. The king's smile left him and he became all business.

King Henry's voice was not reedy like his father's but powerful like the man himself. "This is the Archbishop of Canterbury, who now holds England's purse strings." It was a perfunctory introduction for the most powerful prelate in the land. "Captain James, you served my father and England well in the past." I nodded. The king looked at the archbishop. "What you may not know, archbishop, is that this is the man who was responsible for the capture of Perkin Warbeck and who acted as a spy in the court of King James." I saw the old man's eyes widen. He had not known. "England has need of you again, Captain James."

"And I am ever willing to serve, King Henry, but my face is now known by the King of Scotland and his lords. I cannot return there without arousing suspicion."

"I know. I am not a fool, Captain James." His voice had steel in it. Bearing in mind the fate of his father's two ministers I would have to tread carefully. "I believe that the French and the Scots may well be plotting against England."

The archbishop said, "They normally are."

"I know, archbishop, but I plan on helping my father-in-law, the King of Aragon and I need to know if their plans are imminent. I wish you to travel to France. Go as a sword for hire. I want you to find out if the Scots are at the court. You have spied before and know that it is the whispers you overhear and the faces that you see which will give me the intelligence that I need."

"But I am English, King Henry and if you are right then they will be suspicious of me immediately."

"You speak French and Flemish and I will provide an identity that might explain your presence." He took a ring from his purse. "This is the signet ring of Edmund Dudley. His sons are children and I have taken them and their mother as my wards. You will assume the identity of an illegitimate son. I know he had mistresses and one may have born him a son. This ring will be your way into the French court."

Even as he was telling me my mind was already identifying problems that I might encounter. That I could not refuse was obvious but I wanted to survive and so my mind planned.

He smiled, "I know what you did for my father. I want them to think that you are like Perkin Warbeck and a traitor. I want them to try to turn you into an assassin so that you can come back and try to kill me."

My eyes widened, "But I could not do that."

"You mean, kill me? Of course not. You are English and James of Ecclestone has a wife, a family and land he needs to protect. But they will think you are the illegitimate son of an executed traitor. They will try to fuel your hatred and turn you. That is the real plan. Such a character would be told of any threat to England and yet have the means to return to England." He looked pleased with himself. "Unlike my father, I have devised a means for my spy to return to England."

I nodded, "A clever plan, King Henry." I was not flattering him for it was brilliant. The Yorkists had believed in turning the king's friends to try to defeat him, and the Scots and French, if there was an alliance, would do the same.

"You will travel as soon as possible. You will take a ship from Tilbury to Calais." He casually tossed a purse to me. "Buy a horse when you reach Calais and make your way to Paris. I believe, from my father, that you know your way around that city."

"I did, King Henry, but that was many years ago."

He waved a dismissive hand as though the details did not interest him. I, on the other hand, knew that the details would be important. They would either save or sink me. "Discover where other malcontents are to be found. Watch and listen. If you cannot learn anything within a month then return to England." He nodded to the archbishop, "When you return then report to the archbishop. You will not need to see me again. The fewer people who know of you and your association with me the better. All think that you have come here so that I can heap honours upon you. Let us keep it that way. If you discover nothing then all is well and good but if there is any hint of a plot then return as soon as you can. I do not wish to take an army abroad if the Scots plan on stabbing us in the back." He turned to the archbishop, "The archbishop will tell you anything else you need to know. I have animals to hunt."

He swept from the room. I looked at the archbishop and then the priest. The priest had said nothing but had been taking notes on a wax tablet. As if in explanation the archbishop said, "This is Thomas Wolsey. He is the king's almoner. As you can see there are no secrets from the king's confessor." Wolsey smiled but said nothing and I knew he was more than the king's almoner. "You may be wondering why the king chose you and not some other. After all, any could have gone to the French court and been able to pick up gossip. It is because you are familiar with the way foreign courts work and, having been at the court of King James, it is highly likely that you might recognise Scottish nobles."

"In which case, they might recognise me."

Wolsey spoke for the first time. "If Master James, you shave your beard and moustache, it will change your appearance dramatically."

The archbishop beamed, "A splendid idea. I also have men you might wish to contact when you are in Calais and Paris. They are men who have been useful to me in the past and have been rewarded by the crown. They may well be able to facilitate your endeavours. I will not write their names down for their identity must be protected but you are a clever man and can memorise them." He leaned forward, "We have spread the story that we are looking for an illegitimate son of Edmund Dudley. The king has offered a reward of ten crowns for information." He smiled, "There may or may not be an illegitimate son but word will spread and if people seek to confirm your identity then it is there to be found." I was given the names and memorised them.

I had no need to stay and I mounted Alexander and rode him as hard as I had ever ridden him before. He would not be needed for some time and I wished him to enjoy the ride. When I galloped across my cobbles Jane emerged with the new babe in her arms. I handed my reins to William, "He will need walking to cool off for I gave him a good ride."

William grinned, "He needed it."

As I went into the house I put my arm around my wife's shoulders, "We have but one night together and then on the morrow I leave for London. I am to be the king's spy once more but this time it is in Paris."

When her head whipped around and I saw the fear in her eyes I knew that I had surprised my wife. She liked the idea of my serving the king but to spy in Paris seemed a step too far. I kissed her forehead, "I will be careful. This night I would have you shave off my beard and trim my hair." I told her what I was to do as we went into the room where we sat. It was empty. The other children were playing close to the hogbog, chasing the fowl and teasing the pigs.

"And why do you not shave off your moustache too?"

"I will do but not until I am in France. There may be French spies watching who leaves England. I will change my clothes completely once I leave Calais." I smiled, "I survived the last time by taking few chances. I will do the same now."

After the babe was laid down to sleep, she went to the kitchen and fetched ale, bread and cheese. She closed the door and began to question me further. I did not mind for it would help me to clarify my thoughts. "The archbishop's spies, will they be useful?"

I shook my head, "I have memorised their names but I will only use them if there is no alternative."

She frowned, "Why not use them?"

"It is likely that they will be known to the French. My best hope is to remain at a distance from any who has a connection with England." I patted my sword, "This sword will be my best passport. It is Empire made and not English made. Some may even remember the young man who was at the court of Perkin Warbeck."

She shook her head, "Then they would know you betrayed them."

"No, my love, that is where you are wrong. The ones who knew I betrayed them are all dead. Even Margaret of Burgundy, like the Queen Mother, is now dead. The ones who might remember me were the French faces who appeared at her court. And if they recognise me as the young man from the court at Mechelen then my changed appearance might encourage them in the belief that I am a traitor to England, for they would wonder how I had survived when Warbeck did not." I showed her the signet ring, "This ring will be my introduction and then I will have to use my wits."

She stroked my hand and then kissed it, "And how long will you be away?"

"I hope it will not be too long. The king needs to know if there is an immediate threat. If there are no Scots at the court and if their attention is on other places then I can return quickly. This time I will not be awaiting the decision to invade. I am there to detect a threat and that is all."

James and Walter watched in awe as Jane first trimmed my hair and beard and then shaved it. Elizabeth did not like the change and wept. James just grinned, "Why, father, you look like a different man."

"And I feel like one. I felt like a change and I now have one. Do I look younger then?"

He nodded, "You do."

I had decided that I would not be riding Calliope to London. For one thing, it was too far and I did not want her to be looked after by any other than William. Instead, I would ride her to Warrington and William would accompany me on Goliath. There I would buy a hackney and leave that one at Tilbury. It might add hours to the journey but I would feel happier about it. If William was curious about my journey, he said nothing. With my clothes for the journey packed and my sword and dagger about me, I kissed Jane before the sun had risen and we were at Warrington by the mid-morning. I could not travel anonymously in this part of Lancashire and I knew there would be speculation. I had a story already.

"I have a mind to buy some Lincolnshire sheep. I hear that they are bigger and fatter than those we have here and perhaps my herd might increase."

It made sense and the horse trader nodded. He would retell the tale if for no other reason than to impress others. The road I took south would also go to Lincoln although I intended to take the road that went from Holyhead to London, the old Roman one. I had never travelled it. I bade farewell to William and then headed south. I wanted to make as many miles as I could and disappear into Cheshire. The horse, Jack, was a sound horse and he plodded along quite happily. It allowed me to refine my plans. I had contemplated travelling to Hedingham and thence to Tilbury but even though it would have been good to see Sir Edward, Sam, and Stephen, it might alert others who had long memories. I would visit with them upon my return. I was embarking on a lonely and dangerous life. I had to be ready for the rigours of the road. Making forty miles a day, sometimes more and sometimes less, I made the journey in six days. Jack was not as easy a ride as Calliope and when I found an inn with a stable where I could leave him then I was glad. Calais was now one of the last vestiges of what had been an English empire in France. As such there were many ships that crossed from London. I found a berth on a small cog. The voyage would not be as comfortable as on a larger ship but it would be slightly quicker and my arrival would be more anonymous. I had my plans made and I kept my moustache for the crossing. The clothes I called my French clothes were in my bag and there they would remain until I left Calais. I shaved off my moustache and, having paid the bill the night before, slipped anonymously from the inn. I hoped that my new appearance would help me to disappear.

It was in the evening when I arrived in Calais and that suited me. A shower of rain greeted us and I was able to step from the cog with the cowl of my cloak over my head. I did not look secretive, just practical and others had adopted the same protection from the rain. I headed into the town. The heavy bag and the rain allowed me to stop on my way into the town, and that afforded me the opportunity to see if there was anyone following me or even taking undue interest in me. There was no one and everyone seemed to be like me, eager to get somewhere dry. The words I heard helped me to attune to French. There had been some French crewmen on the cog and I had practised my French there. I headed for the Rue des Gravelines. Jean le Casserole had helped me the last time I had spied. He knew my past and I hoped that he would still honour our friendship. I also hoped that he and his wife were still alive. The plan I had concocted on the road to Tilbury was founded on finding sanctuary with them in Calais.

The pot-making factory and the house that was attached to it were still there. The house had been extended. With water dripping from the cowl I knocked on the door grateful that Jean had fitted a small roof over the entrance. It was neither Marie nor Jean who opened it but an older man with the rough hands of someone who had laboured, "Yes?"

"I seek Jean le Casserole." My clothes were not cheap ones and as he assessed me I added, "I am a friend from the past."

He nodded, "Wait here."

When I saw Jean, I realised he had become an old man since the last I had seen him. He had been much older than me when I had met him but that was just a dozen years earlier. Time had not been kind to him. At first, he did not recognise me and I saw the frown on his face. I said, quietly and softly, "Jean, it is James." I used English but I determined to use French thereafter.

His eyes widened and he made the sign of the cross, "I thought you dead. Come in, come in. Charles, take my friend's bag to the guest room. Come, come."

I took off my cloak and shook it outside. Charles took it from me and hung it from a hook at the side of the door.

A voice called from a room down the hallway, "Who is it, father?"

"Be patient, Jean." My old friend smiled, "Jean has grown."

"And where is Marie?"

His face fell and I saw his eyes well, "My dear Marie gave birth to James, my second son but when she was carrying what would have been my daughter, she became ill and died. I have been a widower these last three years."

"I am sorry, my friend." I had happiness with Jane but he had lost the love of his life.

We entered the room where his sons were eating. A servant was serving food and Jean said, "Another plate, Sophie, for my friend." As the servant hurried off, he said, "Jean, James, this is the man I told you of. This is James the Englishman."

The younger boy's face, he looked to be about seven, lit up, "Just like me."

My old friend nodded, "Yes, for your mother was very fond of James here." He looked sadly at me, "She often hoped you would return. She liked you."

"And I, her."

The servant brought me a plate and Jean ladled the stew from one of the dishes his factory made onto my plate. It was a fish stew and as I dipped in some of the bread, I could not help but remember the taste from all those years ago. I was back in a world I thought I had abandoned. Jean did not ask me about the reason for my visit but instead asked me about my life. I told him of the deaths of my parents and my marriage as well as my children.

He laughed when I told him I had four children, "And that is good, James, for a man cannot have too many children. Had I not met you then I might never have married Marie. Would that I had met you years earlier."

The boys were more curious about my sword and about England. When the food had disappeared and the table was cleared then Jean sent the boys to bed. They were not happy about their dismissal. Once alone he said, "You are here as a spy once more?"

I nodded, "How did you know?"

"After you left, I listened for news about the man who would be king. When we heard he was dead then Marie and I hoped that you would return. When you did not, we both assumed that you had died. When I saw you cowled at my door then I knew this was more than a visit to an old friend." He shrugged, "Yours is a dangerous line of work, my friend."

"My spying days largely ended when Perkin Warbeck died. You are right and I must get to Paris. I will buy a horse tomorrow."

He nodded, "It is better that you do not tell me your purpose. As you know while I live in Calais, which is English I am a Frenchman."

"I know. What I need to know is where I should avoid in Paris and any information you can give me about the politics of Paris."

He poured himself some more wine. From his complexion, I guessed that he was drinking more since Marie had died. "The politics? Louis had his moment of glory when he conquered Naples. That is now over. Although he is well thought of he knows he can never be the emperor. I am not sure. I know that we, here in Calais, worry that one day the French may try to reclaim this land even though it was never French. England brings us all profits and we are happy about that. If you are asking me does France plan a war with England then the answer is no. Since Louis left the Pope's alliance to fight against him then his eyes are firmly fixed upon Venice and Italy."

I took in that information. It seemed I could return to England immediately and then it came to me. Such matters were public knowledge. King Henry would have known of this and so there had to be more to it. I would have to go to Paris and use my eyes and ears to find out the truth.

"What I can do is to provide a disguise for you. I have a wagon which is due to go to Paris. It will not be a quick journey but if you ride on my wagon you will be less visible than if you were to ride a horse."

I did some calculations. If I hired a horse then I could be in Paris in under four days but men might remember a rider rushing along the roads. The wagon might take seven days but who would take note of it? In addition, I would be able to glean information when we stayed at inns along the way. Carters were seen as invisible men.

"Thank you, Jean."

"And hopefully you will not have such a frantic journey when you return." He smiled, "Now tell me about your family."

I was happy to do so and I gave him the story from the moment I met the galleon, Roger de Clifton and the love of my life. He was smiling when I had finished. "Marie would have loved that story. She was as fond of you as any man alive and I include myself in that. You had such an exciting life and she felt part of it." His face saddened, "I miss her beyond words."

"And yet you have two sons. Do not neglect them." I nodded to the empty jug of wine, "Do not drown yourself in red wine. Marie would not have wished you to. It is better that you live for your sons. As I know from my father, a man never has enough time on this earth. I would trade my right arm for another night of conversation with him. His illness came too quickly and I was too busy."

"You are right, James and I shall heed your advice."

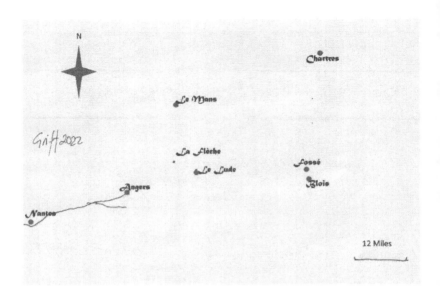

Chapter 12

Paris 1510

Paris had not changed much since I had last been there. Only the clothes and the fashions were different. Paul, the carter, and his son Jacques were good company. Knowing that I was a friend of Jean le Casserole meant they went out of their way to make me welcome and comfortable. I never felt threatened even in some of the places where we stayed. I also picked up a great deal of information. There were many Scottish lords on the roads leading into and away from Paris. They did not leave from Calais but Dunkerque. Of course, one explanation might be that they wished to serve with the French. There was no war with England and since King James had captured the last of the rebels then the isles were secure. The Italian war was the best chance for an honourable fight. I knew from my time with the Scottish knights that they all wished to be better warriors and their one hope was a war with England, a war when their new skills would finally defeat their most hated of enemies.

We halted at Jean's yard in Paris. The men who worked there were not the same ones I had met the last time but Paul's conversation with them left them in no doubt that I was a friend of their master and as such could ask for anything.

"You are welcome to stay with me in my humble home, sir."

The old man who now ran the yard and warehouse, Henri, was a courteous man. The last thing I needed was to embroil him in King Henry's plots. I shook my head, "Thank you for the offer, Henri. When I need to return to Calais then I may well seek you out."

With my bag slung over my shoulder I headed towards the centre of Paris. I regretted not having my billhook for carrying the bag was always easier when hanging from my hook. My time on the road and the talks with Paul had given me a plan. My French was now as good as it ever was. I could not speak it like a Frenchman and everyone would know that I was a foreigner but I had enough conversational French to make them believe that I had lived here. I knew, from Jean, that my accented French could sound Dutch, Flemish or even German. I would save my Dudley connection until I needed it.

That first day was frustratingly unsuccessful. The guards at the palace gates sent me away and left me in no doubt that a return would result in a beating. I sought accommodation. I was playing a part and so I chose somewhere which, whilst cheap, was not a hideout for criminals. The room was clean and the rate was reasonable. Even more important was that it was close enough to the Louvre for me to be able to walk to it quickly. The king was not at home and the guards, it seemed, were determined to keep away everyone that they did not know.

After a disappointing three days, I changed my tactics. I learned, from the innkeeper, where the fashionable parts of Paris lay. I would seek the company of French nobles. I would be playing a part once more but this time it would be an easier part than Thomas of Burscough. I would play the same part that had won me friends at the court of Perkin Warbeck. I would tell a good tale and I would try to ingratiate myself with the nobles. I discovered that the young nobles used the Palais de la Cité on the left bank of the Seine. There were inns nearby and the old palace, now that the Louvre had been completed, was less well used. The young nobles could use the outer bailey to practise the art of fighting. I could not simply try to walk into the old palace, it would arouse suspicion and so I headed for the inns and taverns. As the university was close by then it was a busy place. It was where I had met the Yorkist conspirators. As such, I was more familiar with it than the inns around the Louvre. I gambled that my appearance had changed since I had been the youth who had infiltrated their ranks. I consoled myself with the knowledge that all those who had recruited me were now dead.

I knew, from my time in Paris the first time, that the French, unlike the English, were particular about using taverns to dine at midday. Accordingly, I found an inn that had a slightly more expensive menu than the others, reasoning that the nobles might like to keep away from those with smaller purses and I went there, slightly early. I ensured good service by ordering a more expensive pichet of wine.

"Would you like to order food now, sir?"

I knew that the only food available would be bread and cheese. The kitchens would not produce hot food until closer to noon. I shook my head, "No, innkeeper. This is a pleasant inn and I have time on my hands. I shall enjoy the wine and watch the world go by." It was the sort of remark that a noble might make. Arriving early I had secured a good table and as the inn filled up, I was able, from my vantage point, to scrutinise the nobles as they entered. They wore good clothes but not their best. These were the idle rich whose fathers owned estates and land that allowed their sons to indulge their passion for hunting, gambling, fighting and drinking. It was not the season to hunt and so they were practising the art of swordplay. I saw that they all had a good sword and the parrying dagger that was becoming fashionable in France. I had heard of them but never seen them. Now that knights no longer used shields in battle the idea of an extra blade had become the trend.

I was scrutinised when the next young men entered but then ignored. Their conversations were loud and boastful. They spoke of the blows they had struck and generally crowed about their own prowess. The mercenaries who had trained me had looked down on such boasts but I knew from my time with English knights that the young ones all did the same. As the inn filled up so my isolation ended and men filled the tables adjacent to mine. When they began to order food then so did I. I ordered the same stews as they did and I ate, slowly. The table next to me spoke of the new phenomenon of the Swiss pikemen. They were disdainful of both the formation and the weapon but their distaste was because it negated the power of mounted knights.

"I would not like to charge into a phalanx of such pikes and where is the honour in being skewered by a peasant?"

"Aye, one of my grandsires was pulled from his horse by an English archer when that devil, Henry, slaughtered so many. My family lost a fortune that day. I would rather fight a knight."

"We will not fight the English again. They have lost France."

"What of the Scots? There are many Scottish nobles at the king's court."

My ears pricked up for this was the news I had been seeking.

"King Louis does not need the Scots and they will not fight against the Pope. No, Gilles, if you wish to fight then you must risk excommunication and join in the war in Italy."

"There is neither profit nor honour in that. I am young and I will have time to hone my skills before we fight again."

Two young men entered and looked around the room for a table. They were all taken. Behind them, more men waited to enter for the inn was becoming busier as noon approached. One followed and one led. It was ever the way and the one who led was gaudily dressed. His scabbard was elaborately decorated as was his sword hilt. His hat was richly made and everything about him told me that he was a show-off. I studied my pichet of wine and avoided eye contact. He strode over to the table and placed his hands on it, "You have a table and my friend and I would have it. Move."

I glanced over to the innkeeper who shrugged. The young man before me had money. For all that I knew he came from an important family. The innkeeper would rather keep his trade than an itinerant Englishman who might never return.

I looked up at the young man, "You are more than welcome to join me but I have ordered food and I am staying here. There are other tables for you to use."

I glanced at the follower who tugged at his friend's tunic, "Come, Jean. He is right."

The aggressive young man saw and heard weakness in my words and my manner. "The trouble is, I want this one and he will leave." He reached out to grab my goblet. My hands were faster and my right hand was around his before his hand was halfway to its prize. I spoke as I began to squeeze. Training with a billhook gives a man strength. In battle, a loose grip on a billhook shaft can end in death and I never dropped a billhook. I squeezed and stopped the blood going to the fingers. "Listen to your friend. You are beginning to look foolish and if I continue to squeeze then every bone in your hand will be broken." I was speaking quietly but my eyes never left his. I increased the pressure and saw the pain on his face. Such was my grip that he could not pull away. "Now, if I let go then you and your friend will leave this inn and find another where you can dine." I looked at the follower, "Is that not so?"

The young man looked terrified and said, "Aye sir, come Jean."

I gave an extra squeeze and a squeal of pain was forced from his tight lips. He nodded vigorously. I let go and the one called Jean began to massage blood back into fingers that if not broken would need some time to recover. They hurried out. I was aware that the inn was silent and all eyes were on me. My attempt to blend in was over. I gave a weak smile and then picked up my goblet to drink. A buzz of conversation began to rise. Hopefully, I would disappear back into anonymity.

A voice to my left said, "Excuse me but the inn is full and you have three spare chairs. Might my friend and I join you?"

I looked up and saw two men. They were nobles for they wore spurs but they were older than the four at the table next to me. Not as old as I was, they were dressed more conservatively. I smiled, "Of course. I pray you to sit."

As they sat one said, "You are not French." It was a statement and not a question.

"You have a good ear, sir, I am not."

They waved over the innkeeper and rattled off an order for food and drink.

"Then what are you? Flemish? Dutch? Your sword is Flemish made but your accent..."

I said, as quietly as I could, "English." Even though it was quietly spoken, it attracted the attention of the four diners to my right. All six pairs of eyes studied me.

The noble who had asked the question smiled and nodded, "So what brings an Englishman alone to the heart of Paris? An Englishman who has the strength to frighten off a bully by the mere pressure of his fingers." He drank some of the wine and continued, "This will be an interesting diversion for us, Jean." He turned to the four men at the neighbouring table who were patently watching and listening to us. "And it is the height of bad manners to listen to a conversation to which you were not invited."

They must have known who he was and he seemed to have some sort of reputation for the four nobles whipped their heads around and obeyed his implied order.

The knight shook his head and said, "Young cockerels but you, my friend, look to have the air of a man who has fought in battles. Am I right?"

I was now playing a part. I had concocted a story on the road to explain the sword and part of it had been a history of a man who had fought for hire. I nodded, "I have used my blade in battle, it is true."

"I am being rude. My name is Seigneur Charles of Dreux and this is my cousin Jean d'Ouistreham."

I took a deep breath and dived into the pool of deceit and lies that would now be my world. I played with the signet ring, "I am Edward of Standish and my father was recently executed by King Henry of England. I have fled to France seeking work."

"Work?"

"I have used my sword before now and I am handy with it. I need to earn a living and England is no longer a welcome haven."

The food came and the two men looked reflective as they stopped talking and waited for the server to disappear.

Charles of Dreux put his fingers together, almost as though in prayer and leaned forward. His eyes invited me to close to him. He said quietly, "I see you playing with a ring and I vaguely recognise the crest. The last men I heard who were executed by King Henry were Edmund Dudley and Sir Richard Empson."

"I am the son of Edmund Dudley."

"His sons are children."

"My mother was not married to my father. It was she who gave me the ring before she died."

"If you are not legitimate then why did you need to flee England?"

I had practised the look I gave him. It was a cynical look that bespoke mistrust in authority, "The new king is a vindictive man. My father served the old King Henry well and his execution was a way to gain money. My father's legitimate children are in the Tower. I did not wait for his guards to come knocking on my door and besides," I looked around and lowered my voice, "my father used me as a captain of some of his men. I led and trained them. It would make the king suspicious. I had no desire to see the inside of the Tower."

They seemed satisfied with my story. I knew that one of the reasons that the king had ordered the trial and execution of the two men was that they had raised armies and he had suspected rebellion. I used my involvement in the companies as a lure. They might believe that I had been part of a conspiracy to overthrow the young king. It had happened before. My time with Perkin Warbeck had taught me that you did not use a perfect story. You needed a story with holes in it as they would make it more believable.

Charles wiped his mouth when he had finished eating, "An interesting story. Where are you staying?"

I wondered if the bait had been taken but I had to appear suspicious, "Why?"

The seigneur smiled, "If, as you say, you wish to work then I will need know where you live so that I may contact you."

I nodded and told them, "But I may be leaving soon. I have been here for some days and the prospect of finding a paymaster seems slim. I may go to Italy. There is war there."

"Give me a day or two, young Englishman and do not be so hasty. It may be that there is work here in Paris."

"But there is no war."

He smiled, "I know but you said you wanted a paymaster. What if I could find you a paymaster who did not need you to go to war?"

"Then I would be a happy man."

"Good." He leaned forward, "A word of advice. Do not use this inn again. For one thing it is too expensive and," he looked around at the nearby table, "for another, it is filled with young cockerels who might take it upon themselves to test your skills. Believe me, they are not worth it." He said the last words loud enough for the four young men to hear. I nodded.

I paid my bill and left. I had been there a long time. I headed back to my inn and I knew that I was being followed. The streets were busy but you develop a sixth sense about such things. I was being tested. I did not see the two nobles with whom I had dined but that did not mean they had not come with companions who might follow me. I went directly to my rooms and lay down. I had planted the bait and now I had to wait. I looked at my ceiling and tried to work out what the two men might do. My story had intrigued them but they would need to verify the facts. If they had followed me to the inn, as I suspected, then they would know that part of my story was true. They would then try to discover if I had been seeking work. That would be proved to be true. How they might discover the story fabricated by the king and his archbishop I did not know. That evening, as I ate in the inn in which I was staying I was feeling pleased with myself. I had expected it to be some time before the bait was taken but it seemed to have been taken quickly. To reinforce my story I went, the next day, to the Louvre. As usual, I asked if I could speak to someone about hiring my sword and, once more, I was rejected. I did not return to the inn close to the Palais de Cité instead I went to the market at Notre Dame. It was a dangerous place as there were cutpurses but I had been trained by the best and my purse was well hidden. I kept a few coins in a fold in my tunic. I did not need to buy much but I was guessing that I would be observed. I had been the last time the Yorkists had recruited me. This time I would not have Jean le Casserole endangered. I was truly alone. It was late in the afternoon and the market was ending when I headed back to my lodgings. I looked for my followers but saw none. I took that as a mark of their skill.

For the next three days, my days were remarkably similar. I went to the Louvre and this time, although I was rejected, a sympathetic guard suggested that I might seek employment at the Palais de Cite. I was making progress, of a sort. I visited the other markets, including Les Halles and I ate food sold by the vendors. It was far cheaper than inns and if I was trying to be a sword for hire then I would watch my coppers. I drank sparingly and adopted a sad, hangdog expression.

When I was approached again it was not by Charles but Jean d'Ouistreham. I had left the inn to head to the Louvre when he fell in behind me, "Say nothing, Englishman, but when I overtake you then follow me at a discreet distance."

I obeyed and when the cloaked figure walked beyond me, I began to walk after him. That someone was following me became clear when Jean began to take side alleys as though he was trying to lose a follower. I was completely lost and disorientated. Paris was normally an easy city to use for the river was always in the centre. London only has the river on one side but here, the many bridges meant that the islands in the middle of the river were a thoroughfare. We did not cross one and when the houses began to thin, I realised that we had left the city. We came to a walled house with an armed man lounging outside.

The follower was confirmed when Jean turned and waved forward the scruffily dressed man.

He grinned at me and said to Jean, "He is alone and there were no followers." He saluted me and said, as he headed back to Paris, "Following you was an easy task and I thank you for the coins with which you have filled my purse."

Jean said, as we entered the gates, "Roger has been your shadow since we parted." He shrugged, "We had to be sure. You could have been a spy. We accept that you are not but there is another test yet."

We were nearing the doors to the hall and I said, "A test? For what? I want to hire my sword out. What do you think I wish for?"

He smiled as he opened the door and gestured for me to enter, "It is not what you wish, Englishman, but what we want to happen." He stood aside to allow me to enter, "Your life changed when King Henry executed your father. Embrace this new life for it will bring you gold and power. Perhaps more importantly it will bring you vengeance."

As we entered the hall I said, somewhat grumpily, "I was not close to my father. He barely acknowledged me and he abandoned my mother."

We walked down a long corridor, "Nevertheless you suffered because you were his son." He stopped at a door and gave me a crooked smile, "You know that there is a price on your head? Someone thinks that you are important enough to offer gold to kill you." I feigned surprise. "Oh you are safe enough for the reward is not enough to send one over the seas to find you but it makes you a person of interest to us."

He pushed the door open and there was a table with four men seated around it. I looked at Charles, "Us?"

An older man at the end of the table with a white beard and rings on his fingers as well as a fine sword at his waist stood and said, "An alliance of disparate men who have one thing in common, hatred for all things English. Sit, Edward of Standish, and we shall explain what is needed of you." He had been smiling all the time he spoke but I saw that there was no smile in the eyes and when I sat he said, "You are our man now, Edward of Standish and whether you live or die is our choice. Your fate is no longer in your own hands."

I sat and protested, "But I just want to be a sword for hire."

"What you want and what we wish are two entirely different things. Life is not fair and any fool who thinks it is, deserves to die. Now, let me explain who we are. Each of us represents a different faction who, for one reason or another hates England. We four are a sort of council who decide upon strategy. For obvious reasons, we shall not tell you our names. Suffice it to say that there are Frenchmen with long memories amongst our supporters as well as those who are English and wish for a change of ruler. There are Scots who wish their country enlarged and England diminished and there are those from the Empire who do not like the English aspirations. Your new king has more ambition abroad than his father. Until he came to the throne we talked more than we acted but now we spy a danger and you have been brought to our attention at just the right time."

I looked around the table. The other three were different in appearance and age from the white-haired man. They never gave me their names but I gave them my own names. The first one, Leader, was the white-haired man with the rings. A haughty-looking man with a magnificently oiled beard and moustache spoke to me and as I detected an Italian accent I called him, in my mind, Italian, "Of course, we need to know if you have the skills of which you boast. That will be tested here. Failure will result in death."

A hard-looking man added, with an accent that marked him clearly as Scottish, "As will all failure, Englishman." I naturally called him Scotsman. The aggression in his tone left me in no doubt that he hated Englishmen and he was reluctant to use me. However as I did not recognise him, I knew he would not know me. He had not been with King James and that was a relief. My story and my life would have ended if he had.

The last man who spoke smiled. He looked to be of an age with Leader but I was not taken in by his words. His eyes were cold, "But, my friend, those are the negative side of our arrangement. With luck and hard work you will have vengeance and become a rich man." I had lived long enough at the court of

Duchess Margaret to recognise a Burgundian voice and he became The Burgundian.

The Leader looked at Charles, "You may leave us now. I will send for you when it is time to feed our friend and then begin his training."

Charles smiled and said, "Your account at the inn is settled and your gear is in your new room. See, already you are in profit for you did not need to use your own coins."

As the door closed, I felt like a fool. I thought that I had been so clever and I had woven a good story. They had been the ones who had been looking for one such as I was. I guessed that the inn where I had been recruited had told Charles and Jean that an Englishman was dining. I knew that my accent marked me as English. I had not been in command of the situation, they had.

The Leader said, "Now that you understand the situation let us tell you what we wish. King Louis vacillates too much. He dallies in Italy when he should be using the armies of France to reclaim every piece of French soil that the English hold. When we are satisfied that you have skills then you will be taken from here to the Loire Valley. King Louis prefers it to Paris. We have friends at court and they will suggest a plan to the king. It will coincide with your arrival and even a weak King Louis will think that you are a heaven-sent opportunity to appease his allies and enjoy a victory over England."

It was what King Henry wanted but I was still playing a part, "And what if King Louis does not agree and decides not to use me in whatever this plan of yours is?"

Scotsman grinned, "Then you will die and by my hand. Make no mistake, you are ours now. We own you and your life is in our hands. Your fate was settled once you entered that inn. Fate can be a cruel mistress can she not?"

Burgundian looked at me, "That is the dark side of our agreement but there is no reason why you should not embrace this chance for revenge, However, you will be accompanied now, for every moment of the day and night. The men who watch you will not give a second thought to sticking a blade in your back." he shrugged, "It would set our plan back a little but better that than discovery."

There must have been someone standing behind me, close to the door for Leader said, "Take him to his chamber and guard him until we eat. Now that we have seen him, we need to speak."

I turned and saw a huge, scarred soldier. He was not a noble and I had seen men like him before. He was a Burgundian mercenary. Such men were ruthless killers. I stood and headed for the door. The man's accent confirmed his identity as he said, "Up the stairs." Had I wished to escape that would have been my best opportunity although only a fool would have tried it. There had been guards at the gates and the horses would now be in the stables. The hall had three floors. I guessed it had once been a fortified manor. I was taken to the top floor and given a room that had a bed in it and that was all. My bag took up the remaining space. It showed my status. I was little more than a slave. This would not be the pampered life of the court of Duchess Margaret. My latest adventure was far more dangerous than my first one. What had King Henry got me into? The door closed and I sat on the bed.

Any plans I might have had of heading back to Calais or Dunkerque and seeking a ship home were now in tatters. The Loire meant I would have to cross the whole of Normandy. I would have a bodyguard and that would create a problem. How would I rid myself of my shadow? I doubted that it would be the Burgundian. My bodyguard would be less obvious but skilled.

As I waited to be summoned, I took the opportunity to examine my belongings. They had not been ransacked. Everything had been packed well and I had not been robbed. That had been one thought. I was glad now that there was nothing incriminating amongst my gear. I lay on the bed and closed my eyes. If my first venture as a spy had taught me anything it was to rest while I could. Amazingly, I fell asleep and was woken by a huge Burgundian paw.

My watcher said, "It is time for food."

I followed him down the stairs and we entered the hall. Charles was there as well as one or two other nobles. I recognised none of them and realised from their accents that the majority were French. That made sense for we were close to Paris and in the heart of France. The council might represent different factions but France and Burgundy were the beating heart of it. All the seats were taken; I was not going to be eating with these men. I stood and waited.

The Leader had been in conversation with Charles and when the shadow of the Burgundian loomed up behind him he turned, "Ah, Edward. We have debated what we should do with you and the Seigneur has convinced me that you have potential. Your test will be in the morning. Defeat Albert and we shall start your training."

From his grin, it was clear that Albert was my Burgundian shadow. "And if I fail to defeat him?"

The Leader shrugged, "Then it will not matter for you will be dead. Take him to the kitchens, Albert, and feed him."

A massive paw pushed me in the middle of my back and propelled me from the room. This was a more dangerous situation than the previous two. The Leader and his cronies were the kinds of men who would watch cock fighting or bear-baiting. They would enjoy the spectacle. Watching two men fight to the death would merely add to their enjoyment. I realised that Charles of Dreux must have had great faith in me if he thought I could defeat the massive Burgundian. The kitchen had a table where the servants would eat. They were all busy serving those in the Great Hall and so Albert and I had the whole table to ourselves. We faced each other and a scullery maid placed bowls of food before us. We were not served the swans, capons, wild boar and venison that they enjoyed in the Great Hall, we had the lesser cuts but they had been well cooked and not having eaten all day I was starving. I studied the man who would try to kill me the next day, as I ate. I was not fooled by his size. I knew that big men could be agile. He had been chosen to both watch and fight me as he was skilled. He would be a hard opponent to fight. The Italian mercenaries who had trained me had done a good job with me but then I had been better clay than the sad Perkin Warbeck. They had honed those skills I already had. Since that time I had improved. I was older now and not as reckless as the youth from Ecclestone. I would have to defeat him with my mind as well as my skill.

When I had enjoyed enough food, I began to use my words to fool him and to being to win the battle before the fight started, "So, Albert, you think to kill me tomorrow?"

He looked up at me. His beard and moustache were untrimmed. He looked like a bear with a human voice. His hooded eyes were cold. The man was a ruthless killer, "I know that I shall kill you for that is what I do. I have fought many times …" he shook his head, "and each time I have won." He patted the bulging purse I saw hanging from his belt. "And each time I am rewarded. When I kill you tomorrow then I shall have enough to return to Auxerre and buy a farm. I am glad that my last victim will be an Englishman. My grandfather died at the hands of an English mercenary in Italy. It is fitting that my last victory should be over an Englishman."

"Yet you have not seen me use a sword so how do you know?"

He grinned, "Who says it will be with swords? It is I who will choose the weapons and the ones I choose will suit me. I do not play fair, Englishman. I do not play at all. I simply win. If I liked you, I might make the end quick but I do not like you for there is something about you I do not trust. I will make your end slow and painful." He pushed the empty platter away from him. "Now let us go outside and when you have made water then I will escort you to your chamber." He gave an evil smile, "And lock you in. If I were you, I should say my prayers tonight for tomorrow you might get to see God or perhaps the devil I neither know nor care."

Chapter 13

I had tried to intimidate him with my words and failed. It was a good lesson for me, as it showed me that I was overconfident. This was not the Flemish court. This was a cockpit and I was in danger of being served up as a piece of entertainment for these enemies of England. I had to get back to England for my family's sake but I also had to let my new king know the danger of this conspiracy. That it was secret was clear and the danger was far worse than a political alliance of kings and princes. Their motives were easier to discover and understand. I had always said my prayers each night but the warning from the Burgundian made the ones I said that night particularly pleading. I hoped I would not die but I knew I needed divine help if I was to emerge with my life. I finally drifted off to sleep with the unpleasant thought that even if I won, I might be wounded in the combat and given a warrior's death. I not only had to win but make sure that I was unwounded. My dreams were haunted by the image of a bear tearing my flesh to pieces. It was not good preparation for a fight to the death.

I was awake before Albert unlocked my cell and took me down to the kitchens. After making water and emptying my bowels, supervised by the leering Burgundian, I ate a hearty breakfast and began to get my mind into the forthcoming fight. Albert ate well too but I noticed that while I drank small beer, he drank wine that was unwatered. He might have the capacity to hold his drink but it was a chink in his armour and I would exploit it.

He waved a paw at me, "Come. We prepare."

I did not know what to expect but I hoped for some protection for my body. When we went into the yard where chairs were already being placed by liveried servants, I saw no armour, not even a leather jack. Nor were there any helmets. There were weapons on a table and there were two of each. I still had my sword and dagger on my belt and as they had not been taken from me, I thought it clear that I would be able to use them if I chose. The weapons on display showed me that it would be a mistake. There were halberds and poleaxes, maces and war axes. There were the two handed swords favoured by the Germans but there was not a sign of a shield or a sword such as mine. I saw the amusement on Albert's face. He knew which weapon he would choose and he was enjoying the fear on my face for I was afraid. If he chose a mace or an axe then I might stand a chance for I could discard it and use my own sword. Speed and agility might be the bear's undoing. Any of the pole weapons would negate my sword. Knowing I could do nothing about the choice of weapon, I did the unexpected and sat on one of the chairs.

For the first time Albert the Burgundian looked confused, "Do you not wish to try the weapons out?"

I smiled and then closed my eyes, "Why should I? Whichever one I try will not be the one you will use. You have already picked out the weapon you are going to use. You will use your favourite and as I cannot read the mind," I opened my eyes, "I assume you have a mind?" He scowled and I knew I had scored a point. "The mind of a Burgundian butcher who kills to order, no, I shall rest and set my mind to work out how best to kill you."

"Stand, those chairs are for... our masters." He loomed towards me his intent clear. He would pull me from the chair.

I shook my head, "Firstly, they are not our masters and secondly," I had my dagger out and pointed at his throat in an instant, "I could end the combat here and now with one push of my blade." A tendril of blood dripped from his throat.

"You have courage, Edward, but do not deprive us of our sport." Charles of Dreux pulled back my hand. "Albert, go and prepare." I sheathed my dagger.

I had angered the bear and as he put his finger to his throat to reveal the blood he shouted, "You will beg for death! I will make you die by inches!"

Charles shook his head, "Albert is a killer you know. All that you have done is ensure that I will have to return to the inns of Paris once more to find another who can take your place. I had such high hopes for you. You seemed perfect." I heard the noise of men emerging from the hall and he said, "Now stand for Albert is quite right. The chairs are for our masters."

I stood and then said, "They may be your masters but they are not mine. Even if they employ me I will not be theirs to own. Remember that, Charles of Dreux."

The look on his face told me that I had confused him too.

I walked over to the table with the weapons. Albert had stemmed the bleeding and he glared at me but kept far enough away so that I could not use my dagger again. The Leader took the best seat and the others flanked him. It confirmed that, whoever he was, he was most definitely the Leader. I saw a smile on his face when he saw the wound I had inflicted on the Burgundian. Albert had told me this was his last fight. Did they think that I would win and in doing so would not have to pay their killer? It was hope and a drowning man grasps at any sign of survival.

"Well, Albert, which weapon do you choose to test our latest recruit?" The Leader's choice of words was interesting. The previous night his tone and words had implied that I was to die or Albert was. Now he said '*recruit*' and had used the word '*test*'. Once more hope rose. Albert wished to kill me but would the Leader halt the combat if I was in danger?

Albert went to the table and picked up a poleaxe. It was the one weapon I had hoped he would choose. "This is my favourite for it always brings victory and," he grinned at me, "and the death of my opponent. Let us see if this son of a lord has used one." The poleaxes had a blade, a spike and a hammer head. Like my billhook there was a langet protecting the head of the weapon and, at the bottom was a metal spike so that it could be planted in the ground.

I picked one up and deliberately feigned unfamiliarity with the weapon. In truth, it was as close to a billhook in size and weight as to be indistinguishable. I first held it the wrong way around and everyone laughed. I took a better grip and then made a clumsy attempt at a swing and the laughter rose. The only one who was not laughing at me was Charles of Dreux. He was watching me closely with a half-smile on his lips.

The Leader shook his head, "Come, Edward of Standish, try to make entertainment for us. I have invited guests today to see a battle between Burgundy and England. Do not let me down."

The Scotsman held out a purse, "Fifty crowns on Albert? Any takers?" The others laughed even more.

Their laughter ended when Charles took out his own purse and said, "I will take that bet."

For some reason that angered Albert who said, "Enough of this. Have at you." He brought the axe blade down towards my unprotected head.

If it had connected, even with a helmet I would be dead. As it was the lack of armour and helmet helped me for I was more agile than Albert and I danced away from his clumsy blow. It was predictable and would only have caught out a complete novice. I was far from being a novice. I held the poleaxe balanced so that I could use it to block Albert's blows and, when the opportunity arose, use it offensively. Stepping back encouraged him and he lunged at me with the sharpened spike. I made the move look hurried as I blocked the strike. It was an easy block and I realised that he was not as good with the weapon as he thought or, perhaps, I was a better billman and my training had given me skills superior to a hired mercenary.

"You have luck, Englishman, but you cannot evade me for long. I will soon draw some of your blood."

I did not rise to the bait but watched his eyes. That was one advantage of his not wearing a helmet, I could see his eyes and they told me where his next blow would strike. His eyes flicked to my head and I knew it would be a two-handed sweep at my neck. He had fast hands and he quickly slid them down the shaft of the poleaxe and began his swing. I was already stepping back when he swung and the swing hit the air. It exposed his side and I lunged with the spike of my poleaxe. It struck him in the side and I drew first blood. It enraged him and he rushed at me, holding the poleaxe like a staff so that he could use both the head and the pointed bottom of the haft as weapons. I used to practice with Thomas and Richard every day using staffs and I blocked both his blows as I raced back. It was the Scotsman, no doubt eager to win his bet, who was almost my undoing. As I neared him, he stuck out a foot and I tumbled backwards. Even as I was falling, I had the wit to roll and the blade of the Burgundian's poleaxe buried itself in the earth where my body had been a moment or two earlier. I was on my feet quickly and as he lifted the poleaxe I swung at his middle. He managed to block the blow with his poleaxe but my blade hit below the langet and I saw it bite into the wood. I stepped back and moved away from the spectators.

"That was not well done, sir." Charles of Dreux's comment was aimed at the Scotsman.

The Scotsman shrugged, I saw it from the corner of my eye, "He is English."

It was such a bizarre comment that it almost distracted me from the next frenzied attack from Albert. I think he had given up on a slow lingering death for me and wanted it over as soon as he could. I saw blood on the ground and knew it was not mine. Blood loss would gradually weaken him and I was, thus far, unhurt. The thrust from the spike was easily deflected and allowed me to use the metal at the bottom of the haft of my poleaxe. I smacked it hard into his knee. I did not draw blood but I hurt him. It seemed to give him an idea of how to beat me and I watched as he turned the poleaxe in his hands. He was going to use the hammer head and as I had hit his knee it was no great stretch to work out that he would go for my knee. As he swung his weapon so did I but my blow was aimed at the haft of the poleaxe. It split his weapon in two and the spike tore down his breeches, cutting the flesh and adding to his list of wounds.

I thought that might be the end of the contest for his weapon could now only be used in one hand. I would easily win. No one said a word and so I raised my poleaxe to end the contest.

The Leader shouted, "Hold. We use the rules of chivalric combat here. Englishman, drop your poleaxe. You must now use your swords."

I did as I was told but knew that the advantage now lay with Albert for his sword was longer than mine by a handspan. I was not unduly worried for I had been trained by the best. I did not know Albert's skill level and I would take no chances. Once more he tried to strike the first blow and he held his sword in two hands. Had the sideways strike connected with my neck then I would be dead but I blocked it and deflected it to the side as I drew my dagger. I was not told to sheathe it. He raised his sword above his head and brought his sword down at mine. I made a cross with my sword and dagger and easily held the strike. I then brought my knee hard up into his groin. I had hurt him and he staggered. I punched at his face, while he was distracted, with the hilts and pommels of my sword and dagger. His nose burst like a ripe plum. I knew that his eyes must water. If I was to be of use to King Henry then I had to live. Thus far Albert had not come close to hurting me but as the Scotsman's trip had shown, it was possible. I crossed my arms and brought my sword and dagger across at the same time. Albert's sword pointed at the ground and he was unable to see the two blades as they scythed together to take off his head. His body stood stock still for a moment as the head rolled to end up close to the Scotsman's feet and then, like a felled tree the body fell to the ground.

My victory was greeted with silence until Charles of Dreux's laconic voice said, "And that means, sir, that your purse is mine."

The Leader began to clap, "That was a surprise and no mistake. You were right, Seigneur. He is the right man for us. You men, dispose of the body." As one came to claim the head another four armed guards picked up the body.

As they passed us Charles said, "Hold." They stopped and the Seigneur went to the body and took the purse from it. He tossed it to me. "You deserve it more than these. That was well done."

The Frenchman had done me no favours for the guards glowered and glared at me.

The Leader stood, "Let us retire inside while the yard is cleaned. We can now speak more openly to Edward of Standish. We can easily hire more Burgundian killers but men with the skills of this Englishman are rare."

I was accepted and the first part of King Henry's plan looked to be close to completion. From that moment the attitude of everyone seemed to change. I was still guarded and the two armed men at the stables guaranteed that I would not be able to escape. I still dined in the kitchen but I was not watched as closely and certainly, no one glowered and glared at me. I learned that Albert was a bully. Most of the other guards were frightened of him and he had taken women against their will. While the council still kept its distance from me, the others seemed quite happy to accept me as one of them.

The day after the fight Charles and Jean came to the kitchen where I had just eaten my breakfast. "Get your cloak, Edward, for today we ride."

I was curious and excited. I took the stairs to my attic cell two at a time and returned with a hat and cloak. As we walked to the stables Charles said, "Do not entertain ideas of escape. Jean and I will have the better horses and we are both good riders."

I nodded, "I still do not know my purpose and I might be happier if you confided in me."

"All in good time. This is like a courtship and we need to get to know one another." I noticed that Charles was careful to speak only when we could not be overheard. He was a careful man. The horse I was given was smaller and more docile than theirs. I would not be able to escape. Of course, they did not know that I did not want to escape, not yet anyway.

As Charles led us down a track to the forest I said, conversationally, "You took a chance when you gambled so much on me. I would have backed Albert."

He laughed, "No, you would not. I saw you in the inn when you crushed that foolish young man's hand. I saw your eyes and saw a determination there. As you knew Albert was overconfident and had drunk too much. He assumed you were a poor warrior and he paid the price although I confess your victory was more complete than I anticipated. You have more skills than I expected. Where were you trained?"

"At home." I was deliberately vague. He had to believe that I was the illegitimate son of a noble.

He nodded, "Those skills may prove to be vital."

I shook my head, "Look, Charles, whatever the council wishes of me I will do but I cannot see what purpose it will serve." I sighed, "I can see that you all hate England and that you wish me to, in some way, help you to have vengeance but I cannot see how. There is a price on my head. As soon as I return to England then I will be apprehended. You do not wish to see me in the Tower, do you?"

He said nothing but spurred his horse. The trail he had chosen twisted and turned through the hunting forest. I had to follow and try to keep up. Behind me, I was aware that Jean was close behind me. It took all my skill to not only keep my saddle but to make the docile beast keep up with Charles' horse. We came to a charcoal burners' clearing and he reined in. My horse was panting and sweating.

Charles looked at Jean, who nodded, "He can ride."

I shook my head, "Another test but for what purpose?"

He threw his leg over his saddle and dismounted. I followed suit and we walked our horses to a small stream that ran through the trees.

"You are aware, for you are far from stupid, that the only names you know are mine and Jean's. That is deliberate. If you should betray the cause then the leaders and the council would be unharmed. No matter what happens to you their work will continue. You passed the first test when you slew Albert. We met last night to plan the next phase. The test I just gave you was of my choosing. I like you, Edward, and I want you to survive. When you are cut loose, I wanted to know that you would not be easily captured."

"Captured? Why should I be captured?"

The horses were drinking and, just a few paces from where we stood fallen branches had dammed and made a small pond. It would disappear with the next heavy rain. Charles picked up a stone and threw it up into the air. It landed in the middle of the water. The ripples moved outwards towards the edge. It was the same action Jane's father had sown me when I had visited him. "That is you. The greatest perturbation in the water is in the centre but you can see that even at the edge, the effects can be seen. King Louis has many petitioners at his court. There are those there, not related to the council, who wish to see the Tudor dynasty ended. Jean and I are known to be against the English. It is why you know our names for we cannot be hurt by the divulging of them. King Louis may not be interested in supporting the son of an executed English noble but others will be. They may use you as they did those usurpers to King Henry's crown."

I saw their plan now. I shook my head, "But nothing may happen. What if they do not use me?"

He shrugged, "You have a purse taken from Albert. You will be given a good horse and ten crowns. If you are ignored then consider this the easiest way to earn money. You will not need to hire your sword out for you will be rich."

"Easy way to earn money? Albert could have killed me."

"We both know that is not true, Edward. There is something about you that marks you as different. Perhaps it is the manner of your birth, I know not but I do know that if those who wish a change of king hire you then you will have the best chance of succeeding. My task is to take you to the Loire and make the introductions. That is the end of my involvement."

It all seemed too good to be true. I already had information that was hidden from King Henry. At the court, I would see the petitioners and even if they did not take me on, I would meet King Henry's enemies. I kept a straight face but inside I was dancing.

When we returned to the hall, I noticed that most of the horses in the stables had gone. The meeting that had been convened seemed to be over. Was I the cause of the meeting or was that happenstance? That evening I dined with Charles, Jean and the Leader. I said little but listened to everything. It was not a feast although the food was both well cooked and delicious. I was there for my final instructions. When we had finished and the servants were dismissed the Leader nodded to Charles who pushed a purse towards me. It would have been churlish to count it and when I merely put the unopened purse to one side I saw the smile from the Leader. I had passed another test.

"Tomorrow you will ride to Blois. The King of France has returned from his Italian wars and Charles here will manage an introduction for you. I doubt that King Louis will have much to do with you but there are others at his court who may seek to use you to create unrest in England. If they seek your services then you will facilitate their aims." He was an astute man and he said, "The Council employs many men. You do not know who they are. Failure will result in an untimely end. You have shown yourself to be resourceful. Continue in that vein and there will be more rewards coming your way. You shall never see me again after tomorrow and I will leave this house that was loaned to me. I shall watch from afar."

With that, I was dismissed. When in my room I saw that I had been given ten crowns. It was not enough to begin a new life but, along with Albert's purse, made me a wealthy man. The next morning the three of us took the road to Blois. The two knights had two servants and they led the sumpters with our baggage. We did not stay in homes but in inns and religious houses. I knew the reason for if we had then I might be able to identify the supporters of the leader. I was a small investment and if I succeeded then they would be happy. If I failed then the trail to the Leader would end with Charles of Dreux. We did the journey in three days.

The court at Blois was a hotbed of intrigue and politics. I could see why Charles of Dreux was used as he was not only well known but welcomed as soon as we entered the ancient town. He even had a small hall which we used. There was just one servant, Jacques, and he acted as cook, stablemaster and custodian. With just four bedchambers and a stable that held four horses, I realised it was merely a place to use when he could not stay in the palace at Blois. Jacques quickly made us a meal and then left to make up our bedchambers. When he left us then Charles explained to me the way that the court worked.

"Men come from all over to seek help from King Louis. Some travel from abroad. There are ambassadors who have legitimate motives and others, such as we, who have ulterior ones. I will present myself to Guillaume, King Louis' steward and explain who you are. That should then gain us entry to the court the following day. There we will wait with other petitioners in the antechamber. We might be there for days. If the king agrees to see you then that is all to the good but he may not. If, after a week, no one has approached us then we will have failed."

"And what then?"

He shrugged, "You are on your own. I hear that Italy is the place for hired swords. I should avoid Spain as your king had married the daughter of the King of Aragon."

I was pleased for I had a week only and then I could take my new horse and ride, gently and as a man of leisure to Calais. My work would be done and I would have coins to take back to England to make my family more comfortable and I would have information to give to the archbishop and the king. I began to plan my journey through Normandy and Picardy to Calais.

Chapter 14

Blois 1510

Charles was obviously known and the two of us were given permission to petition the king. The antechamber was like a market the only difference being that in the antechamber at the court there were no women and instead of stall holders there were men of many nationalities each one with a different reason to be there. King Louis had, when he came to the throne, changed the tax system so that the nobles were worse off. More than half of the men I saw were nobles trying to get relief from the king. Charles pointed those out to me and told me to ignore them. It was on the second day when he pointed out those who were of interest to us. He took me across the room to meet Richard de la Pole. His brother languished in the Tower and Richard was the last claimant to the Yorkist crown. I had never met him but as we walked across the floor, I studied all the faces around him. I was looking for one who might have been at Mechelen. I saw no one I recognised and I breathed a sigh of relief. The lack of beard and moustache had helped.

"Your grace might I introduce the son of Edmund Dudley. Edmund this is the Duke of Suffolk, known as the White Rose."

The duke nodded and frowned, "I thought Edmund's sons were younger and are the guests of Henry Tudor?"

I noticed that he did not accord Henry the title of king.

I bowed and held out my hand so that he could see the signet ring with the crest upon it, "I was born the wrong side of the sheets, your grace. My mother was not married to my father."

He looked relieved, "A bastard, eh? Nothing wrong with that. And what brings you here to this cockpit?"

"I am seeking a master to hire my sword."

"Then if you look to me, young man, you will be disappointed. The days of the Dowager Duchess of Burgundy funding rebellion in England died with that great lady. You will have to join the list of beggars seeking crumbs from King Louis' table and since his war with the pope they are few and far between."

The news that the Yorkist threat appeared to be truly over would be welcomed by King Henry.

"However, if you are any good," he looked at Charles whom he obviously knew. Charles nodded, "Then perhaps we can both be swords for hire and join King Louis in Italy. It may well be that valiant service against the pope might result in funding for another attempt on the crown. Where do you stay?"

Charles said, "In my home, your grace."

"I will be in touch." He waved a hand and, with his handful of followers headed off to find the steward.

Charles shook his head, "I do not think the council will pin their hopes on a war in Italy which might, at some point in the future, yield results. We will seek the Scots. They might well need you, your sword and your name."

It was in the early afternoon that the door to the inner chamber opened and four men came out. That was when the White Rose, the Duke of Suffolk, was admitted. Charles said, "I recognise the man who just emerged. He is the Scottish ambassador, James Stewart, the Earl of Buchan. We shall accost him."

The Scot had a grim face and had three men with him. I had heard of him when I had served as Queen Margaret's bodyguard but he had been on his estates and I had not met him. Nor did I recognise any of the men with him.

"My lord."

The earl scrutinised Charles and gave a thin smile and a nod of recognition, "Seigneur, still trying to ferment discord?"

Charles smiled, "We share the ambition, my lord, that one day England and its Tudor usurper will be humbled."

"Hmm. And who is this?"

"This is Edward of Standish, the illegitimate son of Edmund Dudley who was recently executed by King Henry."

The earl's eyes narrowed, "Edmund Dudley was no friend to Scotland. He bolstered Henry Tudor. If you wish coins then crawl off to find another master. You will get none from me."

I did not like his tone and I had come to know this character I was playing. He would not like it either, "I seek no charity, my lord. I am a swordsman and would fight for one who recognises my skill. I owe my father nothing." I held out my hand with the signet ring upon it. "This was the only inheritance I had and that came from my dead mother's finger. I left my home with the clothes I wore and my sword. If you do not wish to hire me then do not insult me when you refuse my service. I do not suffer insults and would as soon draw sword and test your mettle as not."

I saw the men with him bristle but the earl began to smile, "You have spirit and I apologise for any insult. There are many men who come here seeking coins to serve me and not all have the right motives."

One of his men said, "But, my lord, this man is a mercenary. He just seeks coins."

"And that is as good a motive as I can see. It may well be, young man, that I can use you." He came closer, "Do you still have friends in England?"

I nodded, "Aye, and, at the moment, a price upon my head."

He looked at my face and said, "Grow a beard and change your clothes. They will make you a new man."

I knew what he wanted but I had to feign ignorance, "But, my lord, what has my friends to do with hiring me as a sword?"

"You can pass amongst the English and not arouse suspicion. You could spy out their defences and let King James know their weaknesses."

"Be a spy?"

"A spy is still a sword for hire but one that does not draw his sword except in a dire emergency."

"Then King James still wishes harm upon England."

"Not England but those parts of Scotland that they have enslaved, Northumberland." He looked at Charles, "He stays with you?" Charles nodded, "Then wait there while I make enquiries. It may take a week or so for me to verify your identity but if you speak the truth then I have high hopes." He smiled at Charles, "If the Seigneur is your host, then for the present, you do not need Scottish gold."

With that, he left us and Charles shook his head, "You have a natural talent, Edward. I thought your reaction was the wrong one but it seems you are as accurate with your words as you are with your sword point. Come, we will learn no more here. Let us join Jean at my hall."

That night, as we dined, Charles told me that he and Jean would be leaving the next day. He did not tell me where he was going but I guessed it was council business. From the words of the White Rose and the earl, I deduced that Charles was the public face of the council.

"And what of me?"

You will stay here, of course. At the end of the week, if you have not been contacted, then we have to assume that our plan has failed. You will keep the horse and the crowns but quit this house. As I said to you, there is work in Italy and it may well be that there lies your best hope of work." He gave a sad smile, "I confess that I hoped you could be the small stone which starts an avalanche. We get few young men who have your skills. Your French is almost perfect and you do not have the reckless arrogance that marks many young English noblemen. Your skill with weapons is nothing short of miraculous. Tell me, Edward, purely to satisfy my curiosity, are you able to use weapons from the back of a horse as well as you do on foot?"

I was not being arrogant when I nodded. I had skills and I knew it.

"Then let us hope that either the White Rose or the earl recognises your potential."

I was sad when the two knights left the next day. Charles was an enemy to King Henry and England yet I liked him. In a way, I was a little relieved as well as sad for he would not be there when I fled for England. I would not leave for a day or two. I wanted Charles as far from Blois as possible. I had enough information to give to King Henry and the archbishop and I did not think that either the duke or the earl would contact me. I spent two days walking the streets of Blois. The castle and the town were beautiful and I spent the next days enjoying the sights.

It was the second day and having enjoyed a fine meal in one of the inns by the river I was walking back through the town. Replete I headed back to the hall and I saw two of the duke's retainers waiting at the door of Charles' home. Jacques pointed to me as I approached. The two retainers openly sported the white rose on their livery.

"Come, Master Edward. You are needed at the palace."

They headed me towards the palace and I almost had to run to keep up with them. The bait had been taken but I was ready to flee. I liked this not for I was no longer in control.

We were admitted to the antechamber and then, to my surprise, I was allowed to enter the hall where King Louis held court. All eyes swivelled to me as I entered and King Louis' voice carried to me, "So this is the Englishman who keeps a king waiting. Does he speak French?"

I knew how to behave at court and I gave an elaborate sweeping bow and said, "Yes, King Louis and apologies. I was dining."

I had chosen the right thing to say for the king laughed, "Not only can he speak French but he has embraced French customs too. You might have chosen well, Suffolk."

The Duke of Suffolk looked relieved, "I hope so, King Louis."

"The duke tells me that you are a sword for hire and would serve me."

"I am a sword for hire and to put food on the table I will serve any who hire me."

"Even King Henry in England?"

"As the duke will have told you, King Louis, I cannot serve him for there is a price upon my head."

"And are you any good?"

"I have killed men and, as you can see, my face and body are undamaged, as yet. I do not think you will be disappointed."

The king beamed, "I like this man. Then you shall serve the duke and he will serve me. We leave for Italy at the end of the month."

I was a sword for hire and my next question would be expected if not welcomed, "And the pay, King Louis?"

I saw the Duke of Suffolk roll his eyes but the king nodded, "A crown a month until we see your worth."

"Thank you, King Louis."

The duke and I backed out of the court and when we reached the antechamber he said, "You could have asked for the payment later. Why was it necessary to embarrass me so?"

"My lord, you do this to have backing for you and your search for a crown. I seek money, no more and no less."

He nodded, "I suppose I must accept that. I have a house by the river. It is a little crowded but you had best bring your horse and belongings there."

"I have rooms until the end of the week. With your permission, I shall come then."

The duke looked relieved. He gave me the directions and headed towards some Swiss knights who had recently arrived.

"Standish, I have still to receive word from Scotland."

I turned to see the Earl of Buchan and his men, "My lord, I have been employed by the Duke of Suffolk and I will be serving the French king in Italy."

The earl looked disappointed, "A shame, still, the king does not leave until the end of the month. I may be able to offer a higher payment."

"I gave my word, my lord."

He smiled, "We shall see. It may be that King Louis sees merit in having you ferment discord with England." He leaned in, "I have heard word that England seeks an alliance with the pope. If that is true then King Louis will want England distracted and what better way to distract King Henry than with a war on his borders. I will be in touch."

The intelligence I had gathered was now filling my head and I decided to leave for home once my time at Charles' residence came to an end. I wanted as few questions as possible when I left for Calais. Jacques would expect me to leave and the duke would be unworried if I did not arrive for a week or so. I began my preparations. The horse I had been given, Marie, was a powerful beast and so I began to gather provisions for the road. I would stay in inns but I knew that to disappear completely, I had to delay using inns until I was well clear of Blois. I did not expect a hue and cry but if there was one then they would seek me in the inns within a hundred miles of Blois. I used some of the money to buy two skins: one for wine and one for water or beer. I bought a small hard cheese that would last a week or so and I bought a cured ham shank. It would feed me for some days and I could always use it to make soup. To that end, I bought an old pot helmet. It cost me literally coppers but with the arming cap I also bought it would afford me protection not to mention a disguise if I needed it and yet could double as a cooking pot.

With the blanket, spare cloak and grain for Marie that I bought I felt I was well prepared for my flight.

The day I left Charles' hall, Jacques treated me to a fine breakfast and I filled my belly with well-cooked food and bread. I led my horse from the stable and walked towards the north gate. My route took me through a part of the town I did not recognise. I had entered through the east gate. I was lucky that I walked my horse else I might have been seen earlier than I was. It was as I was nearing the gate that I spied some of the Earl of Buchan's retainers.

One called out to me, "Are you leaving Blois?"

I shook my head, "My horse needs exercise. I am taking him for a ride."

"Then call here when you return. The earl has received word from Edinburgh. We have a messenger here."

I smiled and feigned joy, "Excellent. Then I shall begin my ride early.

The gate was just forty paces from me and was open. It was as I threw my leg over the saddle that the earl and another man emerged from the house. I recognised the man but he took some moments to recognise me. It was Andrew Buchanan, the Scottish knight who had taken against me and as I kicked Marie in the flanks, I heard his shout of recognition.

"That is Queen Margaret's bodyguard."

I waved at the two sentries as I rode through the gate. I was not galloping yet and I dared not spin my head around. The two sentries nodded as I passed them and then, as I saw a wagon and some carters appear I spurred Marie to gallop past them. It was as I turned around the wagon that I was able to look back and see Andrew Buchanan speaking urgently to the earl and from his gesticulations I knew that my story was now revealed. There would be pursuit.

I forced myself to be calm. The men were all afoot and could not simply run after me. They would have to find and saddle horses. That would take time. I had to disappear as quickly as I could. In my head, I had a map. Charles had one in his house and after he had gone, I had studied it. To the north lay Le Mans and to the east lay Chartres. Angers was to the west. If I was going to head to Calais then Le Mans would be my choice of route.

Chartres would be my choice if I was heading for Paris. The Earl of Buchan had been introduced to me by Charles and they might think that would be where I would head. I decided to risk fooling them. Less than four miles from Blois lay the village of Fossé. I reined in and played the ignorant Englishman. I asked, in English for directions to Chartres. When I repeated them in deliberately poor French the man pointed to the east. I nodded my thanks and headed along the road. As soon as I found a road that headed north, I took it and then took the next road west. I would head for Angers and then try to get a ship from Nantes. I would disappear into Anjou.

I used the smaller roads and kept the cowl of my cloak about my head. I did not gallop nor thrash Marie for she had to take me more than a hundred miles and I needed her more than food. I did not want to stop in the small villages and hamlets through which I passed and so I watered her at every stream and river that I crossed. While she drank, I took the opportunity to eat. I was grateful for Jacques' breakfast.

It was dark when I reached the Loir. I only knew the name of the river later but I was just grateful for the patch of grass where Marie could graze, the river where she could drink and the overhanging trees that hid us from view. I saw to my horse before I made my bed. She had not suffered hurt but she needed to be rested. As I ate a frugal meal I decided that I would walk her for the first part of the next day. The map I had studied had only had the main towns marked and I needed to know exactly where I was. The sun gave me the direction I would need to take. It would be generally west although I would when I neared it, have to veer south to reach the port of Nantes.

I ached, the next morning, as I saddled Marie. It had been a long time since I had ridden so long and slept on the hard and unyielding ground. I walked back to the road I had left and kept going until I reached a village. I had to find out where I was and that meant revealing my identity. I spoke to the first man I spied. It was a priest. I spoke in Flemish which he did not understand. When I spoke French, fluently this time, he answered my question.

"This is the village of Saint-Pierre-de-Chevillé. Are you lost, sir?"

I smiled, "I must be. I am heading for Le Mans."

He laughed, "Then you are heading in completely the wrong direction." He pointed north and east, "That is the direction you need but," he turned and pointed north and west, "you need to head west until you find a bridge over the Loir. There is one at Nogent. If you reach Vaas or Le Lude then you have gone too far."

I had to be sure of exactly where I was and so I made a joke of it, "And if I reach Angers then I am lost once more."

He joined in the laughter, "Yes, my friend, but as that is another sixty miles along that road then I think you would have realised it. Just keep heading west and then north and you will find it. Go with God."

I mounted Marie and then headed in the direction he had said. If I was unlucky and anyone pursued me then they would head for the bridge at Nogent. The road was quiet and I passed only locals going about their business. I gambled that any Scotsman following me would have to be very lucky to speak to one of those who saw me. When I spied the signs for Nogent and Le Lude, I took the road to Le Lude.

One difference between the spy who travelled the roads now and the one who had done so many years ago was that I was now a farmer. I understood the way that farmers worked. As darkness approached, I looked for an outbuilding close to a field that was some way from the main farm. I had them on my land. Some stored equipment that would be needed to repair walls and fences while others would be shelters for men during the lambing season. I saw one such building as the last rays of the setting sun illuminated the building. The field had been used for cattle and there was a water trough for Marie to use. The grazing was not the best and so I augmented her diet with grain. I would eat ham and cheese. When it was time for sleep, I brought Marie into the crude wooden shelter. I did not want her to be seen. The large structure had lengths of wood inside and I guessed they were to repair the fences to prevent the cattle from entering another field. It suited me.

I had trained myself to wake when I wished and not merely when my bladder demanded it. I woke in the dark and rose immediately. Outside I saw the first hint of dawn in the east. I made water, saddled Marie and was back on the road before dawn. I walked Marie until dawn. I was acutely aware that Marie was my only hope of survival. I needed to husband her strength. As the sun finally cleared the clouds that delayed its arrival, I reached a crossroads and a sign. The better road headed north and west towards a place called La Flèche. I took that road and made good time. The back roads I had used the previous day had been rutted and made my journey longer. This was a well-maintained road and Marie ate up the miles.

There was a market in La Flèche and that suited me as, walking Marie, I blended in with the other visitors to the town. I even risked a meal in an inn. I kept my words to a minimum but the inn was as busy as the town and there was little conversation. I left the town before noon. The signs told me that I had less than thirty miles to travel to reach the largest town in this area, the former capital of Anjou, Angers. As I rode the busy road, I began to adjust my plan. If I was to avoid inns, I would have to find somewhere well short of the large walled town. When I left Angers, I would have sixty miles to travel to Nantes. If I rode Marie hard for that last section I could do it in one day. A night in a stable would benefit Marie and that made my decision for me. I would risk a night in an inn.

I pushed Marie on and we made the gate to the town before the night watch was set. Normally I would have asked one of the sentries on the gate for a recommendation but I did not this time. I did not want them to remember me and I led a weary Marie through the gate with my head down. The watch ignored me for it would soon be the end of their shift. They were ready for wine and food. A weary traveller and a sweating horse did not concern them. I walked through the town and stopped at the last inn before the western gate. I saw that it had a stable and I handed the reins to the ostler.

"She has been ridden hard, sir."

I handed him a silver coin, "Groom her and feed her well."

He beamed, "I will treat her as though she was the king's own animal. Thank you, sir. There are rooms in the inn. We had a large party of men staying but they left this morning." He shook his head, "They were not generous men. They were mean-spirited as well as having tight purses."

The owner looked pleased to see me when I asked for a room. He did as all innkeepers do; he assessed my ability to pay by my dress. I was dressed as a gentleman and the price he quoted was higher than had I been more poorly dressed. I did not mind the extra payment. I had a full purse and even if the Scots had managed to follow me, I would have disappeared and be in Nantes before they could question the innkeeper. I ate a pleasant, hot meal before a fine fire and anticipated a comfortable night in a bed. I awoke early but lay in the bed knowing that I would not be able to leave the town until the gates were opened. I rose, washed, dressed and packed my bags. I went down to a fine breakfast and settled my account. Marie was already saddled and had been well-groomed by the ostler. Her coat shone and both her mane and tail had been not only brushed but plaited, albeit simply.

My thanks were genuine. As soon as we left the town and reached the open road, she seemed eager to open her legs and ride. I was on the last leg now but I was not foolish enough to think I was safe. As we ate up the miles, I pondered the problems I might face. There might not be a ship ready to take me to England and even a day's delay could be disastrous. Andrew Buchanan would not rest until he had found me. He would have told the Earl of Buchan of my other identity. It would tell them that I was a threat to them. There was a chance that they might have swallowed my bait and headed for Calais but I could not count on that. The first thing I would need to do would be to sell Marie. If I tried to take her back to England that would limit the number of ships I could take. More, she marked me as the man who had tried to fool the Earl of Buchan. Once I sold her I would buy new clothes and change my appearance. I rode hard and only stopped for calls of nature and to ensure that Marie was watered. She was weary and I was glad when we saw Nantes' walls appear. I passed through the gates without attracting attention and headed for the river. I spied ships that were tied up and loading but there were just three of them. What would be the odds that they might take me home?

I accosted a lounging sailor who looked to be awaiting orders to cast off, "Is there a horse trader close by?"

He looked me up and down and then nodded towards the church tower I could see. "Just behind the church, there is one."

Just then a voice shouted, "Wake up Pierre, cast off!"

The man hurried to obey the command and then lithely leapt aboard. There were now just two choices of ships and I had no idea if they were about to take the tide. I led Marie towards the church. The horse trader was about to lock up when I reached him. He took in the horse and her condition in an instant. He knew my intention.

"You wish to sell this animal?" I nodded. I would keep my speech to a minimum. "She has been hard-ridden."

"Aye, but she is a fine animal."

The ostler's plaiting had made a difference and as the horse trader walked around her, I saw him calculating how much he could get away with paying. It would look suspicious if I did not haggle and rejected his first two offers. I suggested a price above his last offer and I saw him debating. "And for that, you can have the saddle too."

He beamed for the saddle was an expensively made one, "Then we have a deal."

I took the coins and went to nuzzle Marie, "If I could, Marie, I would have taken you home. Calliope and Alexander would have enjoyed your company."

Slinging my bag over my back I headed back to the river. To my dismay, I saw the other two ships heading downriver at the high tide. I would have to spend a night, at least, in Nantes. If I was pursued then my pursuers could reach the port the next day. I needed to find a place to hide and new clothes.

As it was dark and the ships had gone, I went to the arches that were the entrances to the warehouses. It was dark and there I could think. I needed somewhere close to the river but that normally meant somewhere less salubrious than one with my clothes might use. I had changed clothes since leaving Blois but they were not the clothes of one who would stay close to the river. I had one good cloak and one that was badly stained by horse sweat and the weather. I donned the worn one. Similarly, I had a hat that had endured the sun and the weather and another in better condition. It was little enough to change my appearance but days without shaving had also given me an unkempt appearance. It would have to do.

As I neared the first inn, I heard a loud Scottish voice from within. I did not recognise it and I knew that it might be a coincidence but there was little point in taking chances. With my hood over my head, I hurried on and passed another two inns before I risked entering. Having heard the Scottish voice I was cautious and when I entered, I paused in the doorway. It was not too busy with one of the girls who served at tables, lounging by the bar. The owner saw me and sent the girl to me. She served not only tables but also the men and her face and body showed the ravages of her trade. She might have been pretty once but now her face was marked by puffiness and old pox marks. She had bloated and her thin hair was falling out. She smiled and I saw that she had lost some of her teeth. Rather than recoiling from her, I felt sorry for her fall.

She smiled, "Come, traveller. We have rooms and fine food. We can serve your every need." Her meaning was clear.

I smiled back and said, "Thank you."

"Ah, a foreigner, we have many like you for Nantes is now a much busier port than once it was."

I kept my clothes hidden beneath my cloak and I saw the innkeeper, as we approached him assessing my ability to pay. He had already determined a rate when I reached him. He beamed at me, "Welcome, sir. You wish a room?" I nodded. Sniffing he said, "Have you a horse?" He could smell Marie on me."

"No, I just need a room. I seek a ship."

He wrote a price on a blackboard and I nodded. It was a fair price but then I had not seen the room. I knew that in my position beggars could not be choosers, "Where do you wish to travel to?"

I had created a story on my ride from the Loir. "Anywhere. I fell out with a friend," I leaned in, "It was over a woman, you understand?"

He nodded sympathetically, "Aye, women can do that. We cannot live without them but they make life complicated do they not?" He turned to the girl, "Prepare room three for the man, Jeanne." Then he looked back at me and held his palm out for the coins.

I had a purse I kept visible and the one with my treasure in was hidden beneath my beeches. I counted out the payment in coppers. I saw the smile of satisfaction on the inn keeper's face. He had gauged my purse to the sou.

Taking it he said, "Nantes has ships arriving from many lands. You will have your choice. Why, we even have many men from Scotland travelling here." He shook his head, "They do not pay well." He looked at me curiously, "Are you a soldier?"

I was on my guard, "When I was younger but those days are long gone. Why do you ask?"

"Oh, not long ago we had some Scotsmen in asking for an English soldier. They said he was a friend of theirs but I think they lied."

I affected a smile but inside my heart was racing. Buchanan and his men had reached Nantes, my elaborate escape had not fooled them. "I am Flemish, from Mechelen although it is many years since I lived there." I remembered the comment from the ostler in Angers. Buchanan had been ahead of me. Like a spider, I had come to him.

He looked satisfied with my answer, "I knew you were not French but your French is too good for an Englishman. They butcher our language." Jeanne had arrived back and he said, "Jeanne will take you to your room. Will you wish for food? The cook is still in the kitchen but soon she will leave."

I was a practical man and I nodded for I needed food, "Aye, I am so hungry I could eat a horse with its skin on. I will deposit my bag and then return. Whatever is the special of the day will suffice."

I followed the woman down a labyrinth of a corridor. We passed rooms that were occupied and I heard the sounds of what passed for lovemaking in the whorehouses of Nantes. I knew that every inn on the waterfront would serve that purpose. Sailors who landed after weeks at sea were not choosy and even Jeanne would attract customers. The room was at the back of the inn and tiny. Jeanne looked at the bed and gave me what she thought was a come-hither look, "If you would like me to stay…"

I smiled and shook my head, "I have ordered food. Thank you for the kind offer."

Disappointed she left. I put the bag on the bed and examined the door. There was no lock. I would have to jam the bed against it when I retired for the night. I opened the shutter on the window. There was, of course, no glass and it was a small opening but, in summer it would allow a breeze through what was, in effect, a wind hole. I saw that there was a cobbled yard and I could smell horses. The opening was large enough for me to use. I had my escape route. I left my cloak and hat on the bed and headed back down the corridor.

There were even fewer people in the room when I returned. Jeanne brought my food over and a small pichet of rough red wine. She held out her hand for payment and I played the part of one who counted his coppers. I paid the precise amount. I did not think that even Jeanne would try to get more money from me. There would be no more advances that night. The fish stew was edible but the wine was almost vinegar. Luckily the bread that might have been fresh that morning but was now becoming stale, soaked up both the watery stew and the vinegary wine. My stomach was filled and, as a soldier, I knew the value of that. I had found safety but it was a precarious position. There were no ships and my pursuers were here in Nantes.

As I ate, I pondered my problem. If Buchanan had already visited the inn, he would not be likely to return but I needed to know the number of my enemies. I could not ask how many and so I decided that when I had eaten, I would return to my room. I formulated a plan by the time I had finished and I put it into operation as soon as I reached my room.

Chapter 15

Nantes 1510

I left half of the wine and waved to Jeanne and the innkeeper as I headed back to my room. Once inside I pushed the bed against the door and, taking my old cloak and hat climbed out into the yard. I pulled the shutter closed. The yard was dark and I waited in the shadows to ensure that there was no one waiting. The only sounds I could hear were those made by horses. If there was an ostler he was either asleep or, more likely in the inn. My foray was two-fold. I wanted to investigate an escape route in case I needed it while at the same time, I wanted to find any watchers. If Buchanan did not discover me on his first search, he would not just go away. He would watch for me. I needed to know numbers and I needed to identify the quality of my enemies.

The enclosed passage from the yard led back to the front of the inn. It was not high enough for a rider to ride and a horse would need to be led. At the end of the passage, I halted and peered down the narrow street that led to the river. This was not a part of the town with lighted brands. It was dark and full of shadows; not a place to be alone at night. I waited until I was sure that it was empty and then I headed back to the river. I used the doorways to scurry like a spider avoiding the light and reached the dark and empty waterway. To my delight, I spied the sails of a ship as she headed towards the moorings while the tide was still high. The arrival prompted movement and I saw light from the door of the harbourmaster's house as he and his officials emerged. Money would be changing hands soon. I waited in the shadows of a warehouse.

It was not a speedy event. The ship turned in the river so that it was facing downstream and was secured to the bollards on the empty quay. I had my hood up and my hand rested on my dagger. I would be ready if the Scots returned. I was disappointed when the accents told me that the ship was French. It had been too much to hope but I had prayed for an English ship. However, it was a ship and that gave me hope. It was clear that the ship would not be emptied that night when the harbourmaster, having taken his coins, headed back to his office and all but a deck watch headed towards the inns. I contemplated heading for the ship to find out when it would be leaving and its destination. When the three men strolled down to the ship from the direction of the town, I was glad I had not. They stopped just thirty paces from me and began to examine the ship.

I recognised Andrew Buchanan immediately. He was no spy and dressed for what he was, a Scottish lord. The two men with him were also not in disguise. They were clansmen of the lord. "You two make sure he is not close by and I will visit with the captain of this ship."

I now had the numbers but, as the two men began their search, I realised that, if they searched thoroughly, they must find me. Luckily, they parted to search the warehouses from each end. As soon as their white faces turned, I slipped out of the doorway and headed back to the passage. I would need a better vantage point with an escape route. I had been able to get a picture of the area and I crept back down the alley and then along the road with the inns. I headed up the next passage I found and when I came to the end saw that the two Scots searching the doorways had met and found nothing. Andrew Buchanan was walking from the ship towards them. Their heads came together and then they left. I was now the one following. I needed to know where they were staying.

I used the darkened doorways for cover as the three of them headed back into the town. I could hear the mumble of conversation but not the actual words. I did not want to get too close to them for obvious reasons. When they neared the market square I saw them head towards an inn, The White Cockerel. They entered. Were they asking questions there or was it their lodgings? When they had not emerged within a short time, I realised it was the latter and I headed back to the river. After first checking that no one had been left to watch for me I headed towards the gangplank. The fact that Buchanan had left so quickly made me more optimistic that the captain might be amenable to my request for a berth. Two men were on watch. The ship was laden and nighttime was a perfect time for thieves to undo the captain's good work.

"Yes, friend?"

"Where is this ship bound?"

One of them grinned and waved an expansive hand, "Why, Nantes of course."

His companion thought it hilarious and laughed. My question had made their watch a little more entertaining. I smiled and nodded, "Of course. When you have unloaded your cargo whither are you bound?"

"Calais and we leave tomorrow night on the high tide. Do you want a berth?"

"Perhaps."

"The captain is ashore. He will be here when we unload and then load our cargo." I nodded. "Your friends will be sorry they missed you."

"Friends?"

"Aye, the one who came before speaks French like a German and yours is better but he wondered if you had booked a berth already."

"No, I know no one in this part of the world. They must have been seeking another."

As I headed back to my inn, using a circuitous route and checking that I had not been followed I pondered my problem. By the time I had climbed back through the window I had worked out what to do. During the day I could move about the town freely for they would not risk a fight in a French town. The problem would be that if they returned and spoke to the captain and his crew, they would know I had enquired after a berth. All they had to do was to wait close to the ship until it was time to leave. I had to do something about them before they could get to me.

I rose before dawn and left the inn. Jeanne was wiping down tables, "You are leaving, sir?"

"No, in fact, I will see the owner and book an extra night."

I would not be staying but I was ensuring that if they discovered my lodgings they might be fooled into thinking I intended to stay longer. I headed back down the alleys until I reached the wharf. Already the hatches on the ship were being opened and I heard someone shouting out orders. I checked I was unobserved and slipped across to the gangplank which was unguarded. I stopped at the gunwale and a pot-bellied man, whom I took to be the captain said, "Why do you come aboard my ship uninvited? That is a quick way to a watery death, my friend."

"I am sorry. I seek the captain to pay for a passage to Calais."

"I am the captain and I have a berth but I am choosy about my passengers."

I closed with him and took a chance, "Captain, do you often sail to Calais?"

"Once or twice a month, why?"

"I have a friend there, Jean le Casserole, and I am anxious to see him."

My use of Jean's name worked and he grinned, "Jean often uses my ship. How do you know him?"

He was testing the veracity of my story and I told him the truth, "I once acted as a guard for him, many years ago before he married Marie."

The intimate knowledge satisfied him, "It was a shame about Marie. He married late. Aye, you can have a berth. Fetch your gear now."

I risked further confidence, "There are some men seeking me and I would avoid them."

He looked at one of his men and said, "The Scotsmen who came last night." I nodded. "Bring it now and then we will hide you aboard."

It was still dark when I reached the inn and Marie had finished the cleaning. "Would you like breakfast now, sir?"

I nodded, "Aye."

I had no intention of eating but I wanted no one to know I had left. When I reached my room, I grabbed my bag and cloak and climbed out of the window. The stable door was opened as I passed but the ostler's back was to me. Reaching the street I headed up the passage to the wharf. I sensed a movement behind me when I reached the middle. Instincts took over and I used my bag to block the short sword which was swung at my head. The blade bit into the bag and held. I brought my knee up as I swung my assailant to the side. The move took him by surprise and he cracked his head off the stone wall. He shouted as he fell, "Angus, I have him."

I knew, without looking, that Angus would be at the other end of the passage. I did not turn. If I had learned anything as a warrior it was that you fought one battle at a time. I pushed my bag at the man who was already reeling from the blow to the wall. I whipped out my dagger and brought it up under his ribs. Even as he slid down the wall, I whipped my head around and saw Angus, swinging his sword at me. I had no time to draw my sword and so I blocked his strike with my dagger and used his momentum to push him towards his fallen companion. The pot helmet I had bought and not used was hanging from the bag and I pulled it off and smashed it into Angus' skull. He was rendered unconscious. I had no idea if they lived or died but I could not afford to hang around and find out. I grabbed my bag and ran up the alley.

There at the end stood Andrew Buchanan. He had a sword and a dagger in his hand and was moving purposefully toward me. I kept moving but dropping my bag and cloak, drew my sword. So far as I knew he only had two men with him but there could be another and all my senses were twitching in case there was another attack from the rear.

"I knew you would head for Nantes, spy, you are not as clever as you think. You will spy no more for the Earl of Buchan now knows your identity. Every Scotsman will be watching for you but they will look in vain for you will die here in Nantes and your body will feed the fishes."

His words were empty and normally I would have ignored them but I wanted him angry. "Your two companions are more likely to feed the fishes and I have yet to meet a Scotsman I could not best. To be truthful it is rare to face a Scotsman as all I normally see is their back as they run away."

He came at me as though he was riding a war horse at a tournament. It was a mistake for the passage was narrow and I knew that neither of us would be able to swing a sword fully. I put my right leg forward and held my sword and dagger to block any strike that came at me. He realised his mistake when his sword scraped along the wall. If nothing else he had taken the edge off his blade. His dagger had an easier swing but my crossed weapons blocked the strike and I was able to punch with the hilts of both sword and dagger at his face. The hilt of my sword scratched and tore his face. It was first blood to me and the wound seemed to enrage him. He pulled back his sword and this time aimed it directly at my face. I had fought against spears and pikes. I knew how to move my head to the side and out of the way of a deadly blow. At the same time, I used my dagger to force his to one side and that allowed me to simply punch the pommel of my sword at his already damaged face. Whilst I had been able to move away from the tip of the sword, he could not avoid a second blow and he stepped back. I pushed harder with my left hand and the blade began to edge towards the Scotsman's face. He stepped back again. As I had discovered, when first training as a billman, once you begin to step backwards it is hard to stop. So it was with Andrew Buchanan and as I punched and pushed with the hilts of my weapon, he fell and when he did, I stabbed him in the right hand with my sword and when his face rose in a scream of agony, I punched him hard in the face with my sword's hilt and he fell unconscious. I know I should have killed him but his scream would have alerted others for dawn was but minutes away. Sheathing my weapons I ran back for my bag. Angus was on all fours and reaching for his weapon when I swung my foot and kicked him in the head. He too was rendered unconscious. I grabbed my bag and cloak and then leapt over the body of the Scottish knight. As I neared the ship, I saw the captain and the deck watch watching me.

The captain gave a rueful smile, "I see you met your friends. Are they dead?"

I shrugged, "I did not have time to check but as they attacked me, all three of them, then I think I am in the right."

"If they were French, you would not be but Scotsmen and English men are all foreigners. Get aboard quickly and hide in the forecastle. I will tell you the cost of your passage when we are at sea."

His meaning was clear. I would have to pay whatever price he asked or risk being robbed of everything. I nodded. Everything I had in my purse was pure profit. I would not miss what I had not yet even counted.

One of the crew guided me to the forecastle. It was a cabin and looked like, at a pinch, it could hold four people. I might be lucky and have a cabin bigger than the room in the inn. I stowed my bag as the sailor closed the door. There were louvres and it meant I had a little light. I took a cloth from my bag and my whetstone. An early lesson I had learned was to keep weapons clean and sharp. I first cleaned my weapons and checked them for damage and then put an edge on them. I heard the noise of men working as the cargo began to be emptied. Through the louvres, I saw men coming and going carrying one cargo off and another aboard. If Sir Andrew and his men chose to they might go to the town watch but they would find it hard to explain how one man had caused so much damage. I had to pray that no one in authority would investigate. I knew that if the earl knew of my deception, then he would tell others and word would get back to the council. Unlike Andrew Buchanan, if they made up their mind to end my life then it would be ended. I willed the men to empty and then load the ship as quickly as they could.

Time passed and the ship began to be loaded with barrels. I guessed it was wine. It took longer to load the unwieldy barrels than it had to unload the cargo. I had no idea how long had passed when the door opened and the captain handed me a jug of wine, some bread, cheese and ham. He shook his head, "You are lucky, my friend, one of the men you fought was barely alive and the other two have wounds but as none of the three has made a complaint you appear to be safe."

"Thank you."

"Of course, you know that they will know you are aboard my ship. My crew will say nothing but such matters are out of our hands. They will know that our destination is Calais. They could reach there before we do if they have confederates. If they are waiting for you then you will be on your own."

"I know and I am prepared for that. When we are at sea then one problem is over."

"And as with the sea, the trough into which you descend just means there is an even bigger crest ahead." The captain was a philosopher.

When we eventually set sail, it was pitch dark. I heard the cries of farewell from the shore as we were released and then felt the gentle motion of the river as we headed out to sea. The captain had not said for me to leave the cabin and I did not wish to push my luck any further than I had already. The motion of the ship told me when we were at sea and the door was opened, "Captain says that you can come on deck."

I headed out of the relative warmth and comfort of the cabin. When the salt air chilled me, I turned and retrieved my cloak. I felt much warmer with that wrapped around me. I noticed that the sailors were all barefooted and wore simple shifts. They were hard men. I went to the stern and the captain said, "And now it is time to pay the bill. Four crowns."

It was a high price but his tone told me it was not negotiable. When I handed it over, I saw that he realised he could have asked for more.

"How long will it take us to get to Calais?"

"Two days and nights. If the wind is kind, then quicker and if not then longer. It is wine which we carry and that will not spoil. You will eat when we eat and eat what we eat. We are a working ship."

I nodded, "Then I will go and sleep. I will not be in your way."

I returned to the cabin and slung the hammock. It took a couple of attempts but I eventually managed to climb aboard. The jaunty motion of the ship soon had me asleep. For two days I was safe and then I would have to risk whatever dangers Calais threatened.

To say that the sea was fresh would be an understatement and the French ship was tossed on white-capped waves. I found it more comfortable to stand by the forecastle where I could hang on to the gunwale and forestay and watch the horizon. Staying in my cabin merely made me feel queasy and seeing danger was always better than having it creep up on you. As we stood out to sea to pass the Channel Islands and their deadly rocks, I found myself staring beyond the waves. My mind was as agitated as the sea. Once more I would have to call upon Jean to get me aboard a ship and once more, I would be endangering him and his family. Sir Andrew had been stabbed in the hand. It would not prevent him from riding north and he would be angry. I would have to ask the captain to let me off the ship as soon as he could. Even then I might be spied on.

As night approached, I headed back to the helm. The captain shook his head, "I fear this will not be a swift passage. While the wind helps us the seas hinder us. You know the Scotsman will reach Calais before we do." I nodded. "We are in the hands of God now, Englishman, you more than we."

The next morning was, if anything, even stormier and with my cloak wrapped around me, I watched the seas. The time spent looking at the sea had helped me to predict our rise and fall. It was as we fell into the bottom of a trough that I saw something that should not be there. It was a body. I raised my hand and pointed, "Body in the water!"

The lookout precariously perched atop the crosstrees saw where I was pointing and shouted, "It is not a body. It is a man!"

The captain and crew acted instantly, "Reef the sails. Stand by to throw lifelines."

A sailor ran next to me with a coiled rope, "You have good eyes." I nodded. "The man may be dead but we are a brotherhood of the sea. That could be any of us. Even if he is dead, we will still take him from the sea. We thank you for your eyes."

The hand of the stricken man waved each time we rose and then disappeared as another crest appeared but each time, he was closer. I had a good view of him and I realised that he was not a man but a boy for he had no beard, "He is a youth."

As we slowed so the motion of the ship seemed to become livelier. The captain had to hold the ship so that it was not struck beam on by a wave for that would have been a disaster. The sailor said, "Hold on to my belt."

He bravely straddled the gunwale and I let go of the forestay to hold on to his thick leather belt. I was a human lifeline. He shouted to the boy, we could now see him clearly, and he was distressed. Every wave that crashed over his head threatened to take him beneath the waves. The boy did not seem to respond to the French sailor's words. The crewman hurled the rope and it fell short. The boy tried to grab it and sank below the waves. I feared he would not rise again.

"He may be English. Shout to him and tell him to kick his legs."

Thankfully the boy reappeared coughing and spluttering and I shouted, "Kick your legs and we will throw you a line."

I saw recognition at the words and putting his arm beneath the water he began to kick. The simple action enabled the boy to move closer so that when the rope was next thrown it landed on the boy and he grabbed it. The crew cheered and the sailor used his muscle-knotted arms to pull the boy back. I let go of the gunwale to get a firmer purchase on the sailor's belt. I leaned back and that seemed to help the sailor to pull. Two other crewmen hurried to the side and between them they hauled the boy aboard.

"Let fly the sails!" The captain was eager to move again.

A blanket was brought as well as some aquae vita. The sailor said, "Your cabin is closer and we have work to do. Thank you for your help." He pointed to the seagulls, "Those creatures are the souls of dead sailors. I am happy that this little one did not join them. He may be English but he is a seaman."

We manhandled him into my cabin and put him in the hammock. I made certain that his head was to the side and then sat on one of the chests to watch him. I wondered about his survival. To have fallen from a ship was one thing but to have survived a storm was another. Then I wondered if he was not simply a boy who had fallen overboard but perhaps the only survivor of a ship that had sunk. I felt the motion become easier as the storm abated a little.

It was some time before he began to wake and he shouted, clearly terrified, "Where am I? Am I dead?"

I saw the boy open his terrified eyes and I spoke softly. If he was the only survivor then he would need careful handling. "You have been pulled from the sea and you are safe. I am James, what is your name?"

"Adam." I saw the fear in his eyes fade. He shook his head, "My father will be angry that I fell from the boat."

"You fell?"

He nodded, "It was my first voyage and we were fishing. I did not heed his commands and I fell."

I was relieved I had dreaded him being the only survivor.

The captain sent food and watered wine for him and for me. My actions had made me part of the crew and they all smiled at me. We had finished the food when we heard the lookout call, "Sail ho!"

A short while later the sailor who had rescued the boy came in grinning. He spoke to me, "Ask him if he fell from a fishing boat."

I nodded, "He did."

"Then we have found it. We spied a ship circling and we are approaching him. Better bring him on deck. The captain will try to return him."

An idea began to form and I grabbed my bag. By the time we reached the deck the fishing boat was tied to the French ship. The boat was small. I counted a crew of just four.

"Father! I am sorry!"

I knew Adam's father by the relief on his face. "I care not." He changed to French, "I thank you, captain."

The captain had come to the side and said, "We are all brothers of the sea." He turned to his crew, "Tie a rope about his waist."

I cupped my hands, "Captain, have you room for a passenger?"

Adam shouted, "He helped to save me, father."

The English fisherman nodded.

The French captain smiled, "Lady Luck is on your side, Englishman. Go with God."

Chapter 16

Hedingham 1510

Abel, Adam's father, was too pleased to have his son returned from the dead to question my reason for wanting a passage. He was just grateful for my eyes and my involvement in the rescue. It took a day to sail back to the fishing port from whence they had ventured and it was dark by the time we reached it. With winter approaching the days were now shorter. Adam and his father insisted that I stayed with them for Abel knew that Adam's mother would want to thank me. I felt guilty for I knew I was imposing. There were just two rooms for sleeping in the tiny cottage and Adam's parents both wished me to have their bed. I refused.

"I have slept rough and sleeping before a dying fire is far more comfortable than many a night I have endured. I enjoyed the food and I am grateful for the roof. I will sleep here."

It felt good to use my real name once more as I realised that now that I had landed in England my days as a spy were over, at least until I was needed again. I had a relatively short journey to Greenwich and then I could head home and enjoy my family.

They landed their catch and as the weather was unpredictable, Abel did not go to sea the next day. Instead, he was able to take me to a horse trader. The presence of Abel ensured that I was not robbed and I purchased a hackney. I had barely touched Albert's treasure and I still had the Earl of Buchan's coins. Abel's mother kissed my hand as I mounted my new horse, White Star. Abel gave me a warrior's handshake and swore that if I ever needed his aid I would just need to ask. Adam, to whom I had spoken the most both on the French ship and the fishing boat, had listened to my stories of life as a billman. They had seemed safe enough to tell and kept his mind from dwelling on his ordeal. As I swung my leg over White Star's saddle he said. "I will become a billman, Master James, for I can still be a fisherman and protect my land from enemies."

I nodded, "And that is the duty of every true Englishman. We fight for our land and our king."

I was not sure I believed those words any longer but King Henry was our anointed king and as such God smiled on him. We were his subjects and had to obey him.

I reached Greenwich just before dark amidst a rainstorm that threatened to make the road into a quagmire. The king was not at home but the archbishop was and, I was surprised to see, the almoner, Thomas Wolsey. The priest was obviously more than he pretended for he attended my meeting with the archbishop and made notes on a wax tablet as I spoke. When I had finished, they looked at each other and spoke. It was almost as though I was not even there.

"The news about the secret council is worrying, Thomas."

"It is but it was to be expected. Now the king can send another spy to try to discover their identities."

If they asked me, then I would refuse but then it came to me; the two men thought I was not good enough for the job. That pleased me.

"The problem of the Scots remains." The archbishop looked at me. "What is your opinion, James? You have seen the court of King James and now met his ambassadors."

"They will jump at the chance to bring harm to England's borders. All of them believe that the land north of the Tyne is rightfully theirs. There might be a truce between the countries but it is an illusion."

"You are right. Sir Robert Kerr was killed when there was a truce. There is still much bad blood there on the borders and it is like a trail of gunpowder. It will not take much to ignite it. The Scots will have plenty of excuses for war. They will not endure such provocation for much longer."

"And the king?"

"He has made a peace with France and I think it suits them both. He is now gathering an army to go to Spain and fight the Moors for his father-in-law, the King of Aragon. Your work is now done." The archbishop took out a small purse of coins and added, warningly, "For the present. The king may call upon you again for despite your limitations you are an effective spy. Beware this Buchanan. He will remember your face."

I nodded for the thought had crossed my mind, "England, even close to the borders, is a big country and I will return to my life as a farmer."

Thomas Wolsey did not miss anything and he said, shrewdly, "You are a gentleman and a Captain of Billmen. The king and England can call upon you any time they choose. Remember that."

I stayed the night and then decided to visit Hedingham. I had not seen my friends since I had left to aid my ailing father, ten years earlier. It was time I spoke to them and would only delay my return home by one night. I headed for London and London Bridge before heading into Essex and the home of Sir Edward Cowley.

Once more the shorter days were almost my undoing for I reached Hedingham later than I had expected and the new steward did not recognise me. I was almost resigned to heading for Sam Sharp Tongue's home when Sir Edward himself appeared, "What is it, Ned? There is a draught coming through the door. Whoever it is, send them away."

As Ned tried to close the door, I put my foot in the way, "Is there no welcome for an ex-captain of billmen, Sir Edward?"

He recognised my voice and hurried down the hall. He had aged and the old man at arms looked like he would go to war no more. "As I live and breathe, James. Ned, have Captain James' horse stabled and have his bag taken to the guest room."

"I am sorry to impose on you like this Sir Edward but..."

"You do not impose and I am grateful for the company. Since Captain Stephen married, I live a lonely life."

He led me to a warm and cosy hall but one which was clearly that of a bachelor. When I had returned home, I saw the difference between the home where a woman made the decisions about furnishings and one with a bachelor in residence. There was one comfortable chair, close to the fire and I had to move the other to be near Sir Edward. A servant fetched us wine.

Sir Edward shook his head as I moved the chair, "I rarely have visitors, James, and I think I have forgotten how to live. I am like a grumpy bear who lives in a cave."

"You never married then, my lord?"

"I spent too much time in the service of the Earl of Oxford. Since he ceased bothering about the court I have been left in a void. I serve no purpose."

The man at arms who had helped secure the crown for King Henry was now a forgotten man and it was sad.

The wine was poured and the servant left. The steward appeared, "Would your guest like some food, my lord?"

I shook my head, "I bought some food when I passed through London. I am content with a goblet of wine."

"Then I shall leave you. I have put a hot stone in your bed, sir. The guest room has yet to be used this winter."

I read beneath the words of the steward. It confirmed Sir Edward's words. He had been an important man but he was not born into the nobility. His title was just that, a title and the other nobles looked down on his like. I knew it from my contact with the nobles of England. I was under no illusions; I was useful and so given attention. Once I was of no further use, I would be discarded. It was why I took the opportunity to gather as many coins as I could when I did serve the nobles and the king. I felt no guilt at all.

Left alone he drank deeply and opened up, "I had chances to marry when I was younger but now I am a sad old relic. But you, pray lighten my life, and tell me that you are wed and are a happy father."

I was more than happy to tell him my tale and now it seemed more pertinent. I did not hold back and told him of Jane and her family, as well as my parents. Then I spoke of my children and I saw him beam with delight."

When I had finished, he emptied the last of the jug of wine. He went to a bell pull and summoned his steward. It was moments only before a fresh jug was brought. The steward knew his master's tastes and it partly explained why the former man at arms looked so bloated, red-faced and unfit. This was not the Edward of Cowley who had trained me.

"I should like to see your family, James. You, Sam, and Stephen were all like the children I never had, you especially."

"Then you have an open invitation to come whenever you like, my lord. I have a number of houses and plenty of room for old friends."

He looked up, "You regard me as a friend?"

I thought I had committed some crime of etiquette, "I am sorry, my lord. I was impertinent. I meant room for old comrades in arms."

"That we were but I would like to think of you as a friend."

I was relieved, "Then friend it is."

He poured more wine. I had a sufficiency but whatever I did not drink he would and so I determined to keep up with him.

"And I am guessing, that as you have come from London you have been on the business of another. I will not ask what it was for I know you are an honourable man but was it for the new King Henry?" I nodded. "Tell me what he is like for I knew Henry Tudor well but his son… he was not expected to be given the crown and yet he has achieved it."

I had to be wary in my words. I trusted Sir Edward but I also knew that King Henry would tolerate no words that might be construed as treasonous. "He is young but he knows what he wants and the Queen Mother appointed him sound advisers."

"I envy you. Your life may be dangerous but you know you are alive. I rattle around from room to room. The highlight of my week is Sunday when, after church, Captain Stephen comes to drill the billmen. Then I come alive."

We spoke then of Sam, Stephen and battles past. I learned that both of my friends had families and Sam's son had taken up the bill. Stephen's were young. Sir Edward reminisced about our fights for the king. I realised that he exaggerated our action in each one. I wondered if that was why he was not invited to dine with the other lords and their ladies. Perhaps they tired of an old warrior rambling on with weary war stories.

His steward was a good man and he gauged the intake of wine to the goblet. There was but one goblet left when he entered, "I am sorry, my lord, I thought you had retired."

An irritated look flashed across Sir Edward's face. I stood and said, "Thank you, steward, for I have had a hard few days and I look forward to my bed."

The steward smiled his thanks with his eyes as well as his mouth but said nothing.

Sir Edward stood, "You are right and I am sorry. I have forgotten what it is like to do things that mean something. Of course, you are tired. Serving the king is always tiring."

I saw the steward's eyes widen. There would now be gossip.

"Ned, have word sent to Captain Stephen. Tell him that an old friend is here." Sir Edward looked at me, "You will stay, will you not?"

I was torn. I felt guilty that I even contemplated leaving him yet I was desperate to see my family. Christmas was approaching and I wanted to be there for the preparations as well as the celebration. I compromised, "I am anxious to see my family, my lord, but I can stay until the day after tomorrow."

Both steward and master looked relieved.

Not only Stephen arrived the next day but also Sam Sharp Tongue. Stephen had always been my shadow but when he and Sam rode up the next day I marvelled at the change in him. He was a far more confident man than I had left. He had been afraid to take over as captain of the company and yet now he rode and laughed like a man who was assured of his place in the world. Had I been a stranger I would have thought Sir Edward was the lesser of the two. Sam never changed. You always thought, when you spoke to him, that there was nothing beyond his ability.

Sir Edward and I had been walking around Hedingham partly for Sir Edward to show me the improvements he had made but mainly to spy Stephen when he came. The improvements were barely noticeable and had they not been pointed out I would not have noticed them. I had changed my humble home in Ecclestone far more than this knight. We heard the hooves and their laughter as they approached the walled gate. As soon as they saw us, they threw themselves from their saddles and, leaving their reins trailing, ran to greet me. I felt embarrassed for Sir Edward was ignored. He did not seem to mind and smiled as much as they did.

Stephen just embraced me and said, in my ear, "It is good to see my best friend after all these years."

As we pulled apart, I realised that he was right and I nodded, "Aye, time and distance make no difference to true friends. It is as though we have just parted and yet I know we have much to tell each other. Will this one day be enough?"

His face fell, "You stay but one day?" I nodded. "Then let us not waste one moment of it."

Sam came over to me. He had aged but, unlike Sir Edward, he still looked fit. He was just a little greyer and older. "So you return. All these years and not a word. We might have thought you dead." He wagged a finger at me, "You could have written."

"As could you, Sam Sharp Tongue but we are not men of letters, we are men of the bill."

The morning which had been cold but sunny now became colder as rain clouds rolled in from the east. We all looked at Sir Edward. This was his home and he was the host. He said, "Let us retire to a fire and James can retell his tale. I confess that I relish the second hearing of it." He put his arms around Stephen and me and shouted over his shoulder, "Ned, have the horses stabled and fetch another chair."

It was little things like that which marked the difference between Sir Edward and the three of us. At Ecclestone, I would not have needed to ask for another chair as there would have been sufficient already in place. Before we had left to walk the grounds, Sir Edward had asked a servant to bring a seat for Stephen. There was room for at least six seats in his hall. It was a measure of the loneliness of the man. He had no visitors.

Ned had banked up the fire and there were goblets already on the table. A servant hurriedly fetched a fourth. We watched as Sir Edward, the host, took his usual seat. The other two deferred to me and I sat. The wine was poured and Sir Edward raised his goblet, "To old friends who have made this day, early though it is, as Christmas Day!"

We chorused, "Old friends."

I was about to ask the other two about their lives when Sir Edward said, "Tell them what you told me, James, of your family, your home and your battles with the Scots and the Vikings."

Stephen, who came from the north, raised his eyebrows in surprise as he said, "Vikings?"

"The men of the isles, aye, they still raid but I do not think they were of the same quality as made the lives of your forebears so difficult, Stephen." I related my tale. Even as I told it I saw that we drank but one goblet to Sir Edward's three.

Stephen shook his head when I had finished, "You make our lives here seem dull."

"Yet you both have families and prosper I hear." As soon as the words were out of my mouth, I wished I had phrased them better for they highlighted Sir Edward's loneliness and I saw him empty a goblet and refill it. I had made the mistake of relaxing amongst friends.

That prompted them both to tell me about their lives. It was noon before they had finished and Ned came to tell us that food was ready. I saw his eyes flicker to Sir Edward and a frown creased his forehead.

The food was excellent and well cooked. I enjoyed the meal for good food is always enhanced by good conversation and the three of us ensured that it was lively. Sam had always been the wittiest man I knew and he did not disappoint. He had a fund of both stories and jokes that had all of us laughing. I made the mistake, after one such story, of speaking about the Queen Mother. I did not tell the story as a way of impressing them but of telling them of one of her servants who had been an old lady in waiting.

Sam was shrewd and nodded when I had finished, "So, hobnobbing with the royal family still I see. When Stephen here called at my home to tell me you were back, I wondered at that. Are you on your way to or from another adventure for the king?" He shook his head, "Sam, you are getting old and foolish. He has returned for he would have his mind set on the task and would not call here before he served King Henry." He smiled at his own cleverness. I saw realisation on Stephen's face.

I nodded, "You were always too clever for your own good. Aye, I have just returned from serving the king and now I travel home." I sipped my wine slowly.

Sir Edward smiled and said, "He is a good spy for King Henry as he will not even confide in men he knows he can trust."

I put the goblet down and, looking around to see that there were no servants in the room said, in a low voice, "Sir Edward, we have a young king who is distrustful of enemies and those he thinks of as his father's old guard. Sir Richard Empson and Edmund Dudley were held in special regard by the king's father and yet they both met their end at the block. What you do not know cannot hurt you."

The knight looked sad and said, "I would grasp any opportunity to serve the king again and to relieve myself of this ennui and melancholy."

Sam turned to Sir Edward, "My lord, you are well thought of by all your people. Enjoy that for many lords are hated."

"I thank you for that, Sam, but as James has observed I rattle around in this lonely house."

Stephen ventured, "There are many women who would relish the chance to be your wife, Sir Edward."

"That ship has sailed. I am a bluff old soldier. Who would have me? Besides I am set in my ways." He smiled, "This has been the best of days." His face suddenly brightened as though the sun had broken through the clouds, "Sam, Stephen, bring your families here this Christmas Day and we shall feast as though I was the king for with your families around me I shall be the richest man in the land."

The looks they exchanged told me that both men would prefer to celebrate Christmas in their own homes but I knew that their loyalty to Sir Edward meant they would agree.

The hesitation made Sir Edward think that they were going to refuse, "I will brighten my hall and make it both gay and happy. You and your families will not be disappointed. I shall have presents for you children and wives."

Sam shook his head, "You need not bribe us, Sir Edward, we would be honoured to come."

He clapped his hands together, "Your arrival, James, has been like the first growth of green in spring. You have brought hope to an old man and for that I thank you."

He drank too much in the afternoon and Ned had the servants carry him to his bed. When Ned returned, I said, "I know Sir Edward may not be able to thank you, Ned but we do. You care for our old leader and we are grateful."

"I served Sir Edward as a man at arms and when Wilfred, his squire, and the other men at arms left I stayed. Unlike Sir Edward, I married and like you three captains I am happy. I try to make his life as comfortable as I can." He smiled at Sam and

Stephen, "Your families will give him joy that will last far longer than the visit."

He left us and I walked outside with my two old friends. They had a wintery ride in the rain ahead of them. In the stables, as they saddled their horses we spoke. "It is sad to see him thus. I have invited him to my home in Ecclestone and I hope he comes. I live far from here."

"And we have lives to lead but having seen him today I can see I need to come more often." Stephen was the most thoughtful of the three of us."

Sam nodded, "Aye, you are right and we three should keep in touch. You know, James, that if you ever need us we are at your beck and call."

"And I pray that I do not need you. Do you not see what service to king and country does, Sam? There is no reward for titles and land mean nothing. I cannot think of anyone who served the old king more loyally and yet look at Sir Edward now?" I pointed to the old hay that had been discarded by the horse master, "That is our reward. We are used and then thrown to one side."

"You have become a cynic, James."

I smiled, "Stephen, I prefer the term realist. We cannot refuse to serve our king and the lords of our manors but we should always have one eye on our own future. You two are lucky, Sir Edward is a thoughtful lord of the manor."

"And yours is not?"

"My old one was but I have yet to measure the mettle of his grandson. We shall see."

The parting was more deeply felt than the one ten years earlier. Then they had thought that I might return. This time we knew that it was unlikely that we would meet again.

Chapter 17

Ecclestone 1511

I arrived home a week before Christmas and the joy of my family was unbounded. I was even happier to see them than normal as my visit to Sir Edward had shown me how good was my life with Jane and my children in comparison. William was delighted to have another horse. He had begun to breed from my animals and I was pleased as it was another source of income. I invested some of Albert's treasure in new buildings. I told Jane that Sir Edward had said he might visit. I had an extension added so that we could accommodate not only Sir Edward but, should they visit, my sisters Alice and Sarah and their families. I realised that I had been remiss not to do so before. My brothers-in-law were hard-working men but they were not as well off as I was. I owed it to my family to share my largesse. I had become a man of means and I was duty-bound to make their lives better too.

Christmas was joyous and we began the New Year with hope in our hearts. I was home and safe and as we heard, in March, that King Henry was sending soldiers to fight the Moors, we knew that I would not be going to war. I determined to make Ecclestone, the village rather than just my lands, as prosperous as possible. I encouraged farmers to use my oxen to plough. I did not charge them for I did not need the coin and the improved crops benefitted everyone. I made gifts, when the new lambs and calves were born, to farmers who needed their herds and flocks enriching. Already held in high esteem thanks to my titles of captain and gentleman, my status became almost that of a lord of the manor. I did not want the Earl of Derby to accord me that title as there would be too much danger attached. As lord of the manor, I could be summoned to war in foreign fields. I did not mind defending my land against the Scots but this war the king's men fought against the Moors seemed to me to be ill-advised. I could not see any benefit to England save to give our king a chance of glory.

The bill practice was still enjoyable and I made both Thomas and Robert lieutenants, not only for my company but also for the company of the hundred. The old earl had enlarged my command after the Viking raid so that I now commanded five hundred. I did not train them all but if we went to war then I would be the one to give their orders. I needed two men who could help me and Thomas and Robert had proved themselves to be the most reliable of men. The title of gentleman had given me the chance to have a coat of arms. I might not have availed myself of the opportunity but Jane told me that it would please her mother. I did so and, with the approval of the earl and the old king, I now had a pale blue shield with a red diagonal across it. Using seamstresses from the village my wife had tabards made for my billmen and the archers from the village. It cost barely a crown and made the men and their families inordinately proud. I bought two good helmets for Robert and Thomas and they gave their old ones to the young men who did not have a helmet at all. The one I had bought in France I also donated. William would wear it for now that we had horses he would look after my horse, his, and the ones I allowed Thomas and Robert to ride. My sons came to the practice each Sunday and while they were far too small yet to wield a billhook they enjoyed the presence of so many warriors and the banter. I also think that they quite enjoyed the honour I received from all.

As the crops grew and our new animals fattened, life in my part of Lancashire was good. Then two events happened. One was a messenger from the earl that said there had been trouble in the borders and we should prepare to be called to war and we had news that King Henry's forces had left Spain. They had not covered themselves in glory and were leaving after ignominious defeats. I wondered what the two events would mean to me.

Sir Edward and three men at arms arrived at my home in early August. He had not forewarned me but the new quarters were complete and so it was not a problem. However, the arrival of three men at arms was a worry. I had hoped that when he came, he might bring Stephen and Sam for I was anxious for them to meet Jane but the three men at arms, like the knight, had a sumpter laden with armour and weapons; they were prepared for war.

Sir Edward gushed when he met Jane and my family. He had arrived in the early afternoon and it was not until just before we were to dine that I had the chance to speak with him or rather, he was able to tell me the purpose of his visit.

He looked pleased with his news, "King Henry himself came to speak to me and asked me to help. I am no longer a forgotten man."

He was genuinely happy about the visit but the cynic in me was suspicious. I said nothing.

"He said that while you were serving him abroad you had a run in with some Scotsmen. One of them, a rash knight called Sir Andrew Buchanan has caused trouble on the borders."

The cynical side of me had been correct.

"You know that a couple of years ago the Englishman John 'Bastard' Heron of Ford broke the truce and killed King James Marcher Lord, Sir Robert Kerr?" I nodded. "It seems that a couple of months ago there was a raid on Ford. The raiders took livestock and men were killed. The Scots fled over the border to a stronghold called 'The Merse'. King Henry has asked me to cross the border and arrest him. Sir Andrew Buchanan is to be brought back to England to stand trial."

My heart sank for this seemed to me a venture doomed to failure.

"The king said that we were familiar with the area and you with the man. He thought you would be able to identify him."

The king was a cunning man. He was using Sir Edward, who was patently the wrong man for the job, to get me to do his work. "You know, Sir Edward, that this could lead to war with Scotland?"

"The king does not want the Scots to think that they can get away with this sort of thing."

"But Sir John Heron was the one who began this."

"And we are to ask for his help in the matter."

"You bring just three men with you. That is not enough."

"We go to arrest the knight and that should be enough."

I shook my head. "If there is a stronghold then he will have a number of men to help him. We need more men."

"And I have gold to pay for them." His eyes pleaded with me, "I would have you come with me but if you cannot then I will understand. A man would be a fool to give up on all of this." His words said one thing but his eyes and expression said something quite different.

"Aye, you are right, but a man does not turn his back on an old friend however misguided he is."

He frowned, "Misguided?"

"My lord, you seek an adventure and the king has duped you into taking this on. He knows of our connection and this is a way for him to use me again. Say nothing when we eat. I will tell Jane in my own time and manner. I promise that before we leave I will have given thought to how best to deliver what the king needs."

I took them to the new guest rooms. That they were not fully finished in terms of furnishings would irritate Jane but Sir Edward was impressed. As I headed to the kitchen to speak to Jane, I began to plan what to take. The horse was obvious. White Star was new and would not be known by my enemies. Alexander had been given to me by King James and had been a kingly gift. He would be known and Calliope was just too old. I would need my plate for I knew that there would be fighting. My bill I could leave at home but the rest of my weapons, I would take.

Jane was clever and perceptive. As I approached, she took my hand, "You go away again." It was a bald statement and I nodded. "Where to this time?"

I sighed and almost hissed out the word, "Scotland."

Her fingers squeezed my hand. "It is the king's command?"

I took her hand and led her out to the hogbog. The clucking fowl and grunting pigs would mask our words. "Our new king is a clever man. He preys on Sir Edward's weaknesses to use me to do his work."

"His work?"

I nodded, "I think he means to stir King James into a war." I told her of the murder of Sir Robert Kerr. "Had not the old king been alive then that might have prompted a war but old King Henry knew better than to prod the beast from the north. The new king has joined the alliance with the Pope." I saw the question on her face. "It means the treaty that was signed last year with France is null and void. We are now at war with France. I know from my time in France that the French and...

others, will leap at the chance to reform the auld alliance. Sir Edward is the fuze he lights to ignite a war."

She stood on her toes to kiss me, "I knew I married a hero but I did not know the magnitude of his stature. You do what you must and we will keep your home safe."

The boys were eager to dine with the knight and the men at arms. The three men at arms were all young and, I suspected, had only been hired by Sir Edward in light of the assignment. They looked handy enough but none of them had fought in a battle or a skirmish. The borders were a tough school in which to learn your trade and when it came to fighting these three would be schoolboys. Sir Edward, for his part, warmed when he spoke to my children. He had brought them all gifts but his bachelor status had shown that he had enjoyed little contact with children. Only James' appeared to be appropriate but he meant well and my children showed that they had been brought up well when they thanked the knight.

I was quiet during the meal. I had visited with Thomas and Robert to tell them that I would be away. I did not tell them the details. That was not a matter of trust but I knew they would fret more if they knew everything. Even so, when I said that I was riding with Sir Edward to Ford Castle they became agitated.

"My lord, take us with you. That is a dangerous country and you need good warriors to watch your back."

"I have friends in the area and I will be safe. I need you two to ensure that my home is safe. I trust you two to do that and my family are more important than I am."

They were now fathers and they had understood it.

As the last of the pudding my wife had made was eaten, I plotted our route north. We would ride the way I had first gone to war, through Craven and Clitheroe and thence through Ripon. We would avoid York for I knew that the Scots had to have spies there. Instead of crossing the Tees at Stockton, I would use the bridge at Piercebridge. We would still be seen but the ferry at Stockton would be an easier place to spot us. I had served in the borders, as had Sir Edward when we had hunted Perkin Warbeck. In comparison to what we now undertook that had been an easy task. We would ride the high country between Barnard Castle and Durham. It would enable us to approach Ford

Castle from the southwest. I had already spoken to Sir Edward and asked him and his men at arms to discard their livery and adopt plain cloaks. It would not do to make it easy for our enemies to identify us.

The village knew that something was amiss as the five of us led the two sumpters on the road to Clitheroe. Men came from their farms to ask what was happening. I hated to lie to them but gossip and speculation could be our undoing. I had concocted a story.

"Sir Edward has been asked to visit with the Sherriff and as I am familiar with the road it was thought easier for me to take the visitors."

"There is no war then, Captain James?"

"There is no war, Henry, and we have a prosperous year ahead of us." My villagers looked to me as a weathervane to warn of bad weather.

We largely rode in silence that first day. It would be one of our easier days as the plain was generally flat and we made good time. It was as we climbed towards Clitheroe that our horses struggled. There was a monastery just outside the town and we were given rooms for the night. Sir Edward was a rich man and he made a healthy donation to the monks so that we were well looked after.

As we prepared for bed I asked, "Who was it set you on this road?"

"I said before, the king."

"And who advised him?"

"His new bishop, Thomas Wolsey."

I nodded. He was the new power behind the throne. He had been elevated from almoner to bishop and that was a mighty leap in a short time. He would be a man to watch. The archbishop had been a stop-gap and showed how ruthless King Henry could be. He used men and discarded them. "King Henry is gathering a new guard around him. The old earls were his father's men as was the archbishop. When we return you should watch Bishop Wolsey."

Once we left the Clitheroe and headed towards the main road Sir Edward commented, "You are well thought of James, in your village." He smiled, "Not that I expected anything less but the warmth of your people impresses me."

"They are not my people, my lord. I am not the lord of the manor."

"Do not delude yourself. They see you as the lord of the manor. You have earned the title and have not been granted it. Such a title is more precious than gold for it comes from the hearts of folk."

I did not like attention on me and so, as we headed towards the pass that led from Clitheroe to Blubberhouses I told him of my plan. The men at arms were several lengths behind us and were in animated conversation about the prospect of action. They would learn the reality soon enough. "We will not go directly to Ford. Do you remember when we hunted Warbeck along the Tweed?" He nodded. "There was a man at arms who aided us, Gerald of Etal. We will go there first. If anyone can give us reliable intelligence then it is he."

"What about Sir John?"

"If he knew anything then he would have already acted. We will go to speak to him but that is courtesy." I was not convinced that we would have any help from the man known as The Bastard.

The road to Clitheroe had been a revelation to the three southern men at arms but the road across the hills came as a shock. The sheer drops from the narrow road built a thousand or more years earlier by the Romans were terrifying for them and by the time we reached Ripon all of them were desperate to enter the cathedral and thank God that they had not fallen to their deaths. As Sir Edward and I arranged for rooms and stabling I said, "These young men seem keen enough, Sir Edward, but are they the men to take against border reivers?"

He shook his head, "I know that I was remiss to have allowed the situation to arise. When Wilfred left and Ned became too old, I hid inside a jug of claret. I should have done as you did and kept up my skills."

The change in our relationship was shown when I said, "You may have signed their death warrant by bringing them north."

He looked shocked, "But they wish a chance to gain some glory."

I laughed, "Sir Edward, where is the glory in seeking rats in a rat hole? I have fought against Buchanan and his men. I should have slain them when I had the chance and I am now being punished for my charity. Your men at arms need lessons in survival and for the next days, as we near our prey I shall give them the benefit of my experience."

He looked shamefaced, "I am a knight."

I nodded, "And the last time you drew your sword in anger was when we chased Warbeck across the southwest. That was more than ten years since. I fear for you too, my lord."

He stiffened, "Then do not. I know what I do and I know that I am not the man I was but, with God's help I shall be the man I wish to be."

I looked at the three young men at arms who had the weapons, the plate and the horses but that was all. If they had been any good they would have accompanied the king to Spain. Given time and good training they looked to me to have the potential to be good warriors but the borders were not the place to learn how to fight. If you fought there then you needed skills already. The trouble was that good intentions were not enough. Sir Edward was not the man for this task and he could not suddenly recover all his old skills. The jugs of claret had sapped his strength. From that moment on I made a point of speaking to the three men at arms as we rode. I gave them as much knowledge as I could about our opponents. Ralf, Henry, and John all seemed keen and they did do me the courtesy of listening. I told them if our target resisted, and I was sure he would, then they had to forget about honourable fighting. "His men will use any means they can to kill you. Make sure that you have more than one dagger to hand. Our enemies will use anything to hurt you. If they wear a helmet then beware the head butt. Your strikes and blows must be intended to kill. If we are able we will give King Henry a prisoner to try but I do not wish to travel home with one of your bodies draped over a saddle or leave you buried in some forgotten dell in the borders."

When we stopped and were in public places, I kept silent. I knew the dangers of speaking in places where you did not know the company. Ripon was the last large place we passed through.

Once we crossed the Tees, I intended for us to disappear into the back roads of Durham.

"Before we leave this town, on the morrow, it will be your last opportunity to buy what you need. We may have to sleep rough. I have a blanket, do you? My cloak can serve as a tent and will keep me dry. I have weapons enough, do you?"

Sir Edward's reaction told me that he had forgotten much that we had learned. While I held the horses and sumpters the four of them made themselves very popular with the merchants of Ripon by buying better cloaks, blankets and daggers. The prices they paid were high. That it would be remembered could not be helped. We had more than one hundred and thirty miles to travel and the route I had chosen was a lonely one. We would avoid Durham, Newcastle and other large places. There would be few inns and few monasteries for us to use. If we were lucky, we might find a farmer with a barn to afford us shelter.

The weather both helped and hindered us as we crossed the Tees. Rain swept in from the west. It made our journey less pleasant but folks kept within their homes as we passed through the small villages and our first day helped us to disappear. To avoid Raby Castle we headed west, into the rain to the village of Eggleston. It was a small road but it led us closer to the Wear Valley. A lonely road and a bleak landscape ensured reflective silence amongst us. The farmer whose farm we came across just beyond the village was grateful for Sir Edward's coins and we had not only a barn for shelter but also hot food cooked by his wife. This was the borderland and he neither offered nor requested information. It was safer for all. I was pleased for we had more comfort than I had expected.

We had one night in the open but the rain had stopped by then. I had to give the three young men at arms lessons in building a hovel. To a billman it came naturally and using the billhook I carried in my saddle I hacked down branches and quickly made a shelter against the wind. Theirs took longer and would have taken even longer if I had not loaned them my billhook.

Ralf stated, "Sir Edward said that you were a billman, James, but I would not have expected you to carry a billhook in your saddle bag."

I held the spare billhook in my hand, "This is the best of weapons for it is also a good tool. I carry it for I can quickly make a shaft and fit this head so that if I need to I have a pole weapon."

"But you should not need it on this quest."

I smiled at the young man at arms, "If I have learned anything it is that you never know what you may need or when. I cannot prepare for every contingency but I do my best. It is how I have survived so long."

Sir Edward nodded, "You three would do well to mark James' words. He has done more in his short life than any man I know. I may be a knight but I will heed all that he says and when we find our prey, I will follow his orders. It has been a long time since I gave commands and I will not allow pride to get in the way of common sense." His words pleased me for I wanted no glory hunting from Sir Edward. I wanted him and his men safe so that we could return home.

My plan meant that we had to circumvent Ford to reach Etal. I wanted to speak to Gerald of Etal before Sir John Heron. We would have to ford the River Till and, in hindsight, that was no bad thing as the three men at arms had never had to wade their horses through relatively deep water whilst holding on to the reins of their sumpters. I was able to teach them how to do this and it was another skill they acquired. It was one thing to ford a river but quite another to do so while being attacked. If we had to ford another river then they would know how to do that.

The castle of Etal had a constable, John Collingwood. The gates were barred when we arrived for it was getting on to dark and in this land that was the time when enemies could come with blades and evil intent. Sir Edward's name granted us entry. John Collingwood was not a warrior. Sir George Manners, Baron de Ros, lived in the south close to King Henry and the constable was more of a steward than a defender of the castle. Gerald of Etal was still in the castle, and it was he who commanded the tiny garrison. He greeted us with a beaming smile when we were admitted.

"This is the constable of Etal, John Collingwood."

"You are all welcome. I will have your horses stabled and rooms will be prepared. I fear you will not be feted as Sir George might wish but we shall do our best."

Sir Edward was gracious, "We expect nothing for you should know we are here on the king's business. Sir George would wish you to offer us whatever aid you could."

The constable looked at Gerald. This was not a business with which the constable was familiar. "I will leave you then, with the captain of the garrison, Gerald of Etal."

We were left alone in the Great Hall. It was a misnomer for it could only hold ten or so people at a feast and I knew why the baron lived further south.

Gerald looked at me when he spoke, "Your arrival fills me with disquiet, James. You are ever the harbinger of danger. The king sent you?"

Sir Edward nodded, "Aye, this goes back to the time Sir Robert Kerr was killed by Sir John Heron."

Realisation dawned and Gerald nodded, "And now some Scottish lord has exacted vengeance on the Heron family."

"Just so."

"But that is common around here. True, the Scots waited a long time for vengeance but that is their way. Why should the king bother himself?"

"The king wishes the perpetrator of these crimes arrested and we are sent to arrest him."

Gerald laughed, "Five of you? Sir Edward, you and James are good men, that I know but you do not even know whence came this man or where he has fled. He may have disappeared into Scotland."

I spoke, "It is Sir Andrew Buchanan and we know where he is. He has a stronghold called 'The Merse'."

"I know it. It is, as the crow flies, twelve miles from here but I did not know the name of the man. How come you by this information?"

I looked at Sir Edward who smiled at the three men at arms, "You three are not needed here. See to the horses and then find our chambers. When that is done look around the castle for it may provide a temporary home for us."

Left alone Gerald smiled, "You have been up to your usual tricks, James."

I nodded and told him how I had come across Andrew Buchanan. I did not mention my service to the King of Scotland but just of my mission to King Louis' court."

"And how did you discover the identity of the man who murdered and raided? Are you sure this is the same man?"

Sir Edward smiled, "King Henry has a good man, Bishop Wolsey and he learned the identity. It makes sense for he does not know James' real name. How best to have vengeance on the man who wounded and slighted him than by raiding England?"

"You think he expects you to come for him, James?"

I shrugged, "I know not but he pursued me far further than any might have expected. I should have killed him but did not."

"That just makes you human, James. And what do you wish of me?"

"Whatever aid you can give us. We will ride tomorrow to Sir John at Ford but neither Sir Edward nor I are confident that he will offer us much aid."

Gerald nodded, "Aye, you are right. He lost no family in the raid and he has appointed another farmer to take over the land that was ravaged." He drank some of the beer that had been brought for us. They brewed good beer on the Tweed. "Even if I took every man from the garrison," he gave us a rueful smile, "All five of them, then we could do nothing about taking the tower in which this man hides. It is strongly made. No, your best plan would be to let him know who you are."

Gerald was a clever man. To survive in this land you had to be. I had not thought of that and even as he said it, I began to think about how to do this. Sir Edward was slower on the uptake. "I do not understand. How does that begin to help us?"

Gerald leaned forward, "There has to be a spy in Sir John's castle. How else would this Buchanan have known the best place to raid? When you go tomorrow to Ford, tell Sir John how you know who this man is. Sir John will offer aid but not men. He will give you information. You tell him that you will ride the next day to Norham to seek the help of the constable there."

I nodded, "That makes sense for the Bishop of Durham's constable in the strongest border castle would have to be informed of our quest."

Sir Edward was still confused, "And how does that help us?"

"There will be an ambush. You remember the roads around here, my lord, do you not? Twesilhaugh Castle is still slighted as is Castle Heaton. The ford across the Tweed, where we so nearly caught Warbeck is the place that your enemy will use to cross into England. When you leave Ford Castle then your enemies will be told that you travel on the west side of the Till. They will ambush you at the Ford over the Till. It is a perfect place for an ambush."

I saw that Gerald, a real borderer, had thought this through well. "I remember it well and you, Gerald, will ambush the ambushers."

"I am the only man at arms in the garrison but the others are all skilled archers. No matter how many men this Buchanan brings my archers will reduce their numbers." He paused and looked at Sir Edward, "You, James, and your men at arms must be bait. I can work out roughly the place they will attack but it will not be precise. You will have to hold them off until I can reach you."

I knew it was a good plan but Sir Edward had to be convinced. However seeing that I was convinced he nodded, firmly, "Aye, we shall do so. I trust in you, Gerald, and in God."

The basic plan made, we refined it. We decided to ride to Ford armed and armoured. That meant we would not need the sumpters and would make life easier. We would not tell the three men at arms of the plan until we left Ford. It seemed harsh but I pointed out that they were young and might not be able to dissemble in the same way as Sir Edward and me.

The constable sent a messenger to say that food was ready and the hall needed to be prepared. While Sir Edward went to fetch his men at arms I spoke with Gerald as we walked the walls.

"You know, of course, that you will not be able to take him alive. That is an idle dream concocted in London far from the realities of the Tweed Valley."

"I know that but we will try."

We walked in silence for a moment or two.

"You also know that Sir Edward is not the man he was."

I nodded, "I know that better than any and if I had any powers of persuasion, I would have urged him to stay at Hedingham but the carrot is out of the ground and he is determined for one last glorious fling."

"I just had to be sure. We fought together and are duty-bound to be honest with each other. That is the way of brothers in arms."

"I know. And you, are you happy here at Etal?"

"Life is good and despite the Scots, relatively easy." He smiled, "I am married now, James and have three boys."

"As am I and have children too, and lands. I am a gentleman farmer."

He laughed, "Who spies for King Henry. I am happy with my dull life."

I became serious, "You know, Gerald, I believe that King Henry is trying to provoke a war with King James. If he does so then Norham, Ford and Etal will be his targets."

"And I am a realist as is John Collingwood. We are a token garrison and with these new bombards and cannons that are used, neither Etal nor Ford could withstand a bombardment. We would surrender."

"And Norham?"

"It is a strong castle but it is old. I know not what would happen. If King James is determined and brings the full force of his army then it would need a battle to hold him. The castles have been allowed to deteriorate too much. Do not worry about us. We would surrender and hope that King James is not a vindictive man. Besides, that is in the future, the next two days will determine if we are to live or die, eh, James? Let us hope and pray it is the former but if it is the latter at least we have both left sons. Our blood will continue."

It was at that moment that I fully understood Sir Edward's melancholy. When he died that would be the end of his line. Sam, Stephen, and I would mourn him but that would be all. If Gerald or I fell then our sons would take up weapons and we would be honoured by their actions. I knew that my dead father, in heaven, of that I had no doubt, would be proud of both me and what I was doing with my life.

Chapter 18

We arrived at Ford Castle at noon, having forded the river to approach the castle from the south. If anyone was watching they would assume we had come from that direction. I wanted our connection with Etal hidden. Gerald and his archers might be our only salvation. Ford Castle was a little larger than Etal but not by much although it had a garrison of ten.

Sir John and the captain of his garrison, along with his reeve as well as his butler, were gathered in the hall conducting the day's business when we were admitted. We had left Etal early and that meant we had arrived at Ford just as the business of the day was beginning. None asked us why we were there so early and we did not volunteer the information. Sir John was now an old man and when we were presented to him, he was sympathetic to our request but no more. He spread his arms to the west, "I lost men and land in the raid, true, but if I were to take my men to hunt the perpetrator, even if I knew who he was, I would lose more men. We mourned the dead and we made our homes stronger but that is the extent of my actions. If you wish to hunt the man, I wish you Godspeed although how you expect to find him, I know not."

Sir Edward knew his part and I allowed him to speak as I studied the men in the hall seeking the spy. Any of the four men, including the priest, could have been potential spies and I watched their faces as Sir Edward explained our course of action.

"We know who the man is, Sir John. He is a Scottish lord, Sir Andrew Buchanan. One of my men here met him while on service for the king at Blois." I saw Sir John scan our four faces as did the other men. I kept my eyes on the other men, as Sir Edward continued, "Sir John, we would if you would allow us, stay here the night." The knight nodded. "And tomorrow we will take the road to Norham to seek help from the Bishop of Durham's constable. Four is clearly too small a number to cross the border and ride to the Merse to apprehend this man."

Sir John laughed, "Good luck with that for Norham is not as well defended as it once was but, of course, you are my guests for the night. I would enjoy hearing of how you helped to capture Perkin Warbeck."

Sir Edward's part in the capture was well known. I had not even been introduced to the knight. The three men at arms were seen as my superiors and I was ignored. All of them dismissed me for I was the meanest dressed. I guessed that they thought I was some sort of servant. That suited me for it allowed me to see the spy. It was his reeve, a fellow with cunning eyes. I knew it was he for he asked to be excused as soon as Sir John finished speaking. Sir John's mention of the Merse and Sir Andrew had been enough to frighten the reeve. He was not a very good spy. Had that been me I would have waited longer to make my excuses.

"If I may, my lord, I need to speak to Harold the Pigman. He asked me for permission to build a second hogbog. As it impinges on the land of Walter the Miller, I will need to speak to them both."

Sir John waved an airy hand, "Go for such matters are beneath me. Fetch wine and food while we speak." He smiled at Sir Edward, "Your man there can take your gear to your chamber while we speak."

I was '*your man*'. Sir Edward kept a straight face as he wafted me away. I saw the puzzlement on the faces of the three men at arms and hoped that they had the wit to remain silent. I left the hall and went to the stables where our horses and bags had been taken. As I neared the stables, I saw the reeve mount an old horse and gallop off.

The ostler shook his head as I entered, "It was a good job I had a horse saddled already or Thomas the Reeve would have had to wait and he must have a woman in the village, he rode away so fast." He smiled at me, "And what can I do for you, sir?"

I played the part given to me by Sir John, "I have been asked to fetch our gear as we are staying the night."

He had placed our bags in the corner and he helped me to manhandle them on my shoulders and back. He shook his head, "You are like me, sir, bound to fetch and carry for our betters."

I laughed, "Such is our lot, eh?"

"Aye, but one day we may rise above this, God willing and the Scots do not raid again."

I manhandled the bags and heaved them on my shoulders, heading back into the hall.

We had been given a chamber close to Sir John's. That was not a surprise for the castle was not a large one. There were just two beds and that meant I would have to sleep on the floor. I did not object. I was here for a purpose and comfort was not a requirement. I had marked the direction the reeve had taken and, after opening the shutters, I peered out of the arrow slit to look at the road that headed west, to Scotland. The reeve had already proved himself to be a liar as there were no houses in that direction. 'The Merse' had to be twelve miles or more away and if the reeve rode all the way there and back, he would not return until well after dark. I kept watch all day. It was Sir Edward who was the centre of attention and the mean servant was ignored. I spied him an hour before dusk as he rode back into the castle. His horse was not lathered and that meant he had not ridden far. The message he had delivered must have been given to another for he could not have reached The Merse and returned. I knew that the reeve would have been detailed in his information for he had studied us. The five of us would be described. A second-hand description would not be accurate but I knew that Buchanan would recognise my build. My broader shoulders and rougher hands marked me as Sir Edward's man but to Buchanan, they would confirm that I was the spy he had pursued.

The other four returned to the chamber to wash for the meal. Sir Edward said, "I am sorry, James, but Sir John seems to think you are more of a servant and you dine with the castle servants in the kitchen."

I shrugged, "That does not worry me." The idea appealed for I would learn more about the reeve from the servants than from Sir John.

Ralf said, "But should we not tell him that you are the captain of billmen and that the Sherriff of Lancashire thinks well of you?"

I shook my head, "Ralf, I am content. I pray you not to mention anything about me and certainly nothing about having visited Etal Castle."

He nodded. He was a perceptive young man, "I am learning much, James of Ecclestone, and my fellows and I will keep our counsel. It is sad that you do not trust us but perhaps that is explained by our youth."

Sir Edward said, "We do trust you but you are right, we dare not give you more information. James is the expert and even this dull old knight has the wit to do as he says. Tomorrow, when we leave this castle then we will tell you all."

I added, "And you will be given the chance to leave us if you wish for I have to say that tomorrow will see all of us in harm's way."

John said, indignantly, "I have not slept in fields and barns to spurn the chance of honour and glory. Know that you can trust we three to remain silent and to fight for England and King Henry."

I think that they took my words as an insult but they were not meant as such.

The reeve ate in the Great Hall and that suited me for I picked up much information eating with the servants. I said little and listened more. It was clear that the reeve was unpopular. Indeed, he was the most unpopular man in the castle. The ostler took great delight in telling the tale of the reeve going for the assignation earlier that day. "I hear he said he was going to visit Harold the Pigman. If he did then he went in totally the wrong direction."

The cook, a woman who had enough layers of fat around her chin to tell me that she was not only a good cook but enjoyed her food nodded, "Aye, and he has far too much money for my liking."

The captain of the guard shook his head, "All reeves steal. It is common knowledge."

"As does Thomas the Reeve but that still does not account for the fine clothes he buys for his wife." The cook was a woman and recognised such things. "I know not where he finds another woman." She shook her head, "Still she must be desperate to open her legs for such a mean little runt. For from what his wife says he is poor John in that area." The table all laughed. Poor John was a shrivelled-up dried piece of fish and she was referring to his manhood.

The conversation drifted, without any help from me to the recent raids. The ostler said to the captain, "And I still do not understand why Sir John did not retaliate against the Scottish raid."

The captain shook his head, "A waste of time. We do not have enough men. It would take the garrisons of Etal, Ford and Norham to find the raiders and then we would need Berwick's garrison to reduce it. Sir John is being practical. He is letting sleeping dogs lie. The Merse is too great a morsel for us to take. When King Henry decides to bring an army north then we may have safer borders." I did not like to say that King Henry had greater matters on his mind than the security of his northern borders.

They were all kind people and made me feel welcome. I enjoyed their company more than I would have done had I been in the Great Hall. I had a greater affinity with servants than with nobles. I was in the bedchamber before the other four for Sir John had enjoyed Sir Edward's tales and more wine had been broached. I made a bed of our spare blankets and lay close to the door. I did not suspect treachery for the gates of Ford were firmly closed and Sir Andrew Buchanan would not have had time to reach us. As I lay down to sleep, I knew that he would be planning his revenge. The more I thought about it the more I knew that Gerald was right. Had the reeve not ridden out as quickly as he had then I might have had doubts. Now I had none. I was asleep when they returned but the opening of the door woke me. I feigned sleep.

We did not rise early and Sir John gave us a good breakfast. He came to the outer bailey to see us off, "If the constable in Norham wishes men to help you then I can supply four only. I cannot leave my land undefended."

Sir Edward smiled, "And I hope we shall not need your help. Thank you for your hospitality." He pointed to the north, "We keep on this side of the Till until we reach the Tweed?"

"Aye, and then head for Etal. If you seek men there then you will be disappointed. They have but one man at arms."

Out of the corner of my eye, I saw the reeve disappear. I did not doubt that he had a horse already saddled and would ride to Sir Andrew to confirm our route. We were putting our heads in the noose and no mistake. We were relying on my brother-in-arms and his archers.

We left the castle and headed through the woods to the ford over the River Till. It gave us the opportunity, once we had crossed the ford, to dismount and tighten our girths. It allowed me to give instructions to the three men at arms.

"We are to be bait. A Scottish spy has sent word of our journey to the north and Sir Edward and I expect to be ambushed close to the Tweed and the remains of Twesilhaugh Castle." I paused, "As I said last night you can, with no dishonour, leave us now for I cannot guarantee that we will survive such an ambush."

John shook his head, "We have spoken of this and we are determined to remain faithful to Sir Edward."

Ralf smiled, "Besides, you have a plan, do you not?"

I nodded and told them. I took my helmet and donned it. I took off my cloak and tied it behind the saddle. "Put on your helmets and your cloaks where I have placed mine. Beneath our tabards we all wear plate and that is better protection. A cloak can trap an arm. Be ready to draw your weapons in an instant and listen for my commands. When the ambush begins do not ride in a straight direction but jink your horse from side to side."

They obeyed me and we mounted. I led with Sir Edward behind me. We had spoken of this. Sir Edward wished to lead but he knew that his reactions would be slower than mine. I was attuned to danger and had drunk sparingly the night before. I rode towards the slighted castle of Twesilhaugh. From the moment we saw its ruins then I knew we might be attacked for it afforded shelter to any who wished to ambush us. Memories of the last time we had been here flooded back. Then Twesilhaugh had been under attack and we had faced Scots intent on its destruction. I was wary as we recrossed the Till to head towards the trees and the abandoned houses of Twesilhaugh. One day people might return but that would be years away.

The trail we used towards the Tweed had not been used for some time and the undergrowth had encroached upon it. I remembered the frantic flight the last time as Warbeck and his mercenary guards had fled. Now all was silent except for the sound of rushing water from the River Tweed. My senses were alert. I almost regretted wearing the helmet and arming cap yet I knew I had to. The slight deadening of sound could be the difference between success and failure, life and death. However, it was a mixture of things that alerted me to the ambush. Thirty paces up the trail sparrows and blackbirds suddenly flew up from the ground. Something had disturbed them and it was not us. The second clue was when White Star snorted. The only time my horse had done so before was when we had approached horses coming in the opposite direction and I heard the unmistakable click as a crossbow was loaded. I drew my sword and spurred White Star, shouting, "Ware ambush! Charge the trees! I was just in time for the bolt clanked off the side of my helmet.

Behind me, I heard Sir Edward shout, "Ware ambush! Into the woods!" The message was for Gerald of Etal. We had to pray that he and his archers were somewhere close by. My ears still rang from the bolt striking my helmet. I headed for the place the birds had vacated. I knew from experience that the crossbowman would be reloading. I heard the crack of another two crossbows releasing their deadly bolts. I was just grateful that the enemy were not archers for bows were a silent and deadlier killer. I sensed the bolt coming for me as it crashed through the undergrowth and I lowered my head as I raised my sword. The surprised crossbowman was still using his hook to draw back the cord when my sword hacked into his neck as I burst through the undergrowth. A cry from behind told me that we had not escaped unscathed. Someone had been hit.

"Close with them! I want their heads!" I recognised Sir Andrew's voice. Men suddenly appeared from both sides of the trail. It was both impossible and unnecessary to count them. I just had to kill as many as I could before they got me.

As I wheeled to charge the pikeman who ran at me, I saw Henry's riderless horse career through the woods. I jinked White Star to one side as I stood in my saddle to swing my sword into the shoulder of the pikeman. My sudden move and his lack of familiarity with his weapon of choice meant that his pike struck air and not horse flesh. He was not wearing plate and his leather jack was an old one. My sword sliced through flesh and cracked bone. Turning quickly was my undoing. As I turned to head back down the trail a rogue branch smacked into me as White Star faltered and dropped its head. I felt myself pitching from the saddle. The lessons learned at Mechelen came to my aid. I kicked my feet from my stirrups and tucked my head in. My helmet saved me from a fatal blow as my headgear bounced off the side of a tree. Landing heavily I was winded but I had still retained my sword. I had just risen to my knees when a swordsman wielding a two-handed claymore lurched at me.

"Now I have you, you bastard! Die, you English spy."

I knew I was doomed but I still tried to rise and used the tree to help me to my feet. The tree gave me a stay of execution for the sword hit the tree and not me. I drew my dagger as I prepared for the next blow. His sword was longer than mine and I was still groggy. He began to swing and then stopped. I saw the tip of the bodkin emerge from his chest as he slipped to the ground. Gerald of Etal and his archers had come. As quickly as the man died so I was struck in the back by a heavy weapon that made me stumble forward. I whipped around slashing my sword as I did so. An axeman stared at his axe as though it was bewitched for he had struck my back and I was still standing. My backplate had saved me and his amazement cost him his life as my sword knocked away his axe and my dagger found his neck.

"You have nine lives, English spy. Is that to match your many identities but I have you now?"

I turned to face my next attacker. It was Sir Andrew with two henchmen. I saw that he held his sword in his right hand, the hand I had stabbed. It was a weakness but the other two looked to be useful. One held a poleaxe and the other a two-handed sword.

I heard as they advanced towards me, the sound of a horse crashing through the undergrowth, "I am coming, James." It was Sir Edward.

The movement distracted them and I lunged at the man with the poleaxe. He had on a breastplate but my sword managed to score a hit on his right hand as it screeched and squealed along the breastplate. I flicked away Sir Andrew's sword with my dagger as the two-handed swordsman swung his sword at Sir Edward's horse's head. It hacked into it and Sir Edward was thrown from his mount. I lunged at the swordsman and managed to slice my sword into his side. The warrior with the poleaxe saw Sir Edward lying prostrate on the ground and raised his poleaxe to end the knight's life. Swinging my sword and ignoring Sir

Andrew's sword slash, I ran at him. I managed to reach him when the head was an arm's length away from ending Sir Edward's life. My sword slid under his arm and the poleaxe dropped from his dying hands. The two-handed swordsman took his chance and brought his sword down to split open my head. I saw it coming and, raising my dagger to block it, moved my head slightly to the side. Sir Edward had risen and was facing Buchanan. The two-handed sword hit the side of my helmet and began to slide down the side. My dagger managed to catch the man's hilt just before it sliced into the straps holding my breastplate. The blood coming from the man's side told me that his wound was bleeding and he would weaken. I stepped back to swing my sword. He succeeded in blocking the blow but it was a weak block. A two-handed sword takes some wielding. I heard the clash of steel as the two knights fought. I hoped that Sir Andrew's weak hand would result in victory for Sir Edward but I had the more dangerous opponent for mine was younger and fitter.

My enemy knew he had to finish me before he succumbed to his wound. There were others fighting in the trees but the battle of we four would be the one that determined the outcome. He ran at me with his sword pointed at my head. He had the advantage because his weapon was longer than my sword and all that I could do was block. My training as a billman came to my aid. I knew that holding a long weapon for any length of time made muscles in your shoulders burn and the tip had an annoying habit of moving. So it was with the Scotsman that when I used my sword to deflect the end of the longsword, he could not stop me from doing so. His forward momentum could not be halted and so the long, double-edged sword slid over my shoulder. I rammed my dagger up under his right arm. It is impossible to protect there unless you wear a mail hauberk and even then, a blade can slide up under the mail links. The dagger tore into flesh, sinew and nerves. I felt the sword fall onto my shoulder and I pushed harder to scrape and scratch along the bone there. When the tip emerged, I ripped it out. The blood that spurted told me that it was a mortal blow.

As the man slid from my blade to the ground, I saw that the fight between Sir Edward and Sir Andrew had not gone the way

I had predicted. Sir Edward was wounded and from the way he gasped for breath, I saw that the claret and lack of exercise had done for him. Even with a damaged hand, Sir Andrew was the better warrior. It was sad because in his prime Sir Edward would have disposed of his opponent in a flurry of blows.

I stepped over the body of the long swordsman and that delay saw Sir Andrew's sword slip into the gap between breastplate and fauld. Sir Edward's sword and dagger slipped a little lower leaving him wide open to a final fatal strike. I brought my own sword across to block the strike from Sir Andrew's sword. The Scot had not seen me coming and he whipped around angrily slashing at me with his dagger. Instinct made my left hand block the blow and as our swords locked, I twisted the hilt of my sword against his causing him pain when the metal scraped along his old wound. I was not a knight, fighting with honour and glory in my head. There would be no arrest and Sir Andrew would die. King Henry would have to be content with the body and head of the killer.

"Why can you not just die?"

I smiled, knowing that it would annoy my enemy, "Because I am a better warrior than you and you know it."

I knew that it would be equally galling that I was a commoner and not a knight. He pulled back his hand to stab at me with his sword. He had skill and had been well trained but the mercenaries who had trained me had been better fighters and I riposted every blow and strike that came my way. I was looking for weakness. This was not a back alley in Nantes where we could be discovered or where walls blocked blows. We were in a lonely forest in the Tweed Valley and I could afford to wear him down. I suspected that the reason no more arrows had come to my aid was the simple fact that an archer might find it hard to be certain to hit his target in such a confused fight. It would be Sir Andrew or me who would survive and I had a family that needed me.

When I saw Ralf and Gerald appear along the trail, I knew that we had won. Sir Andrew did not see them but I saw the sweat on his brow and knew that he was tiring. Thus far I had riposted and blocked but now I went onto the front foot and began to drive him back. Each blow with the rondel dagger or sword made him block and I varied the blows. One on high, one horizontal, another to the side, and one from below. He was forced to step back and react to my attack. Such a strategy was bound to result in defeat for it meant he had lost control of the fight and I was the dancing master making him move. In the end, it was the root of the Scots Pine that did for him. He tripped over it and began to fall. I lunged with my sword, intending to wound him in the upper arm but his flailing sword struck my blade and I could not prevent my weapon from sliding into his throat. He was dead.

Ralf, Gerald and the archers appeared, "The rest?"

Gerald said, "Dead or fled. We thought to come to your aid but I can see that you needed it not."

"Sir Edward!"

I turned and ran back to the stricken knight. He was not yet dead and had pulled himself up so that he was sitting upright against the bole of a tree. He gave a grim smile as I knelt, "That was good to see, James. You are a better swordsman than even I was and today…" he shook his head, "I was a shadow of the man who fought at Bosworth but at least I was still of service to my king."

I balled the piece of cloth Gerald handed me. He had torn it from the shirt of the dead axeman. I pressed it to the wound.

"That will not be necessary for I am a dead man already but I thank you for giving me the chance to leave this life with some sort of honour. When you found me at Hedingham I was doomed to die soon enough." He gave a sad smile, "When you begin to pass blood instead of piss then you know your time is limited. Ned has my will. The earl will give the land to another but my wealth is for you, Sam, Stephen and Ned. The last of my brothers in arms will have what little I have."

His hand grabbed mine and he arched his back in pain.

"Thank you, James, may God…"

He said no more and a great knight died in the Tweed Valley. He had died on his own terms and that was good but I could not help but think he had been badly used by Thomas Wolsey and King Henry. He had been sacrificed for a hidden purpose and I did not like it.

I stood and looked at Ralf, "John and Henry?"

He shook his head, "You were right, James, and we were not good enough. They have paid the price and I was lucky."

Gerald said, "There are horses. Let us put our dead and Sir Edward on their backs and head to Etal. Sir Edward and his two men can lie in the graveyard there. I will let the villagers know that their graves are to be tended in memory of English heroes who fought for King Henry."

We buried them the next day and I confess that I wept. I did not feel unmanned by my tears for Sir Edward deserved someone to cry for him and I was all that there was.

We had spare horses now and when we left, with Sir Andrew's body draped over the saddle of one of them, I gave the reins of three to Gerald. "Take these in payment for your services, Gerald of Etal. I pray we meet again but if not, I will see you in warrior heaven."

"Fear not for we shall meet again. King James will not suffer another insult like this. War will come and when it does then you and I will be called upon again to defend the borders."

Epilogue

We rode back to Ford. I was not sure what kind of reception to expect but I think that Sir John was surprised when the two of us rode in with Sir Andrew's body draped over the back of the horse. He made no comment about the three men we had lost. If anything I think he was embarrassed.

"You are the one who was attacked by this man, Sir John. I hand over his body to you. What you do with it is your affair. We have done our duty and we have obeyed the instructions of our king." I emphasised the words duty and obeyed. If he was insulted, I cared not.

"Will you stay the night?" The knight almost pleaded with us but I would not suffer a night in his hall.

"No, but I will give you some information as thanks for your hospitality." My finger darted out to point at the smiling reeve, "That man is a traitor. It was he who told Sir Andrew what we did. Either you arrest him and try him or I shall kill him here and now."

The man's face fell and he turned to run. I drew my sword and galloped after him. He was heading for the burn that ran close to the castle. He had no chance of escaping me but I would not kill him. Instead, I used the flat of my sword to smack into the back of his skull. He fell face down in the water. I dismounted and grabbed his foot. Remounting I rode back to the others who waited open-mouthed. The reeve's face was bloody and scarred by the time I had dragged him over the cobbles. I dropped him at Sir John's feet.

He nodded, "A trial is not necessary for his flight told me of his guilt and I have heard rumours." He turned to his men. "Hang him from my gates." It was as though I had unleashed a dam for Sir John strode to the horse with Sir Andrew's body draped over it and pulled it to the ground. He took his longsword and in one movement hacked through the Scottish knight's neck. "And put this head on a spike over my gate. Let the Scots know the price for treachery."

The reeve was awake when they began to haul him to his death. I heard his feet banging against the stone as he was strangled to death. I did not turn for I had seen enough of death. I wanted to get home to my family.

I nodded and said, "Farewell."

We rode for a mile or so in silence and then, as the road climbed to a ridge, we stopped to adjust the girths on our horses and to rearrange their loads. We had left the sumpters with Gerald and had four good horses with us. Sir Andrew's was a particularly fine animal.

Ralf looked at me nervously. I could see he was summoning up the courage to ask me something. I let him do so in his own time. "May I ask a favour of you?"

"Of course for you have proved yourself to be a valiant warrior and I was proud to fight alongside you."

"I have no master now but I do not wish to seek one until I am a better warrior. Would you train me? I am a hard worker and I am more than happy to labour on your farm just so long as you pass on your skills to me."

I thought back to Sir Edward. He had begun my training and I owed it to him to ensure that Ralf had a chance of surviving his next encounter. Gerald had told me that he had almost come to the same end as his fellows but his archers had been able to save him. Ralf had been lucky and I would ensure that the next time he fought he did not rely so much on luck.

"Of course." Gratitude gushed from his eyes.

We mounted and I surveyed the land. I could see Ford Castle from where we stood and I knew that just a few miles north lay Etal. I spied another ridge and a village to the northwest. As we headed down the road, we met a man driving a small flock of sheep to Ford. We moved to the side and I asked him, "Sir, what is the name of yonder village?"

"Why sir, that is Flodden."

"Thank you."

As we continued on our way Ralf asked, "What is so interesting about the ridge, Captain James?"

I shrugged, "Gerald was right, we will be back here one day and if I were the Scots and wanted to take both Etal and Ford then the top of that ridge would be a good place to mount bombards. Here is your first lesson, Ralf, view everything as though it is a potential battlefield. Who knows, Flodden may prove to be such a one."

The End

Glossary

Carole- a song sung at Christmas and normally accompanied by a dance or a procession

Cockpit- the place where cockfighting took place

Costrel- A wooden beaker with a hook to hang from a belt; used on a campaign to drink

Falchion- a short sword with a curved end. A one-bladed weapon

Fauld- plate armour protecting the lower body

Gardyvyan- a sheet containing all the equipment that an archer needed

Gong scourer- a man hired to empty human dung and dispose of it.

Goose/geese- slang for whores

Goose bite- a euphemism for Venereal Disease

Hackney- a good riding horse, superior to a rouncy

Hogbog – a small enclosure close to the house for pigs and fowl, mainly chickens.

Jack- a padded vest sometimes made of leather and strengthened by metal. Often called a brigandine

Marchpane- marzipan

Mesne- an old-fashioned word for the men who serve a knight

Reiver-men on both sides of the Anglo-Scottish border who raid

Rondel dagger- the most common type of dagger with a short crosspiece and two blades

Rouncy- a good riding horse

Sallet- the most popular type of helmet at the time having a flared back to protect the neck

Terces- the third hour of the day

Twesilhaugh- Twizell Castle in Northumberland

Historical Background

I have made up all the incidents involving James of Ecclestone. As far as I know, while there were raids on the Lancashire coast by pirates none were as devastating as the one I write about. I am trying to entertain. There were Scotsmen and Frenchmen who were trying to ferment war with England and the plots I have concocted are there to reflect that. John the Bastard Heron did kill Sir Robert Kerr and that almost precipitated a war. King Henry's daughter did marry the King of Scotland who finally conquered the isles. King James did not regard the Norse as worthy enemies and, the next book in the series, Flodden, will detail how his overreaching ambition resulted in that most famous of border battles. King Henry VIIIth was also desperate for glory and he went to war alongside his father-in-law, The King of Aragon, to gain glory. He failed. King Henry VIIth had been a frugal king and he left his son more money than was good for him.

James will reappear in at least one more book, Flodden. This whole series evolved from a visit I made to Flodden with two of my grandsons. I have been to Waterloo and Gettysburg as well as Hastings but Flodden is the only battlefield I have visited where you can really see how the battle was almost won and then lost. It is a very atmospheric place and well worth a visit.

Books used in the research
- Tudors- Terry Breverton
- Tudor- Leanda de Lisle
- The Tower of London- A L Rowse
- British Kings and Queens Mike Ashley

Griff Hosker July 2022

Other books by Griff Hosker

If you enjoyed reading this book, then why not read another one by the author?

Ancient History

The Sword of Cartimandua Series
(Germania and Britannia 50 A.D. – 128 A.D.)
Ulpius Felix- Roman Warrior (prequel)
The Sword of Cartimandua
The Horse Warriors
Invasion Caledonia
Roman Retreat
Revolt of the Red Witch
Druid's Gold
Trajan's Hunters
The Last Frontier
Hero of Rome
Roman Hawk
Roman Treachery
Roman Wall
Roman Courage

The Wolf Warrior series
(Britain in the late 6th Century)
Saxon Dawn
Saxon Revenge
Saxon England
Saxon Blood
Saxon Slayer
Saxon Slaughter
Saxon Bane
Saxon Fall: Rise of the Warlord
Saxon Throne
Saxon Sword

Medieval History

The Dragon Heart Series
Viking Slave
Viking Warrior
Viking Jarl
Viking Kingdom
Viking Wolf
Viking War
Viking Sword
Viking Wrath
Viking Raid
Viking Legend
Viking Vengeance
Viking Dragon
Viking Treasure
Viking Enemy
Viking Witch
Viking Blood
Viking Weregeld
Viking Storm
Viking Warband
Viking Shadow
Viking Legacy
Viking Clan
Viking Bravery

The Norman Genesis Series
Hrolf the Viking
Horseman
The Battle for a Home
Revenge of the Franks
The Land of the Northmen
Ragnvald Hrolfsson
Brothers in Blood
Lord of Rouen
Drekar in the Seine
Duke of Normandy
The Duke and the King

Tudor Spy

Danelaw
(England and Denmark in the 11th Century)
Dragon Sword
Oathsword
Bloodsword

New World Series
Blood on the Blade
Across the Seas
The Savage Wilderness
The Bear and the Wolf
Erik The Navigator
Erik's Clan

The Vengeance Trail

The Reconquista Chronicles
Castilian Knight
El Campeador
The Lord of Valencia

The Aelfraed Series
(Britain and Byzantium 1050 A.D. - 1085 A.D.)
Housecarl
Outlaw
Varangian

**The Anarchy Series England
1120-1180**
English Knight
Knight of the Empress
Northern Knight
Baron of the North
Earl
King Henry's Champion
The King is Dead
Warlord of the North
Enemy at the Gate

Tudor Spy

The Fallen Crown
Warlord's War
Kingmaker
Henry II
Crusader
The Welsh Marches
Irish War
Poisonous Plots
The Princes' Revolt
Earl Marshal
The Perfect Knight

Border Knight
1182-1300
Sword for Hire
Return of the Knight
Baron's War
Magna Carta
Welsh Wars
Henry III
The Bloody Border
Baron's Crusade
Sentinel of the North
War in the West
Debt of Honour
The Blood of the Warlord

Sir John Hawkwood Series
France and Italy 1339- 1387
Crécy: The Age of the Archer
Man At Arms
The White Company
Leader of Men

Lord Edward's Archer
Lord Edward's Archer
King in Waiting
An Archer's Crusade
Targets of Treachery

Tudor Spy

The Great Cause

**Struggle for a Crown
1360- 1485**
Blood on the Crown
To Murder a King
The Throne
King Henry IV
The Road to Agincourt
St Crispin's Day
The Battle for France
The Last Knight
Queen's Knight

Tales from the Sword I
(Short stories from the Medieval period)

**Tudor Warrior series
England and Scotland in the late 14th and early 15th
century**
Tudor Warrior
Tudor Spy

**Conquistador
England and America in the 16th Century**
Conquistador

Modern History

The Napoleonic Horseman Series
Chasseur à Cheval
Napoleon's Guard
British Light Dragoon
Soldier Spy
1808: The Road to Coruña
Talavera
The Lines of Torres Vedras
Bloody Badajoz
The Road to France

Tudor Spy

Waterloo

The Lucky Jack American Civil War series
Rebel Raiders
Confederate Rangers
The Road to Gettysburg

Soldier of the Queen series
Soldier of the Queen

The British Ace Series
1914
1915 Fokker Scourge
1916 Angels over the Somme
1917 Eagles Fall
1918 We will remember them
From Arctic Snow to Desert Sand
Wings over Persia

Combined Operations series
1940-1945
Commando
Raider
Behind Enemy Lines
Dieppe
Toehold in Europe
Sword Beach
Breakout
The Battle for Antwerp
King Tiger
Beyond the Rhine
Korea
Korean Winter

Tales from the Sword II
(Short stories from the Modern period)

Other Books
Great Granny's Ghost (Aimed at 9-14-year-old young people)

For more information on all of the books then please visit the author's website at www.griffhosker.com where there is a link to contact him or visit his Facebook page: GriffHosker at Sword Books

Printed in Great Britain
by Amazon

86981779R00133